Jasper Moon, internationally renowned 'seer to the stars', is found dead on his consulting-room floor, his thin skull crushed with a crystal ball. Around him the office is in chaos, a window has been smashed, files on famous clients have been ripped from their cabinets and £1,000 has been stolen from the cash box. It's not every burglar who would cause this much damage and then neatly lock the cash box afterwards, and Inspector Rafferty and Sergeant Llewellyn suspect that this is more than a routine break-in gone horribly wrong.

Jasper Moon usually kept Thursday evenings free for a regular mystery visitor but, according to his cleaning woman, on the Thursday of his death he had a client with him. A client who has never been seen before and who has now disappeared. Then Rafferty and Llewellyn find a highly incriminating video concealed in Moon's flat, a video which, if made public, could wreck more than one life.

Through their conversations with Moon's friends and colleagues, Rafferty and Llewellyn begin to build two deeply contradictory pictures of the dead man. Was the famous astrologer really a generous and forgiving man or a vicious and highly calculating sexual pervert? Gradually connections begin to emerge between Moon and others in the small town of Elmhurst, giving Rafferty plenty of ideas as to who might have wanted him dead. But why is it that all of Rafferty's suspects have seemingly unbreakable alibis?

Death Line

Geraldine Evans

**MACMILLAN
LONDON**

First published 1995 by Macmillan London

an imprint of Macmillan General Books
Cavaye Place London SW10 9PG
and Basingstoke

Associated companies throughout the world

ISBN 0 333 63170 6

9 8 7 6 5 4 3 2 1

A CIP catalogue record for this book is available from
the British Library

Phototypeset by Intype, London
Printed by Mackays of Chatham PLC, Chatham, Kent

Dedication

To George, my husband, Cath, my mother, and the rest of my family, with love, and especially to the newest member, my great-nephew, Alex James David.

Acknowledgements

With thanks to the wonderfully helpful staff at the Irish Embassy in London and to my own 'Ma' for their help with Irish spelling.

Chapter One

Jasper Moon, internationally renowned 'Seer to the Stars', had signally failed to predict his own future. He lay sprawled on the dark carpet of his office at Constellation Consultants with the back of his skull caved in. A small crystal ball – presumably the murder weapon – lay beside him.

A black silk cloak covered the torso, leaving only the head and feet exposed. Disconcerted to see that, like himself, Moon sported a pair of vivid emerald green socks, Rafferty turned his attention back to the cadaver's other end. The waxy, heavy-jowled profile was in ghastly relief to the dyed black hair and the midnight richness of the silk. A crescent-shaped scar under his left eye showed up with a lividity it had lacked in life. Rafferty imagined that the reputedly vain Moon would have been glad that the cloak lent his podgy, middle-aged body a certain dignity, a touch of elegance. An elegance certainly not shared by the room.

Obviously Moon hadn't subscribed to the 'less is more' style of interior design. Even Rafferty, not normally one to flinch from the garish, spared only a cursory, deprecatory glance at the night black ceiling with its mother of pearl stars and scale paintings of the planets and what he assumed were astrological symbols decorating one of the walls.

Unlike Sergeant Llewellyn, whose face evinced its usual Sphinx-like inscrutability, Rafferty had never learned to mask his emotions. He was reminded of this flaw when Edwin Astell, a tall, spare man and the victim's business partner, commented from the doorway, 'You shouldn't judge Jasper by ordinary standards, Inspector. In his own way, he was as much of a star as his clients – they mostly came from the entertainment world. You could say that Jasper shared their showmanship and taste for the dramatic.'

1

So did his murderer, thought Rafferty. There was a TV and video in the corner. The video was undamaged, though empty of film, but the screen of the television had been smashed in; it looked as though someone had taken a hammer to it. The drawers had been removed from the desk and stacked on top of it, dislodging a vase of late roses which lay strewn on the floor in front of Moon's desk, as though thrown in tribute by a mourner. The filing cabinet was surrounded by untidily strewn piles of its contents. Glass from a broken pane was scattered under the window. Rafferty walked carefully round the body and over to the window. The bottom sash had been raised to its full extent and a chill wind teased the curtains over the sill, blowing them about in a frenzied dance as he examined the rear of the premises.

An alleyway ran the length of the parade of shops and flats. The consulting rooms of the partners were on the first floor, above the Psychic Store, the partnership's sideline, which, Astell had already informed him, sold New Age books and trinkets. Adjoining the shop, another door opened on to a flight of stairs that led directly to the consulting rooms from the high street. But Astell had told them that it was seldom used and kept locked. An intercom beside this door was used to admit clients who had an evening appointment. During the day, clients came through the shop and reached the first floor by another, inner staircase; the one they had used. Moon's office was the largest of the three. It shared the back of the premises with a windowless internal kitchen and a small washroom with windows of frosted glass.

Whoever had broken into Moon's office would have found little difficulty, Rafferty realized. Not only had the burglar alarm been switched off, presumably by Moon himself, but even if Moon hadn't admitted anyone himself, access would have been simple enough, as a small, flat-roofed extension from the ground floor of the shop ended just under the window. And, as an additional bonus for any intruder, although Moon's window had a security lock, the key was in it and he guessed that it had been a simple matter for an intruder to stretch an arm through the broken pane and help himself to the key that had presumably dangled from the empty hook less than one yard away.

Rafferty's lips pursed. He could understand the desire to have the key close at hand in case of fire, but surely a man who spent his time peering into the future could find sufficient foresight to put the key out of sight? Unwilling to risk any more mind-reading by Astell, he took the trouble to compose his features before he turned and nodded at the silk-shrouded body. 'You haven't touched anything? Is this exactly how you discovered him? Covered like this?'

Astell confirmed it, adding anxiously, 'I hope none of his client files are missing. They're confidential and it could be embarrassing.'

Rafferty frowned as the words 'confidential' and 'embarrassing' set off warning signals in his brain. The Constellation Consultants side of the business provided clients with astrology and tarot readings, as well as palmistry – hand-analysis, Astell had called it. He had told them that Moon had regarded the crystal ball as nothing more than an amusing paperweight and didn't use it in his work. As it seemed likely that this ball had been the murder weapon, he wondered if the dead man would appreciate the irony? Now, seizing on one of Astell's words, Rafferty repeated it: 'Confidential?'

'Perhaps it'll surprise you to learn this, Inspector, but in this profession one can hear as many secrets as doctors, listen to as many confessions as priests. You might say we're the social workers, marriage counsellors and career advisors of the psychic world. I've often thought Jasper was unwise to keep so much personal information on his clients. My own files are much more circumspect. Of course,' he added, 'I rarely see clients personally, as Jasper did. But even by post people confide the most intimate details of their lives.'

'Are you saying that Mr Moon might have been murdered because one of his clients had told him something and then regretted it? Regretted it enough to kill him?'

Astell looked appalled at Rafferty's suggestion. 'I didn't mean that at all. I was thinking more of an opportunist than a client, someone who thought there might be scope for blackmail in Jasper's files.' Astell nodded at the broken window. 'No client of Jasper's would need to break in. They would only have to use the intercom at the street for Jasper to release the private door.' Sounding a touch put out that Rafferty should suspect the clients, Astell added, 'Surely it's obvious that some intruder attacked him?

Someone who riffled Jasper's files looking for whatever damaging information he could find?'

Rafferty didn't think much of Astell's detecting skills, though he could understand why he found this scenario more attractive than the alternative. Would Moon be likely to turn away from an unknown intruder and present the back of his skull so obligingly for the blow?

Rafferty realized that his face had again betrayed his thoughts. 'Jasper's clients were more concerned with matters financial and emotional,' Astell told him with a cool smile. 'No one has yet confessed to anything worth murdering for.'

Not to you, perhaps, thought Rafferty, as he again forced his face into unnatural immobility. But, suspecting the flamboyant Moon would have been the repository of more such secrets than his reserved partner, he made the observation, 'I imagine Mr Moon would be more understanding of human weaknesses than most.'

Glancing again at the plump corpse, with its Dracula cape and satan-black hair and beard, the late Jasper Moon looked to Rafferty to have had more than his fair share of such weaknesses himself; maybe one of them had caused his death?

Moon was certainly very famous. That his international clientele, many of them household names, should be prepared to travel to an Essex backwater spoke volumes for his ability. Though, Rafferty, with a sceptic's humour, wondered whether Moon's greatest skill mightn't have been for self-publicity.

He remembered seeing Moon during an experimental dally with breakfast television a month ago. Moon had been giving his daily predictions. He had come over as someone larger than life, a creature apparently so running over with love and concern for his fellow man that he had called them all 'darling'. Such showbiz mannerisms always jarred with Rafferty. He had immediately switched off and gone back to Wogan and Radio 2.

He moved away from the window as he heard the scenes of crime officers clattering heavily up the stairs, weighed down with their professional paraphernalia. Glancing at Edwin Astell, Rafferty asked him to wait in his own office.

Once Astell had left the room, Rafferty had a word with Adrian Appleby, the head of the SOCOs. 'Can you get Moon's appoint-

ments book and the filing cabinet and its contents dusted asap?'
He would need to speak to all Moon's clients. Of course, most of
them would be quickly exonerated. He had had a quick flick
through the diary earlier, and, even though Astell had briefly
mentioned the names of some of Moon's more famous clients, it
had revealed names from the film, music and literary world that
startled him; people like Shane Dalton, the teeny-boppers' idol;
Sian Silk, the hottest property in Hollywood at the moment; even
Nat Kingston, the well-known writer and literary critic. If the rest
of Moon's clients were even half as well known as these, a fair
number probably wouldn't even have been in the country – never
mind in Elmhurst – on the night Moon was killed, which should,
once their movements had been checked out, lessen the load a bit.

He had earlier noticed several threads of black material with
glittery silver bits caught on a rough section of Moon's desk and,
as he drew Appleby's attention to them, he heard from the
stairwell the unmistakable sound of pathologist cum police surgeon Dr Sam Dally's Scottish tones muttering about 'bloody
women drivers'. Rafferty went down to the shop to speak to him
while Sam got into his protective gear. 'Here at last then, Sam?
What delayed you?'

Dally raised his head. There was a lump on his forehead the
size of a hen's egg. 'Some damn-fool woman. She was racing away
from town here, way past the speed limit, overshot the lights and
ploughed into me. She didn't stop, of course.' He gave Rafferty a
grim smile. 'Got her number, though.'

'Are you OK?'

Sam nodded. 'Banged my head on the windscreen.'

'As long as you didn't damage anything vital.' Rafferty peered
at him. 'Sure you're all right? You ought to get yourself looked at.
There might be concussion.'

'I popped into old Boyd's, the optician here in the High Street.
Luckily he lives in the flat above his business and I got him to
give me the once-over. After gazing lovingly into my eyes for a
bit he pronounced me fit, so I suppose I'll live. It would happen
the day I forgot to put my seatbelt on, of course. You can be sure
that blasted insurance company'll make something of that if I go
ga-ga in the next day or so.' Having finally struggled into his gear,
Sam thrust his outer clothing at Smales, who was still guarding

the door, with the instruction to mind it, before stomping up the stairs. 'Got a new toy, I see,' he said to the video-camera-toting photographer as he pushed his way into Moon's office. 'Nearly finished, I hope.'

'Just waiting to film the star.' Lance, the photographer, who had ambitions beyond policework, grinned as he got Sam in focus. 'Scowl nicely for the camera. That's it. It's a wrap.'

With a 'Hrmph', Sam's stout body bustled past the SOCO team, bent over the corpse and got to work. 'Rigor's well established,' he remarked a few minutes later. He took the temperature of the room and the rectal temperature of the corpse, frowning as he made his calculations. 'He's a fine figure of a man, isn't he? Tends to slow the onset of rigor down a bit. Did you know, Rafferty,' he threw over his shoulder, 'that some particularly fine-figured specimens *never* develop rigor at all?'

Rafferty frowned. 'Are you trying to tell me that he's too fat for you to give me an idea of the time of death?'

Sam, whose figure was at least as 'fine' as Moon's, tutted at Rafferty's want of sensitivity. 'Certainly not. He probably died some time yesterday evening, say between 7 p.m. and 11 p.m. Of course that's a rough calculation. But I can tell you that he was definitely killed from behind by a right-handed person plying our old friend, the blunt instrument.' Sam paused and added teasingly, 'Unless it was a southpaw masquerading as a right-hander. Modern killers are getting very crafty about hiding their tracks. It's all those crime programmes on the telly – gives 'em ideas.' He glanced at the crystal ball lying on the floor next to the victim's head. 'And by a Holmesian process of deduction, I'd say this cute wee thing was the weapon.'

Rafferty shook his head in mock admiration. 'Amazing. How do you do it?'

'Och, it's just a little skill the Almighty gives to fine-figured men in their prime, Rafferty.' Sam swept a disparaging glance over Rafferty's skinny frame and bright auburn hair, before adding, 'You'll need to get some extra flesh on your bones, a higher forehead and some wise grey hairs before he invests you with similar abilities.' Having satisfactorily put both Rafferty's comparative youth and thick auburn mop in their place, Sam bent his balding pate back to its work.

6

'Anything else you can tell me, O wise one? Like whether he was hit by a man or a woman, for instance?'

'Could be either, Rafferty.' Sam spared a glance for the murder weapon as one of the SOCO team placed it in a protective bag and smiled. 'Perhaps, if you ask Appleby here nicely, he'll let you have a peer into that crystal ball before he takes it away.' He got to his feet, picked up his bag and, after a few words with the scientific team, advised Rafferty, 'As far as I'm concerned, you can pop him in his Jiffy bag now.'

After checking with the Coroner's officer, Rafferty gave the instructions. Moon's head, hands and feet were encased in protective plastic bags and his body lifted on to polythene sheeting and secured before he was placed in the usual fibreglass shell.

'Any idea when you'll be doing the PM, Sam? Only—'

'Trying to queue-jump again, Rafferty?' Sam paused, considering. 'I'll maybe squeeze yon cadaver in this afternoon. About five. Is that quick enough for you?'

Rafferty blinked in surprise and nodded. He watched as Moon's body was carefully manoeuvred round the bend in the stairs, and, with Sam in the rear, retrieving his clothes from the constable, the little procession disappeared through the front door.

With the removal of the body, Rafferty relaxed a little. 'Right,' he said to Llewellyn. 'Now that Sam has given us the benefit of his great wisdom, we can get on. Let's get back to Mr Astell.'

He led the way through to Astell's office. It was a large, airy room. After the hectic busyness of Moon's office, Astell's was bare and clinical. There was nothing on the desk but a computer, which Astell presumably used to compile the natal charts. There was nothing on the walls, apart from several stark, simple but exquisite Japanese brush paintings.

Astell had evidently been thinking about what Rafferty had said earlier, because, as soon as they entered, he returned to the theme of their previous conversation. 'I wouldn't want you to think that Jasper ever went beyond the bounds of prudence during the consultations, Inspector. Although it's true that he had a way of drawing people out, he was sensitive to his clients' privacy and would never probe in delicate areas without being certain the client was happy for him to do so.'

Rafferty gave a diplomatic nod.

7

'I deal solely with postal clients, making up the computerized natal charts from their birth details. Jasper taught me himself. I've learned quite a bit about hand-analysis also, but I have nothing to do with that side of things. I suffer quite badly from eczema on my hands and I find clients don't like my touching them.' Rafferty had already noticed that Astell wore thin cotton gloves. He could see some greasy ointment already beginning to seep through. 'Jasper, of course, loved the more personal aspect of private consultations. He said if he was to help his clients he needed to meet them, see what made them tick. He liked people, you see.'

Rafferty pounced. He couldn't help it. Taken with Moon's other vices, from what Astell had said the man sounded like a prime victim. 'You're saying he was inquisitive?' he asked sharply. 'In fact a bit of a nos—' Rafferty stopped abruptly as he saw Llewellyn wince. In his eagerness, he had forgotten that Superintendent Bradley's latest baby was a PR number entitled *Politeness in Interaction with Members of the Public* – PIMP for short, though luckily Bradley had yet to tumble to that aspect. Rafferty was rather pleased with the title. After all, he *had* suggested it. At least it was the most accurately named in a long line of Bradley's schemes. And like pimps the world over, Bradley got the benefits and the team; his public relations officers, as he had taken to calling them, or PROs for short, got – well, they got what PROs usually got. The jargon phrase for this little programme was 'Politeness Costs Nothing'.

Rafferty had, as a matter of principle, offended against several of Bradley's previous arse-licking exercises aimed at winning for himself even more friends at Region, and PIMP wasn't something he could lightly ignore. Not that he had anything against being polite to the public; far from it. It was just that the Superintendent's man-management methods tended to pettiness, deviousness and, when these didn't work, outright bullying. His favourite pastime was reducing the younger WPCs to tears.

Thankfully, Edwin Astell wasn't aware of the Super's newly tender approach to public relations, and, although his nostrils pinched slightly, he didn't contradict Rafferty's description of Jasper Moon's character.

'I wouldn't have put it quite like that, Inspector, but yes, I suppose he was inquisitive. Though a competent, experienced palmist could discover much about a person without them saying a word. I'm merely a knowledgeable amateur as far as hand-analysis is concerned, but even I need only to study a person's hands for a short time to discover if they are generous or mean, passionate or placid, creative or practical. Jasper, as a professional, was, of course, far more skilled.'

Perhaps he'd caught the look of scepticism on Rafferty's face, for Astell went on: 'If I might be permitted to provide you with an example?' Rafferty nodded. 'Although I've just met him and we've exchanged no more than a few words, I'd say your sergeant's a highly intelligent, analytical person, with refined tastes and a certain sensitivity. Of course, this is just a cursory appraisal.' He turned to Llewellyn with an apologetic smile. 'You must forgive my using you as a guinea-pig, Sergeant. I hope I haven't offended you.' Not surprisingly, after such a glowing character reference, Llewellyn seemed more than happy to reassure him on the point.

Rafferty was shaken that his prejudices had been challenged and trumped with such ease. Although unwilling to second Astell's appraisal of his sergeant's virtues, he found himself admitting, 'You're right. That's Llewellyn to a "T". How on earth did you do it?' Next he'd be telling him, à la Sherlock Holmes, that Llewellyn was contemplating marriage and the production of 2.4 children.

Astell's smile had a certain diffident charm. He was quite a good-looking man, Rafferty realized. Along with his distinctly old-fashioned manners, he had the kind of face that, for some reason, made Rafferty think of tragic First World War poets; all planes and angles and shadowed melancholic hollows.

'It's not magic, Inspector,' Astell told him. 'Merely observation and rather elementary observation at that. Any student of palmistry could tell you as much. Your sergeant's hand is long, slim and full of lines, what we term a Water hand. It invariably points to sensitivity and an interest in the arts. The intellectuality is indicated by the long, straight head lines on both palms and the length of the topmost phalanges on his fingers. I told you, nothing can be concealed from an experienced palmist.'

Hastily, Rafferty put his hands behind his back, in case Astell was tempted to point out certain aspects of his own character. He doubted their revelation would render his expression as smug as that of his sergeant. 'And Jasper Moon was an experienced palmist?' he queried.

'Oh yes, of course. Don't let Jasper's esoteric taste in decor give you the wrong idea. His knowledge was wide. I only dabble, though as I said, astrologically, Jasper has taught me a lot. Of course, my real training is on the business side, which is why Jasper originally employed me before he offered me the partnership. I still take care of the administration side of the business.'

Rafferty felt out of his depth with all this hocus-pocus, as he thought of it. Whether Moon had been murdered by one of his clients or not, it sounded to Rafferty as if Moon's profession could offer lucrative opportunities to the unscrupulous. Judging from the quantity of files that had been scattered about Moon's room, he had a lot of clients, and, as his charges were, in Rafferty's opinion, extortionate, none of his clients was likely to be poor. They would all have to be questioned and eliminated. Rafferty sighed and asked, 'How soon could you let us know if anything's missing, sir?'

'As to the files, I'll have to go through the client list and match it up with the individual folders. It'll take a little while.'

Rafferty nodded. 'You can do that as soon as the forensic team have finished with them. What about the rest of Mr Moon's stuff? Did you notice if anything was missing?'

Astell's narrow face was apologetic. 'It was a bit difficult to tell. Jasper liked a lot of clutter about him.'

'What about money, sir?' Llewellyn put in. 'Do you keep much cash on the premises?'

'Not usually, but, as a matter of fact, Jasper asked me to draw a thousand pounds out of the bank only yesterday morning. It should still be in the cashbox.'

'Where do you keep this box?' Rafferty questioned.

'In one of the drawers of Jasper's desk.'

'If you'll just wait here, sir, I'll check.' Rafferty quickly put his gloves back on and opened the door to the waiting room. There was another door on the other side connected to Moon's office. He opened this too, and after a quick word with Appleby, walked over to the desk. The cashbox, a large, black affair, squatted in the deepest of the drawers sitting on Moon's desk. After lifting the other two drawers from on top of it, Rafferty attempted to raise its lid with a paperknife, but it was obviously locked. He shouted through to Astell, 'Have you got the key, sir?'

Astell appeared in the doorway. 'Try the smallest drawer, Inspector,' he suggested. 'That's where he usually keeps it.'

Rafferty checked. Astell was right. Careful to touch nothing, Rafferty inserted the key and turned it, raising the lid with the knife. The usual coin tray was on top. It must have contained about £50 in coins and, with difficulty, Rafferty raised this, too, and peered underneath. Apart from a few folded sheets of stamps, the bottom of the cashbox was empty. 'You said there should be a thousand pounds in notes?'

Astell nodded. 'All in brand new fifty-pound notes. I always insist on new notes.'

'Apart from the coins, there's no money here now, sir,' Rafferty told him. He lifted up the cashbox. 'See for yourself.'

Astell's shocked face peered over Llewellyn's shoulder. 'I warned Jasper that having such large sums of cash was dangerous. Of course, I was thinking more about him being attacked on the street. With the entryphone and window locks, I assumed he'd be safe enough here.'

'How many keys are there to this box?'

'Only two. I have one and Jasper had the other. Though, of course, our staff have daily access to it.'

'Mr Moon wouldn't have taken the money himself and spent it already?' Rafferty questioned. 'You said you took the money out of the bank yesterday morning.'

Astell shook his head. 'When I warned him to be careful, he told me he wouldn't even be removing it from the premises. It would stay in the box till tomorrow – or rather today, as it wouldn't be wanted till then. I take it from that that whoever he wanted the money for would be coming to the office for it.' His lips thinned. Apparently that pleased him little more than that Jasper should walk about the streets with it.

In spite of his insistence that an intruder was responsible for the crime, the discovery of the robbery seemed to have shaken him. A case of the smaller shock helping the larger one to sink in, Rafferty guessed. He had seen it before. Though Astell seemed to find no incongruity, to Rafferty there were points about this so-called burglary that struck him as peculiar. Although the money was missing, several other obviously expensive items on Moon's desk had not been taken; small silver, easily pocketable knick-knacks, for instance. If a burglar had taken the money, why hadn't he taken these also? Just as odd was the fact that there was no sign that he had entered the other offices. Even Astell had reluctantly admitted that he didn't think anything had been taken from them and their filing cabinets and desks were undisturbed.

Another thing; Moon's cashbox had been locked. Even if the key had been taken from Moon's desk, why would a burglar bother locking the box up afterwards, never mind replacing the key? Rafferty doubted that this careful burglar was the same person who had vandalized the office and murdered Moon. He relocked the box and stood up. After telling Appleby that the box was another item for priority fingerprinting, he made a mental note to check with the bank to see if they could let him have a list of the notes' numbers. It would be interesting to see if any of them showed up; even more so to discover who disposed of them. Back in Astell's office, Rafferty resumed the questioning. 'He didn't tell you who he wanted the money for?'

'No, but I can hazard a guess. Oh, not a specific identity,' he added as he saw Rafferty's quick interest. 'I don't mean that. Jasper was a bit of a magpie, Inspector, and more than a little extravagant.' Astell's lips pursed. 'If he saw something bright and shiny he had to have it. This money would undoubtedly be required for some gewgaw. Though it's strange that Jasper arranged to see the seller here. As far as I'm aware, he never had before, yet he asked me to withdraw such large sums three or four times a year.' His gaze fixed on Rafferty. 'You – you don't think this person could have killed him?'

'I doubt it, sir. If this person did business fairly regularly with Mr Moon, as seems likely given that he had invited him to his office, why would he kill such a valued customer?'

'Why were these transactions always in cash, sir?' Llewellyn queried what Rafferty – brought up by his off-the-back-of-a-lorry, bargain-hunting ma – had already guessed. 'Surely he could have written out a cheque or paid by credit card?'

Astell hesitated, shifting his gaze from Llewellyn's ascetic fea-tures to Rafferty's more accommodating ones. 'The legality of some of Jasper's purchases was a little – *suspect*, shall we say? I gather he invariably dealt with the same man, and he insisted on cash. That's why I wondered if this person mightn't have killed him. Obviously, he's some kind of criminal.'

Rafferty nodded. 'I see your reasoning, sir, but I still feel there is a lack of motive for murder. As I said before, if this acquaintance of Mr Moon's had been doing business for some time, he would be unlikely to kill a long-standing and prosperous customer like Mr Moon.'

Astell admitted that, put like that, it sounded improbable. Rafferty paused, before softly posing the question that was guaranteed to get under Astell's skin. 'Was Mr Moon seeing a client last night, do you know, sir?'

As expected, Astell's lips thinned. 'Most unlikely, Inspector.' Rafferty deduced from his tone that Astell felt the partnership's clientele should be out of bounds to the police investigation. 'Jasper rarely saw clients on Thursday evenings,' he told them. 'He liked to keep them free for other work. But if he had made an appointment it would be in his diary.'

There had been nothing booked later than 4 p.m. against yesterday's date, Rafferty knew.

Astell was sufficient of a realist to add what the police would have anyway soon discovered from another source: 'Occasionally, if a client needed to see him urgently for a consultation, Jasper would make an exception, but that happened rarely. He was working on another book. You know that as well as more generalized works he wrote astrological forecasts every year for each of the sun signs?'

Rafferty nodded. He'd seen them on sale in the shops – his ma bought one every year, as did his sisters. They seemed very popular. But then Jasper Moon had been a popular astrologer. The walls of the waiting room beside Moon's office displayed the monthly forecast columns he supplied to various women's glossy magazines. Rafferty persisted. 'Might he have forgotten to enter a later appointment? If the client rang after everyone else had gone home, say, and intended to arrive within a short time?'

Reluctantly, Astell admitted it was possible. 'Jasper could be careless about such things. But he's been better lately as I've impressed on him that if he doesn't enter the details I can't bill

13

the clients. Jasper preferred to have his regular clients invoiced rather than charged cash at the time of the consultation. He felt financial transactions then were unprofessional.'

Too much like having his palm crossed with silver on the end of the pier, Rafferty sardonically translated before he could stop himself. Luckily, Astell was staring thoughtfully into space and unlikely to guess at Rafferty's latest breach of the PIMP code.

'You could ask our cleaner, Mrs Hadleigh. She was working here till about 7 o'clock. She'd be able to confirm that there *was* no client with Jasper.'

Astell seemed anxious to dispel the idea that one of Moon's clients had killed him. Understandable, of course, Rafferty reasoned; the more sensitive souls amongst their customers wouldn't be reassured to discover that Moon numbered a killer among his clientele. Apart from any other considerations, it was hardly likely to improve customer confidence when the famous half of the partnership had failed to foresee and avoid his own murder.

Chapter Two

There were two other doors off the landing, and Rafferty asked where they led. Astell placed his begloved hands together in the precise manner that was already getting on Rafferty's nerves and nodded towards the first of the doors on the left. 'This office is used by one of our staff, Mrs Virginia Campbell. The other one is used as a storeroom for any overflow of stock from the shop.' He opened each of the doors in turn. The second room contained books and fancily packaged bottles of oil, CDs, records and cassettes, all stacked on wall shelves, along with many other items. An old easel, stained and shoved just inside the door, was balanced precariously against the wall and Astell straightened it with a gesture of annoyance. 'I must throw this old thing away. I don't know why Jasper insisted on keeping it.'

'Not yet, please,' Rafferty cautioned. 'I don't want anything discarded until the case is concluded.'

Astell nodded and went on. 'As you know, the room between my office and Jasper's is used as a waiting room.'

'Do you employ a receptionist?'

'No. The nature of the work hardly warrants it. Mrs Mercedes Moreno, the woman we employ in the shop, directs our clients to the waiting room. She's from South America.' Astell explained the unusual name. 'Peru.'

'And they're the only other people who work here?'

Astell nodded. 'Apart from Mrs Hadleigh, the cleaner. She normally comes in at about seven every morning.'

Rafferty frowned. 'But she didn't work this morning?'

'No. Mrs Hadleigh had a hospital appointment yesterday morning so I agreed she could do her chores in the evening, from five to seven, and not come in this morning. My wife and I had a few

15

guests last night and Mrs Hadleigh came over afterwards to help out. Unfortunately, she was only there a short time before she began to feel unwell. I sent her home just before eight o'clock. Naturally, though she seemed to want to, I told her not to bother coming in this morning. I tried to ring Jasper last night to remind him that if he made his usual mess he'd have to clean it up himself. He can – could be rather untidy. This morning I had an early booking with one of my few regulars – she likes to see me on her way to the station.'

'You say you tried to ring Mr Moon? At what time?'

Astell nodded. 'I'm sorry. I suppose I should have mentioned it before. I didn't get through. The first few times I tried, Jasper's phone was engaged, and then, when it did ring, no one answered.' His eyes widened, aghast at the implication of what he'd just said. 'God, I never thought . . . So many things going round and round in my mind. I suppose he must have died around then. How – horrible.'

'What time would this have been, sir?' Rafferty asked again.

'What?' Although still obviously stunned, Astell managed to pull himself together sufficiently to answer Rafferty's question. 'It was at eight-twenty. That's right. I'd just made Mrs Moreno – she was one of our guests – a cup of coffee. She'd forgotten her gloves and returned about ten minutes earlier. I remember as the clock in the hall had just rung the quarter chime; it tends to be five minutes slow.' Rafferty made a mental note of the time. As Astell had surmised, it could be important. Whether Moon's killer had called someone from his office, or whether the phone had become dislodged from its rest during the attack and the killer had replaced it, British Telecom should be able to tell them.

Astell, his voice slow and disjointed after this latest shock, explained, 'I didn't want-want his first client to turn up and encounter Jas-Jasper's usual shambles, you see.' He broke off and, after glancing at his watch, said in a more normal voice, 'It hardly matters now, does it? Still, I suppose I should ring and put them off. Though what I can possibly say to them . . .'

'Don't worry about that, sir. One of my officers will contact them.' Rafferty nodded to Llewellyn, who disappeared. 'You mentioned you had a client this morning. Did you ask her to leave when you found the body?'

Astell shook his head and looked cross with himself. 'Sorry. No.

Didn't I explain? She rang to cancel, so I decided I might as well get on with some work. It was then that I found Jasper's body. I needed some stamps. As you saw, they're kept in the cashbox.'

After obtaining this client's name and address, Rafferty went on, 'You said Mrs Hadleigh would have finished cleaning at about seven o'clock yesterday evening?'

'That's right. She usually did a full two hours. One hour on the consulting floor and the other in the shop.'

'And how long has she worked here?'

'Only about three weeks, but I've known her for some years. As well as helping out when we entertain, my wife and I employ her to clean our home. When our last cleaner left I offered her this job. I knew she needed the money, you see. She was pleased to accept.'

Rafferty glanced at his watch and was surprised to find that it was nearly 9.15. 'What time do your other employees normally arrive?'

'The shop doesn't open until nine-thirty, so Mrs Moreno doesn't arrive till then, but Mrs Campbell starts at nine.'

Virginia Campbell should have arrived by now. So where was she? Rafferty wondered. 'Has she got the day off today?'

'No.' Astell frowned. 'At least, if she has I was unaware of it. She was off yesterday. Jasper might have agreed to her having today off as well. He didn't always remember to tell me if it was a last-minute thing.'

'I'll need her phone number, sir. If she is coming in today and hasn't already left home, it would be best if she didn't come in at all. The forensic team will be working here for some time yet.'

'Of course. You can use the telephone in my office.'

Rafferty followed him back along the short corridor, and through the comfortable anteroom. Like Moon's office, this too had a television and a video, presumably for amusing waiting clients. This television was undamaged. 'I gather Mrs Campbell's a professional astrologer?'

'That's right. She and her husband had their own astrology consultancy but their business folded when they divorced. She brought a few clients with her when she joined us, but she mainly helps me on the postal side. She also covers in the shop when Mrs Moreno is at lunch or has a day off.'

'And Mrs Moreno? Tell me about her.'

17

'Mrs Moreno's a widow. She works in the shop and has nothing to do with the main work of the consultancy.'

'Have Mrs Moreno and Mrs Campbell worked here long?'

'No. I've worked with Jasper for five years, three as a business manager and two as a partner, but it's only in the last twelve months that the postal side has really increased. We took Mrs Campbell on a year ago, and Mrs Moreno six months later when we were able to take over the lease downstairs.'

After Llewellyn had returned and confirmed that Moon's appointments had all been cancelled, Rafferty got him to phone Virginia Campbell and Mrs Moreno. There was no answer from Mrs Moreno and Llewellyn quietly advised Rafferty that he'd tried Mrs Campbell's phone but had got only the unobtainable signal. When he'd contacted BT they'd told him that her phone had been disconnected.

Rafferty raised his eyebrows and quietly commented, 'Let's hope she's not done a flit. Get someone round there quickly to check it out, Llewellyn.' Frowning, he turned back to Astell. 'I wouldn't have thought there would be much of a market in Elmhurst for New Age trinkets, sir.'

'There isn't. We sell mainly by mail order.' Astell opened a drawer and handed a glossy catalogue to Rafferty. 'I thought it would be a good idea to give our regular clients the opportunity to browse at their leisure, and Jasper agreed we should test the market.' Rafferty could see that a few browsing pop millionaires could be good for business. 'Growing numbers of people are looking for alternative ways to improve their lives, and some of the lines are very popular.'

Five minutes later, Appleby popped his head round Astell's office door. 'Inspector. Could I have a word?'

Rafferty excused himself. Llewellyn had returned and he and Rafferty followed Appleby back to Moon's office. Appleby led them over to the wall behind the desk, careful to avoid the chalk marks outlining where Moon's body had so recently lain. There were some bright green daubs on the wall. It was blood, Rafferty knew, though looking more Martian than human. The colour was an idiosyncrasy of one of Appleby's chemicals. Another turned blood to the most delightful pink.

'These marks showed up by the victim's head when I tried the orthotolidine test,' Appleby told them. 'They're not very clear, I'm afraid. Looks like somebody tried to wash them off. Any ideas?'

Rafferty couldn't make much of them and said so. 'What do you make of them?' he asked Appleby.

'They were definitely drawn rather than splashed, and drawn by the dead man, most likely. I noticed his right index finger was bloodstained.'

Llewellyn hunkered down beside them and studied the marks for a few moments before he ventured an opinion. 'Could be an attempt at a name. Ian, say, or Isaac, and Moon never got beyond the first letter.' Llewellyn pointed. 'See? The first "I" is fairly weak. The second is a better attempt.'

Rafferty contradicted him. 'I doubt it's a name. If it was, and it meant anything significant, Moon's killer would only have needed to pick up Moon's finger and alter the lettering, to a "J" for John.' He glanced slyly at Llewellyn. 'Or "L" for—'

Llewellyn didn't give him a chance to go on. 'The murderer seems to have considered the marks important enough to have made an attempt to get rid of them.'

'Probably just rattled by the sight of the bright blood on the white wall. Even killers can have weak stomachs, you know. Moon had just been hit on the head. I doubt his brain was functioning sufficiently to write anything meaningful.' He stood up, pulling rank and closing the discussion, and his workaholic Catholic conscience immediately began to berate him. *Do you have to be so childish, Rafferty?* it asked him. Yes, he snapped silently back. I do. Why don't you mind your own bloody business?

The trouble was that Llewellyn could be such an all-fired know-all. And he was so often right in his deductions, and Rafferty so often wrong, that he frequently got on Rafferty's nerves.

Defensively, he reminded himself that, although Llewellyn might have more education and brain-power he had yet to solve a case, and immediately felt better.

'Maybe you're right. Look into it,' he now magnanimously invited Llewellyn. 'See how many people Moon knew with names beginning with "I".' Llewellyn gave a stiff nod in acknowledgement. Personally, Rafferty doubted there'd be any such acquaintances. Or, if there were, there'd be none who'd had the opportunity to murder Moon.

19

'Seeing as you've spurned the first of my clues,' Appleby broke in, 'how about taking a look at the second? You'll like this one,' he promised. 'There are several nice bloody fingerprints on the outside of the window sill. Definitely *not* the dead man's. Fraser's taken an impression of them.'

Rafferty waved another olive branch at Llewellyn's poker-face. 'That sounds more like it, hey, Dafyd? Something to get your teeth into.'

'If you say so, sir,' Llewellyn replied woodenly.

Irritated all over again, Rafferty opened his mouth, but, before he could say anything, a sudden commotion from the stairway stopped him.

A voice yelling, 'Come back! You can't go up there,' was followed by the pounding of heavy copper's feet on the stairs.

Rafferty strode across the room and flung the door open. 'What the hell's going on?' he demanded.

A woman of about thirty stood at the head of the stairs. Looking sheepish and flustered, PC Smales stammered his apologies. 'She sidled past me when I was looking the other way, sir.'

Rafferty guessed she was the Latin American woman, Mercedes Moreno, that Astell had mentioned. Dressed completely in black, a long flowing creation, covered by straight midnight-dark hair, her skin was very pale, unnaturally so, he thought, as if she was ill or had deliberately powdered it that way for effect. She looked like an extremely exotic witch.

Smales, putting as much authority into his voice as his twenty years could muster, said, 'Come along now, miss. You've no right to be here.' His colour deepened when the woman ignored him. There was an air of suppressed excitement about her, and although she was doing her best to conceal it, the fluttering muscle in her cheek gave the lie to her efforts. She had still said nothing. Her silence only disconcerted the young officer even more. He gripped her arm, but she shook him off as if he were no more than a minor irritation and he stood irresolute and uncertain until Rafferty took pity on him and dismissed him.

The woman fixed her great dark eyes on Rafferty. 'Jaspair is dead, is he not?'

'You are Mrs Mercedes Moreno, I take it?'

'Of course. Who else would I be?'

Who else, indeed? Rafferty asked himself. 'Would you mind telling me how you knew Mr Moon was dead?' Dispensing with Superintendent Bradley's preferred brand of crawling civility, he demanded sharply of Astell as, in response to the noise, he came out of his office, 'Did you ring Mrs Moreno to tell her of Moon's death while you were waiting for us to arrive?' Astell denied it.

'Edwin has told me nothing.' Her expression haughty, as if she considered the answering of police questions to be beneath her, she added, 'I read the Tarot for Jaspair yesterday during my lunch break. Each card told of sudden happenings and great changes. First, he drew the Death card.' Showing a gift for timing the late Olivier might have envied, she paused dramatically, waiting for a reaction. When even Rafferty failed to oblige, she went on, 'Admittedly, this card indicates the end of a natural cycle rather than death itself, but even so . . . Next, it was the Ten of Swords, which warns of trials and tribulations, and the Tower, which represents the defeat of false philosophies, and, finally, the Page of Swords, which warns of a deceitful person.' She paused once more and gazed from face to face, before telling them with a proud toss of her head, 'I am *vidente* – fey, I think you call it. But, even without the warnings from the cards, I sensed danger for Jaspair; negative auras surrounded him and I warned him to take care.' Solemnly, she added, 'It is a pity he did not listen to me.'

At a loss, Rafferty was careful to avoid Llewellyn's eye. He was still fumbling around for an appropriate response when a prolonged bout of wheezy coughing from Astell saved him the trouble.

'Sorry.' Astell apologized, and explained, 'Bronchitis. Suffered from it for years.'

'You should live in a warmer climate, Edwin,' Mercedes told him with a silky concern that, in Rafferty's jaundiced view, sounded overly effusive. 'Have I not told you this before? Always you will have this problem until you do.'

'A sensible suggestion, if lacking in practicality,' was Astell's terse comment. 'My life, my wife, my work are here.'

'None of them are of any use to you if you are dead,' she told him prosaically. 'And I thought you were so much improved yesterday.' She felt his forehead and he backed away in irritation. 'You are very hot. You should go home and go to bed.'

21

If anyone could blow their nose in a manner that said clearly Mind your own business, Astell did so. He put his handkerchief away. 'How can I, with-with Jasper dead? Someone's got to keep the business afloat. Or are you suggesting I leave you in charge?'

Mercedes Moreno's eyes glittered angrily at the rebuke, but she said no more. After a few moments' uncomfortable silence, Rafferty asked, 'And how did Mr Moon take your, er, your warning, Mrs Moreno?'

Disdainfully, she told him, 'He accused me of, how you say, fixing the pack. He never take me seriously. As if I would do such a thing. I was upset that he should think I might. He thought I made practical joke.' Her voice was shrill with outrage, though whether at Moon's accusation, Astell's rebuke, or his own scepticism, Rafferty couldn't say. 'I never joke.'

Rafferty could believe it. She reminded him of sombre, history-book portraits of long-dead and fanatically devout Spaniards at the time of the Inquisition. As a lapsed Catholic, such obsessive ntensity always gave him a shiver of dread.

Nostrils flaring, she declared, 'El Señor Moon and La Señora Campbell seemed to think that because I have none of their pieces of paper that my skills are the second rate sort, fit only for selling trinkets in the shop. Is not true. In my own country I was highly thought of, but here—' She made a noise of disgust.

Half expecting her to stamp her foot and burst into a flood of incomprehensible Spanish, Rafferty wondered why she hadn't stayed in her own country if they had thought so highly of her. She had made no comment about Astell's opinion of her skills, but it was clear he didn't rate them very highly. If he had, he wouldn't have been so sharp with her.

She was clearly a highly excitable woman, fond of dramatizing herself. It was unlikely they'd ever get to the bottom of her outlandish claims, and Rafferty, refusing to let her wrong-foot him, ushered them all into Astell's office and shut the door.

'Perhaps you would both like to tell me when you last saw Mr Moon?' he suggested. 'You first, Mrs Moreno.'

'I left at ten past six, a little later than usual as I had to get changed. I went upstairs to say goodnight to Jaspair. He was in his office.'

'Was he alone?'

'Yes. But the cleaner, she was in the kitchen. Jaspair tease me again about my warning. I was upset that he made mock of me and told him so. I went straight from work to Señor and Señora Astell. Señora Astell had invited me over. Yesterday was the anniversary of her beloved father's death,' she explained. 'She wanted to mark it properly. English people, I find, have little feeling for such rituals, but not Señora Astell. She has the proper respect for her family, and although she is not Catholic, she knew that in my religion we show the dead due reverence; we pray for them, light candles for them to lessen the time they must spend in purgatory. She has a little shrine to her father and she asked me to come to share the evening with her, her husband and an elderly lady friend of her father's. It was an honour to be asked.'

'What time did this, er, occasion start and finish?' Rafferty asked Astell.

'It started about six-thirty and ended quite early, about eight. Clara Davies, my late father-in-law's old friend, is quite elderly now, and doesn't enjoy late nights, not that these affairs have ever gone on very late.' Suddenly, as if sorry about his earlier sharpness, he smiled at the Peruvian woman. 'Mrs Moreno was concerned that my wife would be anxious and came a little early. She knew my wife planned to serve a light buffet afterwards, and wanted to help.'

'Is the least I could do,' she told him softly. 'I am very fond of Señora Astell and it was an important occasion for her. I offered to help clear up before I left the first time, but Mr Astell would not hear of it.' She smiled a smug smile. 'But I got my way in the end. That is why I leave the gloves,' she explained. 'So I have an excuse to return. The cleaner had gone home sick and is not right that Mr Astell should have to do women's work.'

Astell seemed to find her outdated attitude embarrassing. 'I only had to load up the dishwasher,' he explained. 'Not such an arduous task, after all.'

'Even so,' she began. Rafferty, tiring of this dish-talk, interrupted her to ask, 'I gather you finally left a little before nine p.m.?' She nodded.

He turned to Astell. 'And you, sir? What time did you last see Mr Moon?'

'About five-thirty. Jasper's four o'clock client had left about half

23

an hour earlier. He'd have been alone once Mrs Hadleigh left at seven o'clock. Although Jasper was healthy enough, he wasn't a particularly fit man, Inspector. He'd have been easy prey for any violent intruder.'

Rafferty sighed and glanced at Llewellyn. Edwin Astell seemed determined to believe that an anonymous intruder had killed Moon, as if convinced that repetition of this belief would incline the police to share it. Rafferty wished he *could* share it; he didn't relish the thought that one of Moon's well-known and probably litigious clients had killed him. If they had, and Rafferty failed to nail them thoroughly, he foresaw claims for wrongful arrest flying around his unprotected head. For he could be sure that Bradley would promptly disown him.

Get a grip, Rafferty, he warned himself. Worry about making an arrest when you've got a firm suspect, not before. Still, that locked cashbox was interesting. To lock up afterwards was the natural instinct of the security-conscious owner, or conscientious employee, not of a thief. It was possible that the murder was an inside job and the window was broken and the money taken afterwards in order to deflect suspicion. He said nothing of this to Astell. 'And you went straight home?' he asked.

'Yes. I bathed and changed into my dinner suit. As Mrs Moreno mentioned, my wife regards these anniversary evenings as special, so I like to make an effort. My wife is a semi-invalid, Inspector. She doesn't get out much and does very little socializing, so these evenings are that much more important to her.'

Rafferty nodded. 'I didn't realize, sir. It must be difficult for you.'

'Oh, she's not in a wheelchair or anything like that, Inspector.' Astell frowned. 'It might be better if she were. If she had a specific *physical* problem then at least the doctors might be able to do something for her. As it is, beyond saying she's highly strung, over-anxious and prone to the muscular aches and pains and exhaustion brought about by her anxiety syndrome, they are unable to tell me much.' He enlarged a little more on his wife's poor health, as though pleased to find a sympathetic audience, before he carried on with his explanation. 'Anyway, we hold this little remembrance service every year for her father, Alan Carstairs. Usually, we have more guests, but my wife didn't feel up to the extra effort this time, so it was just the four of us.'

24

After a few more questions, Rafferty let Mrs Moreno go. 'Would you accompany my sergeant so the fingerprint man can take your prints?' he asked. 'Simply for purposes of elimination,' he explained before she could protest. Having expected her to make a fuss, he was surprised when she agreed with no difficulty. When she had gone with Llewellyn, Rafferty turned back to Astell. 'I'm afraid you won't be able to use the premises until the forensic team have finished their work. Could be a day or two.'

Astell nodded. 'Probably little point in opening, anyway, Inspector. With Jasper gone, the only people likely to want to make appointments will be the usual ghouls.'

From Astell's drawn features, Rafferty guessed that Moon's death signalled a serious downturn in the business. Moon – to a large extent – apparently *was* the business. 'We'll do our best to keep the ghouls away, sir. I'll ask the forensic team to work as quickly as possible so you can get back to some kind of normality. One more thing. Which of your staff have keys to the premises?'

'All of them. Mrs Hadleigh, the cleaner, starts work before anyone else gets in. And, of course, the shop stays open till six o'clock to catch the returning office workers, so Mrs Moreno has a key. When Jasper is away on working trips abroad there would otherwise be no one to lock up the shop.'

'But wouldn't you or Mrs Campbell still be working?'

'No. As I told you, both Mrs Campbell and myself concentrate more on the postal side, so we work mainly office hours. Because of my wife's ill-health, I like to leave fairly promptly. She becomes upset if I'm not home when expected. Anyway, most people who require a personal consultation naturally want to see Jasper. He's the one they've heard of, you see.'

'You don't mind?'

Astell shrugged. 'We both had our niche. Some of the clients can get very emotional, very demanding. I'm better applying my skills at a distance, as it were. But Jasper is – was – splendid at dealing with such people. Besides, I spent a large part of my time on the book-keeping, and so on.'

'I understand Mr Moon was a wealthy man.' Astell nodded. 'Do you know if he made a will?'

'I've no idea.' He gave them the name of the firm of solicitors used by the business, adding, 'Though I doubt he used their services for writing a will. Knowing Jasper, he would be more likely to write it himself, particularly if the document was a simple one.'

Rafferty expressed his surprise at this, and Astell explained, 'Jasper told me that many years ago, when he first attempted to set up on his own, he had several unfortunate experiences with solicitors. The first one he tried was soon after charged with embezzlement; the second was so slow that Jasper lost the chance of leasing a property he'd set his heart on. And the third one was not only slow, but thoroughly incompetent. Consequently, Jasper had a somewhat jaundiced view of solicitors, and only used them when he had no choice.'

Llewellyn popped his head round the door. Rafferty said, 'You won't forget to check that none of Mr Moon's client files are missing before you go, sir? I'll assign one of my officers to help you.' Astell nodded.

'Llewellyn, check that the SOCOs have finished with the filing cabinet and diary, will you, before you take Mr Astell for his prints?' He turned back to Astell as Llewellyn vanished. 'There is one more thing before you go, sir. Could you let me know the name of Mr Moon's next of kin? Was he married?' Astell shook his head. 'So, who would his next of kin be?'

'I don't know. His parents were both dead and he had no brothers or sisters. He never talked about having any close family.'

'He lived alone, then?'

'Actually, Jasper didn't live alone. He, um, he lived with another man, by the name of Farley. Christian Farley.'

Rafferty stared at him for a moment before what Astell had said sank in. 'I see. Have Moon and this Mr Farley lived together long?'

'About five years, I believe.'

Rafferty felt a sinking sensation at this news. Moon and Farley's relationship had lasted longer than many modern marriages and his stomach tensed at the thought of the embarrassment and difficulties to come.

No matter how hard he tried, homosexuals always made him feel awkward; it was something else for which he could thank the Catholic Church. Although consciously he'd rejected their teachings on most things, some aspects had evidently taken *subconscious* root. Even now, he still felt a twinge of guilt whenever he used a condom, the Catholic Church having long frowned on

26

any sexual act that wasn't purely and simply for the procreation of children. And their views on homosexual unions were like something out of the Middle Ages, full of fire and brimstone warnings that unnatural practices earned an eternity in a devilish barbecue pit where they never ran out of charcoal. Rafferty wondered how he would have coped after such indoctrination if he had found his sexual inclinations to be other than male–female? Back came the answer: badly. He supposed, with all the givens, he should be thankful that awkward was all he felt in their company.

He cleared his throat. 'Is, er, is Mr Moon's . . . Is this Mr Farley likely to be at home now, do you think?'

'I imagine so. He doesn't have any kind of employment. Hasn't had any for the last two years. I'd-I'd break the news gently, Inspector. Christian can be a little emotional. Of course, he's a Cancer sun with a Pisces moon, so it's understandable. Two water signs prominent in his chart, you see.'

Rafferty stared at him in dismay. Homosexual *and* emotional. He just hoped this Farley didn't fling himself round his neck and burst into tears. He couldn't be sure that his reaction would be as sympathetic as Farley's loss warranted and Llewellyn was unlikely to be much help.

The Welshman had confided to Rafferty at the beginning of their very first case together that, when he was a boy, his minister father had insisted on him accompanying him to break news of death. His distaste for such tasks had increased with the years, and, now, such occasions rendered him even more awkward than Rafferty among homosexuals. It was one of the intellectual Welshman's more human weaknesses and Rafferty liked him the better for it.

By the time Rafferty had checked a few more points, Llewellyn had returned, and he let Astell go. After ringing the station and organizing the house-to-house team, he nominated several officers to make a start in listing Moon's client files as soon as Astell had confirmed there were none missing.

Virginia Campbell had still not turned up, though the officer assigned to check her address said a neighbour had confirmed she had been about that morning, so Rafferty ruled out the possibility of a flit. If she had reason to flit, last night would have been the time to do it. Maybe it was as Astell had said and Moon had given her a second day off without mentioning the fact. Hopefully she would return home at some point during the day, because he would need to get her statement.

'Right.' He turned to the hovering Llewellyn. 'Let's go and see Moon's boyfriend.' Rafferty told him what Astell had said, and, as he had expected, Llewellyn's long face grew appreciably longer. 'Farley has two water signs prominent, according to Astell,' Rafferty told him. 'So I reckon we can expect plenty of waterworks. Cheer up, Dafyd.' Rafferty couldn't resist the dig. 'With such sensitive palms you should have no trouble mopping him up. Let's get moving.'

Chapter Three

On the way out, Rafferty stopped to read the words painted in white Gothic script on the smoky glass of the Psychic Store. 'Personal consultations in Tarot, Astrology, Palmistry by internationally renowned reader, Jasper Moon. Make the fates work *for* you, not against you.' Oh yeah? thought Rafferty. Since when were the fates open to argument, however persuasive? Like self-employed plumbers, the fates followed their own idiosyncratic course.

The consultancy and the store seemed to offer something for everyone; the latest New Age books, charms, crystals, oils, incenses – even gemstone amulets in agate, chalcedony, jade, and so on, which possessed the power to attract 'beneficial influences' such as good luck, healing and protection.

'Seems friend Moon failed to take advantage of the beneficial influences,' Rafferty observed. 'Maybe if he'd worn the jade he wouldn't have ended up on his own consulting room floor with his head bashed in.' Llewellyn made no comment and Rafferty went on, musing more or less to himself for want of any input from the pensive Welshman.

'He must have made someone madder than hell for them to just snatch up the victim's own crystal ball and brain him with it. No finesse, no cool planning, just angry emotion.' He mentioned his earlier thought that Moon might have used the information he acquired from his clients to further enrich himself. 'It would certainly explain the type of murder and the panicked attempt to make it look like the work of a burglar. Of course, it still doesn't explain why the box was locked.' He glanced at the still quiet Llewellyn and said, 'Come on, Dafyd, give your brains an airing. Think it's likely Jasper Moon was into blackmail?'

29

'I doubt it. Why would he put his lucrative professional career in jeopardy for the sake of a dangerous sideline?' Llewellyn's dark eyes were thoughtful. 'Still, he catered for those likely to have more to hide than most: rock stars, actresses, and so on. If he was into blackmail, the famous would be the obvious target.'

Contrarily, now that Llewellyn seemed to be taking his black-mail angle more seriously, Rafferty changed his mind. 'I'm not so sure now I've thought about it. Let's face it, showbiz types tend to rattle their skeletons at the flash of a camera, on the principle that any publicity is good publicity. If you read a *decent* paper on a Sunday instead of those dreary highbrow ones, you'd know that. Every week sees them pouring their hearts out to the sex-obsessed Great British Sunday tabloids. Great stuff, it is. You don't know what you're missing.' Rafferty put on a falsetto voice. ' "I long for my lost love child," cries sexy soap star; "I'm ashamed of my promiscuous past," confesses born-again ex-porno queen; "Toyboys were my downfall," admits ageing theatre dame.' He paused, lost the falsetto, and demanded, 'How likely is it that people like that would leave much for Moon – or anyone else – to rake over?'

Llewellyn shrugged absently, said, 'Not very, I suppose,' and lapsed into silence again.

Exasperated, Rafferty sighed, surprised to find he had been looking forward to thrashing out the pros and cons of the case with the intellectual Welshman. Not that he'd admit that to Llewellyn, of course. He already confounded Rafferty's favourite theories; God knew what heights of contradiction he'd achieve if encouraged. But Llewellyn's reluctance to enter into the spirit of the thing was frustrating. Rafferty knew what the trouble was, of course. The sooner they broke the bad news to Moon's boy-friend, the better. 'No.' Rafferty was pensive. 'I think we'll find this murder's an inside job. Have you ever known a burglar lock up a cashbox after helping himself to the stash? Even less to return the key to where he found it.' Llewellyn muttered something noncommittal. Rafferty gave up, turned and made for the car.

It was October, the weather wet and windy. Barely a month ago they'd been roasting in a heatwave; now, soggy leaves from the tree-lined High Street made the pavements treacherous. Rafferty leaned on the car roof, nodded back at the Psychic Store, and confided, 'Ma's into all this, you know. Astrology, palmistry, tea-

30

leaves. You name it, she's into it.' He grinned. 'I think she's hoping to see a tall, dark handsome wife for me.'

'I wouldn't have thought Mrs Rafferty would approve of such practices. Doesn't the Catholic Church frown on that sort of thing?'

Rafferty snorted. "Course. They frown on most activities that don't involve kneeling and praying, making Catholic babies, or getting their hands on the dibs. But, on that sort of thing, Ma and the Pope have taken independent lines. And as she says, if Catholics didn't have some vices, the priests would have nothing to rant about from the pulpit. Doing them a favour, really.

'My father now, he preferred to patronize the turf accountant. But he was generally sorry after. Great one for confessing, he was. A regular Mr Micawber.' He paused and looked at Llewellyn. 'Yes, a regular Mr Micawber. Only with him it wasn't the money he liked to balance out, it was the sins. Like the sensible Dubliner he was, he made sure he got the current week's sins cleared away at confession before he got started on the next lot. That way he could be certain he'd only have one week's sins to account for when he met his Maker. Balancing the heavenly books, he called it.'

'Sounds eminently practical, if a little blasphemous. I wonder in what light the Almighty would regard it?'

Rafferty shrugged. 'I don't reckon my old man ever considered that. For all the priest's efforts, I think he regarded God as some kind of superior bookie who would be too pleased to notch another short-odds soul up on the winners' board to quibble. He'd have died happy; he was well up on the odds at the time he fell off that scaffolding, as he'd only been to confession three days be—' He broke off abruptly. 'Hell's bells. I've just remembered. I promised to take my ma to see a bloody clairvoyant next week. I wouldn't have agreed, only she caught me at a weak moment. Isn't that just like a woman?'

'Weak moment?' Llewellyn echoed.

'All right, I was drunk. A pre-birthday celebration. Ma wants to get in contact with the old man. Gives me the creeps. I could do without the star man's murder at the same time.'

'Why does she want to contact him now?' Llewellyn asked. 'Surely your father died many years ago?'

'He did. One of his cronies moved abroad and recently came

over on a visit. He found out Ma's address and looked her up. He told her the old man had had a big win on the gee-gees a month or two before he died. Apparently it coincided with one of his periods of remorse. Anyway, to cut a long story short, this crony reckons the old man invested his winnings in some kind of insurance policy. Ma's been through the house like a dose of salts, turned the place upside down, searched through a lifetime's accumulation of papers, but she hasn't been able to find this policy. I told her that he either cashed it in five minutes after taking it out, or that it got left behind when we moved down here, but she won't have it. That's why she's going to this clairvoyant. She wants to ask Dad what he's done with it.' Rafferty grinned. 'I wouldn't mind, but he never told her anything voluntarily when he was alive. I can't see him starting now.'

He was about to open the car door when he noticed an elderly woman arguing with Smales outside the front door of Constellation Consultants. As Rafferty approached, he heard him tell the woman firmly, 'I'm sorry, madam, but you can't go in. There's been a death on the premises and . . .'

The woman swayed slightly, clutched the constable's arm, and, in a shaky voice, asked, 'Do you know when? How?'

Rafferty interrupted her questioning. The woman hadn't asked *who* had been killed, he noticed. It certainly hadn't taken long for the news of Moon's murder to travel round the town. He was surprised they weren't already fighting off Fleet Street's hordes.

'This lady wants to get into Mr Moon's offices, sir,' Smales explained. 'I told her—'

Rafferty stopped him. 'It's all right, Smales, I'll deal with it.' He turned to the woman. 'The constable's right, madam. You can't go in there.' He couldn't help but wonder why she should *want* to. She hardly seemed the type to be interested in oils and incenses, never mind the other services they offered. For one thing, she didn't look as if she'd be able to afford them. She was cheaply dressed in a coat of man-made tweed-look fabric, and, to judge by her swollen feet and ankles, she would prefer Radox bath salts any day. Surely she wasn't one of the consultancy's regulars?

After Rafferty had introduced himself and Llewellyn, he suggested they sit on one of the wooden benches that lined the semi-pedestrianized High Street.

'So, madam,' he asked her once they were seated, 'what is your connection with the Psychic Store? Do you know Mr Moon well?'

'No. I couldn't say I knew *Mr Moon* well. Hardly at all, in fact. I always finish work before he comes in. It's Mr Astell I have dealings with. I do the cleaning,' she explained, as she saw Rafferty's puzzlement.

'You're Mrs Hadleigh!' he exclaimed. 'It's lucky I bumped into you as I wanted a word.'

She clutched her shabby shopping bag to her bosom and asked defensively, 'Why? Why should you want to talk to me?'

Rafferty was gentle with her. The news of Moon's death had obviously shocked her. 'It wasn't a natural death, Mrs Hadleigh. Jasper Moon was murdered. It's usual to talk to anyone who knew the murder victim. There's really nothing for you to worry about. We can leave it till later today if you'd rather.'

This seemed to reassure her. She relaxed her grip on the bag and shook her head. 'No, no, that's all right.' Hesitantly, she asked, 'Have you any idea who killed him?'

'It's early days yet,' he told her. 'But we're hopeful.' She gazed back at him, nodding, as if reassured by his confident words. He wished he was. He should at least have armed himself with a good luck agate amulet before coming out with such a rash statement.

'When will I be able to get in to clean?'

'It'll be a few days yet. But I understood from Mr Astell that you cleaned there last night. You weren't expected in this morning.'

'It's all right for Mr Astell to tell me not to come in. He's got a rich wife. I can't afford to lose two hours' pay just because I had to go to the hospital yesterday. Besides, Mr Moon made enough mess, on his own, to keep half-a-dozen cleaners busy, so Mr Astell needn't think I expected to be idle.'

Rafferty nodded as though he found her explanation eminently reasonable. Yet he couldn't help wondering how she had expected to do her cleaning when, but for Moon's murder, the shop would now be open and clients arriving? Perhaps she had expected to be able to hoover round them? 'I believe you've only worked for the consultancy for a few weeks?'

She nodded. 'That's right. As I said, yesterday I worked here from five o'clock to seven o'clock. Then I went on to Mr and Mrs Astell's house to help clear up after their little do. He gave me a glass of sherry in honour of the occasion, though he probably wished he hadn't after.' She glanced at Rafferty in some embarrassment. 'I don't normally drink, you see, and I came over all dizzy. Of course, because of Mrs Astell's ill-health, they keep the place terribly over-heated and I'd been on my feet all day. Anyway, Mr Astell ordered me a taxi and persuaded me to go home. And after he paid for the taxi, I could hardly expect him to pay me for the evening as well. That's why I thought I'd come and clean this morning, only, what with the hospital appointment and then working so late on top of my other jobs, it was a long, tiring day.' She had yet to get over it, Rafferty thought; her face seemed drawn, and her eyes had deep smudges under them. What a way to have to eke out a pension. 'Of course, this morning I overslept. That's why I'm so behind today,' she told him. 'I just rushed straight round here and never gave a thought to the shop being open, or else I'd have left them till last.'

Rafferty nodded, glad to have one puzzle solved. Anxious not to alarm her, but conscious of the fact that she could have been the last person to see Moon alive, he asked casually, 'I gather Mr Moon was still working when you left the offices.' She nodded. 'Was he alone, do you know?'

She didn't answer immediately. Rafferty was about to repeat the question when she said, 'Sorry. It's been such a shock. Mr Moon was in his office when I left. But he wasn't alone.' She paused and added quietly, 'He had a client with him.'

Rafferty's sharp demand of, 'A client? Are you sure?' made her jump. Quickly, he apologized. But it was their first lead and to get it so early in the case was more than he had hoped for. She confirmed it. Trying to control the excitement in his voice, Rafferty asked, 'Do you know this client's name, Mrs Hadleigh?'

She hesitated, bit her lip and gazed across the road as if seeking inspiration. Rafferty's hopes began to subside. But then she told him firmly, 'Mr Moon called him Mr Henderson.'

'Did you see him, Mrs Hadleigh?' Llewellyn questioned. She nodded and Rafferty began to get excited again. 'A description would be useful,' the Welshman prompted.

A faint flush coloured her cheeks as, haltingly, she told him. 'He was about fifty, I'd say, with thinning grey hair. Quite a stocky build. His clothes were shabby, so I'm surprised he could afford

Mr Moon's fees. He seemed nervous. He almost dropped the tea Mr Moon asked me to make for them.'

Rafferty was astonished that she had been so observant. Most people barely noticed what day it was, never mind anything else. Still, it was fortunate for them that she had. 'These cups – I gather you washed them up?' There had been none on the desk or in the sink.

She nodded. 'Washed, dried and put away. Mr Astell's always very firm about the place looking clean and tidy.' Rafferty was surprised that she should interrupt a consultation simply to collect the dirty cups. Surely Moon, or his client, for that matter, would have objected? However, before he could broach the matter, she gave a violent shiver, as a cold wind whistled along the High Street and he realized that he could scarcely have chosen a place less conducive to questioning a witness. The wind lifted the previous night's litter and whirled it in a fitful dance about their ankles. Someone had discarded a blue and red striped umbrella in the gutter; the material fluttered in the wind as though trying to rise – its spine broken if not its spirit, thought Rafferty whimsically as he watched it – only to sink back again after each abortive effort. Then the wind dropped and the umbrella accepted its fate and lay still. Rafferty made a mental note to tell the SOCOs to pick it up, just in case.

Mrs Hadleigh shivered again and Rafferty took her arm. 'It's too chilly here to chat. Could you come to the station and help our photo-fit expert to construct a picture of this client? What you've told us is very important. Apart from the murderer, this Mr Henderson may have been the last person to see Mr Moon alive.'

She hesitated again, and then gave an anxious little nod. Rafferty guessed she was concerned about being late for the next cleaning job of the morning and he reassured her. 'I'm sure it won't take long.' He helped her up and led her over to the car. 'I'll arrange for a car to take you home – or wherever else you need to go – afterwards. Llewellyn.' He tossed the car keys to the Welshman. 'You can drive.' Rafferty only hoped it would help take his mind off their next appointment.

As soon as they had deposited Mrs Hadleigh with the photo-fit man, and Rafferty had uttered further assurances, they left them to it. There was too much work ahead of them to spare any of it holding a witness's hand.

'Right,' he said. 'Let's get on with it. I want you to send WPC Green along to the local Astrological Society. Astell said he and Moon were both members. I also want her to go to the TV studios where Moon did his morning show. Tell her to ask around and see what she can find out. About Moon, Astell, the rest of the staff and the set-up there.' Liz Green was good with people, Rafferty knew. Had a way of drawing them out, just like Moon. 'Get someone to contact the editors of the magazines he supplied with astrological forecasts. He'd worked for several of them for some time. Might learn something interesting.' He paused, thinking. 'Oh, and get Moon's phone checked out. I want to know what numbers were called on it. Come back when you've got all that organized and we'll go and see the boyfriend.'

Rafferty could almost believe that the wind, which had seemed to quieten while they were in the station, had waited for them to re-emerge on to the street, before reasserting itself. Its icy breath was bitter and shrieked painfully in his ears. He tugged his coat collar as high over his ears as it would reach, and put up with it. It was only a short walk to Moon's home in Quaker Street, not worth a car ride. Moon's flat was in the old Dutch quarter of town, a chic, expensive area, which confirmed that star gazing was a profitable line.

The man who opened the door to their knock was fat, fair and fiftyish. Rafferty was surprised. He had expected a much younger man; the equivalent of the bimbo that successful heterosexual males liked to hang from their arm. 'Mr Farley?' Rafferty queried.

He nodded and gave them a hesitant, questioning smile that didn't reach his eyes, which were a flat green colour and reminded Rafferty of those of a snake. They slid rapidly from Rafferty to Llewellyn and back again before he asked politely, 'What can I do for you?'

Farley's voice was well modulated, though Rafferty got the impression it was practised rather than natural. Rafferty showed him his warrant card and introduced himself and Llewellyn. 'Perhaps we might come in?' Rafferty suggested. 'I'm afraid we have some bad news for you.'

Farley stared at him. His skin flushed and then the colour receded, leaving two stark pink blotches high up on his cheeks. Surprisingly elegant fingers clutched at each other as he exclaimed, 'Oh, God, something's happened to Jasper, hasn't it?' Anxiety had made his voice curiously high-pitched, and now it became even higher. 'Tell me, tell me, for the love of God. Has something happened to Jasper?'

Rafferty, mindful of Astell's warning, suggested again, more firmly, 'If we could just come in?'

Farley remained planted in the doorway, his expression uncertain, then he stood back to let them in, carefully shutting the door behind them before he clutched Rafferty's arm. 'Tell me. Please. What's happened?'

Resisting the impulse to throw off the clinging hand, Rafferty steered him towards what he hoped was the living room. It was a spacious flat, as colourful as Moon's office had been, but without the solar system decor and spread over the upper floor of three of the narrow houses, Rafferty estimated. 'I think you should sit down, Mr Farley.' He waited till Farley had perched on the edge of a stark black leather settee before he sat down in the armchair opposite. 'I'm afraid Mr Moon is dead. He . . .'

Christian Farley's hands flew to his face and he stared at them over his fingers, shaking his head all the while. His shock seemed genuine, Rafferty noted. What he could see of his fair-skinned face was pasty. Small fists now pressed against his mouth, Farley moaned, rocking to and fro on the leather settee. It creaked protestingly with each movement.

Rafferty glanced at Llewellyn for moral support. As expected, the Welshman avoided his eye and stared determinedly over Farley's head. Rafferty struggled on, silently cursing Llewellyn and wishing he'd brought a WPC with him. 'I'm afraid it's true, sir. He was found dead in his office this morning by his business partner.' He paused to gather strength and then said quickly, 'I have to tell you that he was murdered.'

Farley's hands came away from his face. His mouth fell open, and, silently, he repeated Rafferty's last word, before he recommenced his rocking, his movements accompanied by the off-key complaints of the settee. Rafferty, at a loss, instinctively followed his ma's usual response in a crisis and ordered Llewellyn to find the kitchen and make tea. With an alacrity to obey his orders that under other circumstances would have been gratifying, Llewellyn went. He was gone some time, and, if Rafferty hadn't known better, he would have suspected he was hunting for a bottle of Dutch courage.

By the time Llewellyn returned with the tea Farley had quietened. He sat huddled in the middle of the big settee, looking lost, making no response to Rafferty's awkward sympathetic overtures. Llewellyn gave Farley's shoulder a tentative pat, put the tea on the table in front of him and retreated to the far side of the room. Rafferty, who had confidently predicted tears, noted that Farley's eyes were dry. They appeared puzzled, his forehead faintly creased, as if he was thinking through what he had learned. He turned questioning eyes to Rafferty. 'Have you any idea who killed him?'

Rafferty shook his head. 'Not yet. It's possible Mr Moon disturbed a burglar, as his office was broken into.'

Farley exclaimed, 'Not again!'

'I'm sorry?'

'We were burgled here earlier this year. While we were on one of Jas, Jasper's regular trips to the States.' He worried at his bottom lip. 'And I thought . . .' He broke off. 'It's almost as if someone has a grudge against us.' The possibility, not unnaturally, seemed to unnerve him. As he picked up his tea, the cup rattled against the saucer, betraying his agitation.

Rafferty had never liked coincidences. And although there had been a spate of burglaries in the town in recent months, he felt that this coincidence might be of more significance than most. 'What was taken from the flat, sir?'

Farley glanced up with a start. 'Very little, that's what was so surprising. They even left the video and the TV. Jasper's study desk and both bedrooms had been gone through, but apart from some jewellery nothing else of value was taken. What was taken from Jasper's office?'

'A sum of money.'

Farley's gaze narrowed. His green eyes, accentuated by the daylight that streamed in at the windows, looked more snakelike than ever, as he asked, 'How much?'

'Mr Moon's business partner says a thousand pounds.'

Farley digested the information silently for a few seconds. 'But, surely . . . ?'

'Yes, sir,' Rafferty encouraged. 'You were saying?'

'Nothing.' Farley glanced quickly at him before shaking his head. 'It doesn't matter.' He lapsed into silence, but he couldn't seem to help himself, and burst out, 'It's just that it seems – odd. If Jasper was-was working, the lights would be on. At least—' He broke off again, before asking hesitantly, 'Were they on?' Rafferty nodded, and Farley sat back, his eyes calculating. 'Would a burglar break in under such circumstances?'

Unwilling to share his suspicions concerning the burglary with Farley, Rafferty gave him the line he had prepared earlier. 'I'm afraid the modern criminal often doesn't care if premises are occupied, sir. Could be a drug addict, desperate enough for money not to bother with the usual precautions. But, at this stage, I'm keeping an open mind.' As he said this, he became conscious of Llewellyn. He was standing, his gaze now fixed on the floor, but Rafferty sensed the thought waves emanating from him. Keeping an open mind? they commented ironically. That must be a first.

After projecting a few strongly worded thought waves of his own in return, Rafferty concentrated his attention on Farley. 'You said you wondered if someone bore Mr Moon a grudge. Do you know if he had any enemies? Someone who had threatened him, perhaps?'

Farley shook his head. 'None that I know of. But Jasper was very successful and success always breeds envy, particularly in this country. I'm afraid the British have always found failure a more attractive trait.'

Rafferty had thought he had detected a slight accent. 'I take it you're not British, Mr Farley?'

'No. I'm from South Africa. The Cape. But I've lived here for more than twenty years.'

'I understand you've known Mr Moon for five years.'

Farley gave a twisted smile, as though he found Rafferty's biblical phraseology amusing. 'Yes, it would have been five years on the eighteenth of next month. Our Wooden Anniversary. I was going to get Jasper a small carved sculpture of our sun signs, intertwined. Like a lovers' knot, you know?' The thought clearly upset him, for now his eyes held the hint of moisture that thus

39

far had been missing. Turning away, he blew his nose with a feminine neatness.

Rafferty shifted uncomfortably, as the thought struck him that, in Farley's eyes, if not society's, he had been widowed; widowed, moreover, without any of the support a legal widow might expect. He opened his mouth to say something sympathetic, but, realizing that anything he said would sound, to Farley, either patronizing, trite or insincere, he gave up and waited for Farley to get control of himself, then gently resumed the questioning.

'I gather you and Mr Moon lived here together?' Farley nodded. 'You must have been concerned when he didn't come home last night.'

'I wasn't here.' He seemed to feel he had to defend himself. 'I was visiting a-a friend for a day or two. I only got back this morning. Naturally, I assumed Jasper had gone to work. Of course, if I'd looked in his bedroom I'd have seen his bed hadn't been slept in.'

So they slept apart. Rafferty wondered if that was usual in their circumstances. Or whether, like ordinary married couples who chose to sleep separately, it hinted that their relationship had cooled? Had they had an argument? Was that why Farley had gone to see this *friend*? he wondered, and why the tears had been so long in coming and so sparse? Yet Farley had been planning to buy Moon an expensive anniversary gift, a gift that showed thought and care, albeit presumably bought with Moon's money. 'I'm afraid I'll have to ask you for the name and address of this friend, Mr Farley.'

As he realized the significance of the question, Farley's face flushed, and he opened his mouth as if to protest. But then, presumably thinking better of remonstrating, he told them, 'His name's Turner – Andrew Turner.' He added the address.

'I don't like to ask this, Mr Farley, but as Mr Moon's been murdered it will be necessary for us to look through his things to see if we can find anything that might help our investigations.'

Farley frowned. 'What sort of thing?'

'It's hard to say. Could be a letter, or a diary. Anything that might help us discover if anyone did have a grudge against him. Where would he be likely to keep such things?'

'In his bedroom or study, I imagine.'

The study was small, no more than twelve feet square. Rafferty guessed this was where Moon had given consultations for intimates. Apart from a computer of the same make as the one in Moon's office, it contained similar books, works by past, presumably revered practitioners of their art; a chap called Cheiro seemed to feature prominently, Rafferty noticed. As soon as Farley left, they began their search in earnest.

Moon was a hoarder. They found piles of circulars, newspaper cuttings featuring the dead man, as well as a yellowing reminder from the Blood Donor Centre to somebody called Hedges.

'Hedges,' Rafferty murmured, as he showed the reminder to Llewellyn. 'Reckon that was Moon's real name?'

'Possibly. It shouldn't be difficult to find out. Farley must know.'

Rafferty nodded and put the letter in his pocket. Eager to shake off the feelings of inadequacy he had felt in Farley's presence, he joked, 'Reminds me of one of the old "Hancock's Half Hour" series on the telly. The one about the blood donor. Do you remember the bit where he says to the doctor—'

'I rarely watch television,' Llewellyn interrupted. 'But I think that was before my time, anyway.'

Reminded that another birthday was looming, Rafferty said tartly, 'It's available on video. You should get it. Tony Hancock might be dead, but then so are those ancient Greeks you're so fond of quoting, and at least he's a damn sight more entertaining.' Disgruntled, he carried on with the search.

In one of the desk drawers he found a stack of autographed photographs of Moon. His signature was written with such an exuberant flourish that Rafferty's lip curled. '*Jasper Moon*,' he snorted. 'What sort of a name is that, anyway?'

'Mr Astell said it was originally the victim's professional name. But I gather he legally adopted it as his own years ago.'

'What did he want with a professional name?' Rafferty scoffed. 'The man was nothing more than a glorified end of pier charlatan.'

'Your prejudices are showing, sir,' Llewellyn remarked laconically. 'Have you forgotten the Superintendent's politeness programme? I suspect that when he finally realizes the descriptive qualities of that acronym with which you provided him, like Shylock he'll be satisfied with nothing less than his pound of flesh. *Your* flesh. If you don't want to supply him with an extra knife, it might be wise to keep such opinions to yourself.'

Rafferty knew he was right. It had been idiotic of him to give in to the impulse when Bradley had asked for suggestions. But he had a perverse, anti-authority streak, which he guessed stemmed from his schooldays. Ironic, really, that he had fallen – or been pushed – into the police force, the most authoritarian career of them all. The trouble was that the pompous Bradley brought this perverse streak out in spades.

'I'll be careful, don't worry. Anyway, if he doesn't like being considered a pimp, he shouldn't act like one.'

Llewellyn shrugged, as much as to say, Don't say I didn't warn you, before adding, 'It'll probably amuse you to know that Moon chose the name Jasper because he thought it singularly appropriate to his skills. It means "Treasure Master", the treasure, in this case, presumably being knowledge.'

Rafferty's lips turned down. 'More likely to refer to his talent for acquiring booty. Look around you,' he invited, as he pointed out the expensive knick-knacks scattered around the room. 'This place is more like Blackbeard's den than a study.' He stuffed Moon's stack of photographs in his jacket pocket. At least they'd come in handy for the house-to-house enquiries.

They turned up the dead man's passport. As expected, it was in the name of Moon. There was no sign of a will or a birth certificate. Probably sprang to life from under a moonbeam, thought Rafferty sourly. His rummaging dislodged yet another photograph, this time a dog-eared black and white snapshot featuring a smiling, gummy-mouthed infant. The year 1956 was inscribed on the back. Rafferty thrust the photo back in the drawer. 'Let's take a look in the bedroom.'

The bedroom contained a television and video, with a stack of popular film tapes stored underneath. Surprisingly, he found a single tape in Moon's wardrobe. It was right at the back of the top shelf, stashed behind some shoe boxes. It looked different from the rest. It was in a plain, but distinctive emerald green video case with an advertising sticker from a firm called Memory Lane Videos, who specialized in transferring old cine film to video.

Curious to discover why anyone should attempt to conceal one tape, Rafferty switched on the TV and video and inserted it.

'If we're to catch the killer, we'd better try to learn something more of the victim,' he commented, as he sat on the edge of the bed. 'Perhaps this will tell us something useful?'

From the name on the box, he had expected some footage from Moon's youth, but as the film started to roll and he realized that the film didn't contain happy family memorabilia at all, his stomach muscles tightened in embarrassment. It was one of those terribly arty, sensitive films about homosexual love. Amateurishly done, it had a dated, forties look. The two naked young men caressing each other under the trees sported short back and sides haircuts. One had the kind of profile that belonged on Roman coins; the other seemed as keen on making love to the camera lens as to his companion. Rafferty was disconcerted when the Narcissus on the grass stared unselfconsciously back at him, and he dropped his gaze. Neither of them was Moon, who, anyway, could have been no more than eight or ten years old at the time.

The car visible through the shrubbery also had a dated look. It was parked in front of a large country house, the edge of which was just visible in the film and provided a backdrop for the embracing figures.

'Isn't that an old Wolseley?' Rafferty mumbled idiotically, unwilling to turn the film off and reveal how embarrassed it made him feel.

'A Wolseley 14/56.' Llewellyn, the car buff, quietly confirmed it. 'A favourite of the police force in the forties.'

Constrained by his awareness of Llewellyn's strongly moralistic upbringing, Rafferty felt unable to ease his embarrassment by making the kind of coarse crack he might have made with anyone else. Llewellyn tended to have the effect of making you feel cheapened by your own prejudices, and Rafferty reflected that the Jesuits had hit the nail on the head when they had roundly declared, 'Give me a child to the age of seven and I will give you the man.' Because with Llewellyn, neither public school nor university, nor the police force, had made any deep dents in that ingrained sense of right and wrong, that high-minded morality that was so out of step with the modern world and its easy option attitudes. It was rare to meet and uncomfortable for the more morally lax of his colleagues, among whom Rafferty, in a periodic burst of introspective self-knowledge, had certainly included himself. As they had got to know one another on a deeper level, he had discovered that, instead of the expected censure, Llewellyn often displayed a deep compassion for the failings of weaker-minded mortals. He did so now.

'Sad, isn't it,' he remarked, 'that young men should have so little self-respect that they should allow their bodies to be used for others' entertainment?'

Rafferty grunted and returned his attention to the flickering images on the screen. In silence they watched the short film through to the end. Rafferty rewound it, turned the machines off, and replaced it in its box, snapping the lid closed with a relieved sigh.

They found nothing else in the bedroom and returned to the living room, with Rafferty clutching the video. There had been little else of interest in the flat, but he found Moon's possession of such an old, obviously amateur film curious to say the least. Where had he got it from? *Why* had he got it? And why had he hidden it? Although on the face of it the film seemed unlikely to have anything to do with Moon's murder, Rafferty, aware that in a murder case curiosities, especially *concealed* curiosities, often rewarded investigation, thought the answers to his questions might prove interesting.

'We'll be going now, sir,' he told Farley. 'I'm afraid we'll have to take this. Llewellyn, write out a receipt, please.'

Farley looked up. 'A video? It doesn't look like one of ours. Where did you get it?'

'In Mr Moon's wardrobe.' Rafferty showed him the cover with its 'Memory Lane' motif. You don't recognize it, sir?'

Farley shook his head. 'But what's on it? Why on earth would Jasper keep it in his wardrobe?'

On an impulse, Rafferty played the tape through again for Farley's benefit. 'Do you know either of these young men, sir?' he asked when the tape had finished playing.

Farley shook his head again, and Rafferty felt sure he was telling the truth. 'No. I've no idea who they are.' He seemed puzzled rather than upset that Moon should have kept such a film and concealed it from him. 'If Jasper wanted to watch porn films, I'm sure he could have done better than that.'

Rafferty nodded. That was what he had thought. 'By the way, sir.' He pulled the Blood Donor reminder letter from his pocket and showed it to Farley. 'Is Hedges Mr Moon's real name?'

The question seemed to disconcert Farley. His expression anxious, he blurted out that he didn't know, and then immediately looked even more anxious.

And here's another little mystery, Rafferty thought, not for a moment believing that Farley wouldn't have known Moon's real name. Rather than tell an out and out lie, Farley had foolishly, impulsively, decided on a midway course, and had immediately regretted it as he realized the police could easily discover Moon's real name from other sources. No doubt there was some peccadillo in Moon's past which Farley hoped to conceal. But, Rafferty reflected, he'd find out soon enough that the pasts of murder victims were as thoroughly gone over as those of their killers. He'd often thought it appalling how little privacy they or their families were left. He didn't press Farley any further on the question of the name. Instead he asked, 'Could you pop into the station in the next day or so, sir? As soon as you feel up to it.'

'Why?' By now, Farley looked even more lost than before, and his question was half-hearted, as if he had other things on his mind.

'I imagine you spent some time in Mr Moon's office?' Farley nodded. 'In that case, we'll need to eliminate your prints. It's just routine, sir, nothing to worry about.'

Llewellyn finished writing out the receipt and handed it to Farley. 'Would you like us to arrange for anyone to stay with you, sir?' he asked. 'A friend or a member of your family, perhaps, if they live here? All this must have been a great shock to you.'

Rafferty scowled as he realized he should have made the offer. Trust Llewellyn to remember the simple courtesies, he thought.

Farley, after a glance at Rafferty, shook his head. 'I don't want anyone. I'm better alone.' With a simple dignity, he added, 'But thank you for asking, Sergeant. I appreciate it.' Glancing again at Rafferty, he said, 'Most policemen seem barely able to conceal their distaste for my kind, never mind show consideration.'

Rafferty was grateful for the rush of cold air that attacked them as they let themselves out of Moon's flat and retraced their steps. It blew away the shame that Farley's dig had made him feel. Judge not, lest you yourself be judged was undoubtedly what Llewellyn would have said to him if he had been foolish enough to mention it.

Rafferty was irritated that his awkward attempts to be understanding had gone unnoticed. He'd done his best, dammit, he thought. It's not as if I licked such prejudices off the street. It was only fair that the Pope and his many battalions took their share of any censure going.

Chapter Four

Like most of his moods, Rafferty's feeling of irritation quickly passed. And with the news-breaking behind them, Llewellyn, too, seemed happier, his earlier, cello-length features reverting to their normal fiddle proportions.

'Glad to see you're back to your wise-cracking self again,' Rafferty teased.

Llewellyn parked the car precisely in the centre of the marked lines of the police station car park and turned off the ignition before he replied. 'I've never considered murder to be a joking matter, sir,' he quietly rebuked. The words 'unlike you' hovered unspoken between them.

Rafferty, defensive in turn, retorted, 'We all have our ways of coping with the strain, Dafyd. Just because I find it helps to keep my sense of humour intact doesn't mean I'm some kind of flinty-hearted dog. Surely you know that by now?'

Llewellyn studied him silently for a few moments before, with a nod of his head, he acknowledged the truth of this.

'You could do with lightening up a bit, you know,' Rafferty advised, as they got out of the car and headed towards the station. 'With all your psychology training, you must realize that your way of coping with strain is bad for the health. You're in serious danger of going doolally before you're forty.'

'Do you think that will be before or after you're admitted to the coronary ward owing to *your* unhealthy lifestyle, sir?'

Rafferty, who liked a drink, loathed exercise, and, until recently, had been a thirty-a-day man, grinned, said, 'Touché,' and slapped Llewellyn between the shoulder blades. 'Come on, fiddle-face. Let's see if we can't catch ourselves that murderer before Bradley's PIMPmobile comes for me.' Digging in his pocket, he pulled out the letter to Hedges. 'The first thing is to find out Moon's real name. Farley seemed a touch bashful about revealing it. Maybe Moon's famous clients aren't the only ones with skeletons rattling in the closets?'

Mrs Hadleigh hadn't taken long over the photo-fit and had gone by the time they returned. Having instructed one of the junior officers to type up her statement, Rafferty, feet on desk, read it through before asking Llewellyn, 'What do you make of the cleaner's evidence, Dafyd? Think Moon saw someone else after this Henderson bloke? Would he be likely to kill Moon when he knew the cleaner had seen him and could identify him?'

Llewellyn's bony fingers stroked his chin thoughtfully. 'Not if it was a premeditated killing. But, from what you yourself said, the *type* of murder indicates it was done on the spur of the moment. A sudden rush of blood to the head, you might say.'

'And a sudden rush of crystal ball to Jasper Moon's.' Rafferty nodded. 'The killer didn't bring the murder weapon with him. Astell told us it belonged to Moon and that it usually sat on his desk.' He was silent for a moment, contemplating the rest of the cleaner's statement. 'Mrs Hadleigh implied that Henderson was worked up about something, as if he was—'

'She *said* he seemed nervous,' Llewellyn corrected. 'That could mean anything. Perhaps only that he was consulting Moon about some pressing personal problem. Confiding in a third party would be enough to agitate most people. At the moment, he's merely *one* possibility,' he reminded Rafferty. 'Perhaps when we find out Moon's previous identity we'll discover many more.'

Llewellyn was right, of course, and Rafferty told himself to slow down. As usual, he was rushing ahead of the game. He often wished he had Llewellyn's calm, rational approach to crime. The logical, Holmesian process of deduction might – jokingly – have been claimed by Sam Dally, but Dafyd Llewellyn was the true practitioner of the art. Rafferty had never been able to work that way and doubted he ever would. He put it down to his genes, inherited from generations of hot-headed, impulsive Irishmen. When he saw a clue – even when he only thought he saw a clue – he wanted to be up and at it, clutching at it and the straws that came with it. He knew it was inefficient, but it was the way he

48

functioned. And it seemed to work most of the time – eventually.

He smiled ruefully at his sergeant and decided to show him that he *could* go about things in a logical manner. 'It strikes me that the quickest way to find out if this Henderson *was* a client is to ask Astell.' Llewellyn picked up the phone, but Rafferty waved it away. 'No. Let's pay a visit. I want to speak to Mrs Astell, anyway. There are a number of points I want to check.'

The Astells lived in some style. Of course, Ellen Hadleigh had mentioned that Mrs Astell was well off, Rafferty remembered, so Astell presumably wasn't dependent on the business for income, which, from what he had said, was fortunate in the circumstances.

The house was on two floors and detached. Mid-nineteenth century, according to Rafferty's knowledgeable guess, it stood in its own small grounds and, while not by any means ostentatious, it was one of those irregularly built old houses which incorporated bay windows, a gabled porch, steeply pitched roofs and tall chimney stacks, which together gave the house a picturesque charm.

Ellen Hadleigh opened the door. After his initial surprise at seeing her there, Rafferty remembered Astell had told them she cleaned for them. He explained that they wanted to speak to Astell and she stood back, gesturing for them to enter the square hall. 'He's not here at the moment,' she told them. 'I don't think he'll be long, though, if you want to wait.'

The hall was lined with photographs, and Rafferty remembered that Astell's late father-in-law had been a well-known society photographer. He recognized a lot of the faces; many of them still featured in the gossip columns today. 'Maybe we could have a word with Mrs Astell while we wait?' Rafferty suggested. He felt sure that, being female, Mrs Astell might have some interesting insights into the victim. Besides, he needed to get her statement.

Mrs Hadleigh frowned. 'She's lying down at the moment. She doesn't usually see visitors.'

Rafferty forbore from remarking that they were scarcely visitors in the accepted sense. 'We won't keep her long, tell her. Mr Astell mentioned that his wife's a semi-invalid. Some kind of nervous ailment, I gather?'

'Too much time to think and not enough to do.' Bluntly, Ellen Hadleigh gave them her opinion. 'And I don't think all those pills help any. A little job would do her more good, get her out and about, seeing people. It's not as if she's got anything physically wrong with her, yet she's become worse rather than better since she had Victoria five years ago. Still.' She pursed her lips. 'It's none of my business. If you'll wait here for a minute, I'll ask if she'll see you.'

It was hot in the hall, and Rafferty was grateful for an opportunity to ease his shirt collar away from his neck without being observed. Ellen Hadleigh opened one of the doors to the right side of the hall. It led into a small sitting room that overlooked the shrubbery.

Rafferty edged forward and caught a glimpse of Sarah Astell through the open door. Her eyes were closed and she was stretched out on a chaise-longue beneath the old-fashioned french windows. Long, stick-like wrists and ankles protruded from beneath the brown mound of the blanket; pale beneath the soil-rich colouring of the cover, like the bones of a recently disinterred skeleton, they looked unused to sunlight. The shrubs bordering the house, already denuded of leaves, appeared to crouch over her body like so many under-nourished triffids ready to devour her. Their stems, whipped back against the window by the strengthening east wind, tap-tapped a staccato, vaguely Hitchcock-ian rhythm. Beneath their eerie tapping, the house was hung about with an almost monastic silence.

Ellen Hadleigh's brisk voice shattered the silence to announce the visitors. Mrs Astell's head swivelled towards them. It was a pinched, unhappy face, mauve-shadowed under the eyes.

Passing them as they entered, Ellen Hadleigh cautioned before closing the door behind them. 'Please try to keep it short or I'll be in Mr Astell's bad books. He won't have her upset.'

Even before the door had closed, the hot-house atmosphere of the room engulfed them. Rafferty had felt stifled in the hall, but this room was far more oppressive and must be several degrees hotter, and he remembered that Mrs Hadleigh had mentioned that the temperature was kept high for Mrs Astell's sake; she was certainly thin enough to need the extra warmth. Rafferty knew she was only thirty-eight, but she looked much older, her skin covered with a network of fine lines which gave the impression she might crack at any moment.

50

Quickly, aware he had been staring, Rafferty introduced himself and Llewellyn, shuffling forward cautiously, feeling out of place in the dainty room. What with bottles of sleeping pills, and tranquillizers and stomach mixtures littering one table, and photographs and delicate knick-knacks crowded on another, he was scared he would blunder into one of them and break something precious. Strange, Rafferty mused. Why was it that women who seemed to have everything – film stars, models, leisured wives – often found their easy, pampered lives difficult to cope with? So many seemed to develop nervous problems behind which they nursed a drink or drug habit. Rafferty had never understood it. His mother had had more pressures to contend with than most. Widowed with six kids to support, she had never turned to anything more than the occasional bottle of Babysham to sustain her. Of course, she had barely had enough money to pay the bills, never mind indulge expensive tastes. He started to sweat; the deodorized male odour mingled with the smells of sickness, of menthol, cough syrup, liniment, and were swallowed up as efficiently as a snapping dog swallows a fly.

Sarah Astell gave them a wan smile. 'Do please sit down, gentlemen,' she invited, voice weak, the words well spaced out between shallow breaths. 'I imagine you're here about Jasper Moon's death?'

'That's right, Mrs Astell,' Rafferty replied quietly. The heat and the smells in the unventilated room brought back painful memories of his wife's stay in the hospice. Angie's had been a lingering, painful death, the pain not always, at the end, successfully alleviated by drugs. His shoulders hunched as he remembered the rows he'd tried to avoid, the smouldering resentments they had both felt, in his case compounded by guilt that he no longer loved her – if he ever had. He shouldn't shut his mind off from them, his doctor had advised, they should be faced, but Rafferty didn't agree. Dwelling on that time didn't help him come to terms with it; perhaps it never would and now he closed off that section of his brain. Such memories were better confined to the mental dustbin, the lid banged firmly on.

Rafferty forced a smile and glanced round for a seat more sturdy than the small, flounced boudoir chair at the end of the day bed. The only other choice was a scarcely more substantial

51

spindly legged settee. It didn't look strong enough to support him and Llewellyn, and he lowered his lanky body gingerly.

'It's Louis Quinze,' Llewellyn whispered in his ear, in tones of admiration as he sat beside him.

Louis was welcome to it, thought Rafferty, as he shifted his buttocks on the inadequately stuffed cushions. Style was all very well, he thought, but did it have to be so bloody *uncomfortable*?

'My husband told me what happened, Inspector. Most reluctantly, I need hardly add. He's always trying to shield me from unpleasantness.' She directed an anxious smile at them, as though doubtful that they would be as considerate of her feelings as her husband. 'I'm sure Mrs Hadleigh thinks I'm very spoilt. Of course, he was worried it would upset me.'

If she was upset by Jasper Moon's murder she hid it well, thought Rafferty. After all, Moon had been her husband's partner for two years and had worked for him for three before that; she must surely have known him quite well. 'Perhaps you'd like to tell me what you knew of Jasper Moon,' he invited. 'In a murder investigation, it always helps to get as many views and opinions as possible.'

She sighed. 'Speaking ill of the dead is not something I would normally do, Inspector.' She paused, glanced briefly at him and then went on. 'But I can see that I must put aside such scruples.' Her brown eyes shadowed, and she admitted, 'I never felt comfortable with him. His homosexuality – repelled me.'

Rafferty was glad to learn that he wasn't alone in his political incorrectness. He noticed her voice had now become firm, the invalid's quaver vanished or forgotten as she put aside the rest of her scruples and warmed to her theme.

'But aside from his . . . homosexuality' – once again she snapped out the word as if she wanted it said as quickly as possible, as if the very word offended her – 'I always felt he took unfair advantage of Edwin; the times he left him holding the fort while he jetted off round the world seeing his star clients. And *careless*; in the years he and Edwin worked together, he never managed to send his birthday card on the correct day. It was always late.' Her mouth turned down, 'Just because he'd written a few books and appeared on television, he seemed to believe he was a major celebrity. He was always so full of himself he probably thought Edwin should be grateful he bothered at all.'

She sat back with a twisted smile. 'Edwin insisted he didn't mind, and of course, as I made a point of avoiding Moon, I hardly had an opportunity to point it out to him. Not that I would have done, anyway. Edwin warned me it would only embarrass him if I did so, so, for Edwin's sake, I put up with the annual irritation it caused me.' Her expression self-deprecating, she added, 'Like my dear father, I've always believed a wife's role to be a secondary, supportive one, Inspector. I'm sure you agree.'

After a wry glance at Llewellyn, whose girlfriend inclined more to the feminist persuasion, Rafferty nodded politely. Personally, he agreed with Llewellyn, that women who always put themselves second were fools. No one respected a doormat. But Sarah Astell seemed proud of her boot-wiping quality.

Rafferty remembered now that Astell had told them he put a lot of his wife's trouble squarely at her father's door. 'Sarah adored him,' he had told them. 'But he was seldom at home and even when he was he paid her scant attention. She became anorexic in her teens, but that's been under control for years and her weight's steady, though she doesn't seem to improve at all. Still,' he had added on a bright note, as if that were all he could hope for, 'the doctors are pleased with her.'

Looking at her now, Rafferty concluded that Mrs Astell's doctors must be easily pleased. She couldn't weigh any more than eight stone, low for someone whose long limbs looked as if, standing, she'd be about 5′8″. She must still eat like a sparrow.

'No,' Sarah Astell continued. 'I didn't like him. I made a point of meeting him as little as possible, that's why I never went to my husband's business premises. Even when Edwin first started to work for him there was something about him that made me uneasy. Oh, he was pleasant enough to me then, went out of his way to be attentive, even insisted on drawing up a natal chart for me. But lately, he had begun to make disparaging remarks about my father. I think he was jealous of him, of his reputation. I don't suppose he thought they'd get back to me, but they did. He might have brought in a lot of business, but money has never been that important to Edwin or me.' She smiled her taut smile. 'We live simply. Neither of us is extravagant. We have each other, our daughter and our lovely home. What more could anyone want?'

'It's certainly a beautiful house,' Rafferty agreed.

He had evidently hit the right note, for she smiled warmly at him. 'Yes, we're lucky. This house has been in my mother's family for generations. Of course, the grounds used to be more extensive, but land had to be sold to pay death duties. My mother's now married to a well-set-up man and lives in Scotland. She gave this place to me when she remarried, and, of course, as I was an only child – my parents waited ten years for me – I had no brothers or sisters to demand their share.' With an unconscious arrogance, she added, 'Perhaps you know that my father was Sir Alan Carstairs?' She nodded at a framed colour photograph which held pride of place on one wall. Under flopping dark hair, Alan Carstairs stared back at them from clear blue eyes. He had been a handsome man and his expression implied that he had been well aware of it. 'He was a very successful society photographer in the fifties and sixties,' she told them. 'I'm sure you've heard of him.'

They nodded in unison, and while Llewellyn proceeded to draw her out, talking knowledgeably of photography in that reserved manner that women seemed to find so endearing, Rafferty let his mind and his eyes roam. Astell had told him she had adored her father even though he had neglected her. Rafferty could see why. The photograph was of a man in his prime, self-assured, good looking, vigorous. A man who turned heads and attracted admirers with no effort at all. A man who was perhaps a little spoilt, a little selfish, but understandably so. A fast-living extrovert, Carstairs, when he wasn't racing round the world snapping the famous of the day, had been the subject of other photographers' lenses. Newspaper snaps had invariably featured him in some exotic part of the world, beautiful women draped around him. The man had seemed to trail an ever-changing harem, and Rafferty wondered what his wife had thought of her husband's lifestyle.

Carstairs might have paid his daughter scant attention, but at least he appeared to have left her well supplied with filthy lucre. And, he noticed, for a woman who didn't like visitors she seemed to have blossomed under Llewellyn's attentions. The invalid's rug had been completely discarded and she sat forward, her face animated, hands expressive as they discussed her father's genius. Rafferty returned from his wool-gathering just as Llewellyn's social skills gave out. Now he asked, 'I understand you and your husband were at home on the night Mr Moon died?'

'That's right. I imagine Edwin's told you it was the anniversary of my dear father's death. I kept the gathering small this year, just my husband, myself, Mrs Moreno, whom my husband employs, and Clara Davies, an old friend of my father. She was a very talented designer and often went on location with him. But even though the gathering was small, I still insisted on black tie. I like to mark the occasion with a proper respect. I even managed to persuade Edwin to buy a new suit this year from Cutts, the tailors, while we were in Elmhurst, though, of course, he kept putting it off and left it too late to get his usual made-to-measure.' Unexpectedly, she glanced at Rafferty in his tired suit and gave him an arch smile. 'You men and your comfortable old clothes. How you do cling on to them.'

Ruefully, Rafferty looked down at his best brown suit. Perhaps it *was* past its prime, he thought, as he stretched his legs out and studied the worn, shiny hillocks that stood away from his knees.

Edwin Astell appeared in the doorway. 'Inspector. Mrs Hadleigh said you were here.' He glanced at his wife. 'Are you all right, dear? You look rather flushed. My wife tires easily, Inspector, as I told you. I hope you've not been wearing her out.'

'Don't fuss, Edwin,' she chided, though Rafferty noticed she looked pleased at his concern. 'We've been having a nice little chat about my father.' She drew her lips back. 'And that business with Moon, of course.'

Rafferty turned to Astell. 'I meant to ask you before, sir. I gather Jasper Moon was the victim's professional name. Can you tell me his real name?'

Astell studied his wife's flushed features with a frown before he told them, 'Sorry, no. I've always known him as Jasper Moon. I've no idea what he might have been called before.'

Rafferty was surprised. 'He never mentioned it?'

Astell shook his head. 'I did ask him once, but it was clear he wasn't interested in discussing it. I never brought it up again. It was none of my business.'

'We found a letter addressed to a Peter Hedges amongst his personal effects,' Rafferty remarked. 'We wondered if that might be it.' Neither of the Astells had any comment to make on that and Rafferty went on. 'Never mind, we'll no doubt soon find out his real name.'

Sarah Astell's brief spurt of energy hadn't lasted long. The flush in her cheeks had now vanished, leaving her paler than before. Rafferty, feeling a little guilty that their visit should have such a tiring effect on her, remarked pleasantly, 'Rather unfortunate that Mr Moon should have been murdered on the anniversary of your father's death, Mrs Astell.'

She gave a brief, strained smile. 'Yes. It was my birthday also, you know. I always felt that gave me a special bond with my father.' Her smile faded. 'But as you say, now I'll have other memories.'

'I hope it won't mar the occasion too much for you in the future?'

No longer chatty, Sarah Astell merely bobbed her head in acknowledgement.

Rafferty turned back to Astell. 'I just want to go through one or two points, sir. I hope you'll bear with me. I gather you and your guests were all together for most of the evening?'

'That's right,' Astell told him. 'As I told you, our guests left around eight o'clock or just after. Mrs Hadleigh left a little before then as she was feeling unwell and obviously unfit to do any work. She sounded quite dreadful when I rang her later to see if she was all right. She lives alone,' he explained, 'and I was concerned for her. But she wouldn't hear of me calling the doctor.' He shrugged. 'People of that age are very independent. Anyway, once our guests had gone, I made a start on clearing the dishes to give my wife a little time alone with her memories of her father. She always likes some quiet time on anniversary evenings.'

'But Edwin came in several times to see I was all right, didn't you, dear?'

Astell stared at her for a few seconds, as though his thoughts were miles away. 'Sorry. Yes, of course. I didn't think you'd noticed. I popped in at about ten past eight, just after Mrs Moreno returned for her gloves and then again, at about twenty-five past. As I told you, Inspector, we chatted in the kitchen for about forty minutes and she left at about ten to nine.'

'Really, Edwin, you might have told me she had come back,' Sarah Astell put in. 'I needn't have—' She stopped and glanced at the two policemen. 'I'm sorry. How rude of me.' She told her husband more quietly, 'You shouldn't have entertained her in the kitchen. What must she have thought of us? You should have brought her in to me or made her comfortable in the drawing room. I hope you at least made her some coffee.'

Edwin Astell smiled. 'Calm yourself, my dear. My reputation as a host isn't quite ruined. I made her coffee. I even offered to ring for another taxi, but she told me not to bother. Said she enjoys walking in a storm.' He turned back to Rafferty. 'When she left, I joined my wife in here, before suggesting she had an early night. It's such an emotion-charged day for her, you see, and that and the unaccustomed entertaining can leave her exhausted.' He lowered his voice and murmured, 'She's not feeling too well today, actually, so, if you don't mind?' Without protest, and after making his goodbyes to Mrs Astell, Rafferty let himself and Llewellyn be ushered out of the room.

'I'm sorry,' Astell apologized as he opened the front door. Rafferty sucked in the cool air gratefully as Astell continued, 'I'm afraid my wife won't always admit how easily she tires, and I know that this business with Jasper has upset her. She was quite fond of him. In many ways they were surprisingly alike.'

'Really?' Rafferty wouldn't have thought the flamboyant Moon and the sickly Sarah Astell had anything in common. He was astonished to discover that Astell should be unaware of his wife's true opinion of Jasper Moon. Most wives wouldn't hesitate to shout their opinion of their husband's colleagues and friends from the rooftops. It was interesting that she hadn't done so. But perhaps it was just another symptom of the dutiful wife syndrome? thought Rafferty cynically. 'I got the distinct impression that your wife *didn't* like Mr Moon, sir. In fact, I'd say she detested him.'

Astell looked taken aback. But he recovered quickly. 'You mustn't take everything my wife says at face value, Inspector. You must understand she's not well. It makes her behave irrationally at times. Admittedly, Jasper could sometimes be a little insensitive, a little pushy, but, for all that, they got on well enough.'

Rafferty wondered why Astell felt it necessary to pretend? His wife had seemed to know her own mind very well. Rafferty paused. 'Was Mr Moon aware that Mrs Hadleigh would be working yesterday evening rather than in the morning, as usual?'

'I did mention it to him, but Jasper had a habit of nodding at you as if he was listening when he was actually somewhere else completely, so I can't be sure.'

Rafferty realized he had nearly left without asking the main question. He hoped Llewellyn didn't realize it. 'Did Mrs Hadleigh tell you that Mr Moon had a client with him when she left yesterday evening?'

'A client?' Astell's voice was sharply interrogative, his body stiff, as though determined not to voice resentment that Rafferty should continue to suspect the partnership's clientele. 'No,' he said. 'She didn't tell me. But I've seen very little of her since it happened. I've been shut in the study answering calls from Jasper's clients. As you can imagine, most of them are very shocked at the news. Did Mrs Hadleigh tell you this client's name?'

'She said his name was Henderson,' Rafferty told him, but it was apparent it meant nothing to Astell. 'I've got an officer checking through Mr Moon's files now. Hopefully, he'll be quickly traced and exonerated.' He gave Astell Mrs Hadleigh's description of Henderson, but he didn't recognize him. 'I understood Mr Moon rarely saw clients on Thursday evenings. Could he be a special new client for whom Mr Moon made an exception?'

'No. Jasper was famous enough to do business on his own terms. He would only ever make an exception for long-established clients and this Henderson is certainly not in that category. Have you questioned the staff about him?'

'Not yet. I've still to speak to Mrs Campbell, and Mrs Moreno had left by the time we found out about him. One last thing. I know you told us you knew nothing about any will that Mr Moon might have made, but I wondered if you'd had any thoughts on it. It seems likely a man as wealthy as Mr Moon would make one, yet we didn't find one at the flat, and the business solicitor had never drawn one up for him. Like you, he seemed to think Mr Moon would be more likely to do the job himself. We've spoken to the other local solicitors and none of them acted for him in the matter.'

Astell massaged his jaw thoughtfully. 'The consultancy used to be based in London – Soho. I suppose, for what it's likely to be worth you could try the solicitors in that area. Rafferty nodded. It gave them another avenue to explore and Rafferty thanked him for the information. 'What about his bank? Have you tried them?' Rafferty nodded again. Astell paused, then asked curiously, 'What happens if there is no will?'

Rafferty wasn't entirely sure and glanced at Llewellyn. As

expected, the Welshman was his usual fount of information. 'The laws on intestacy come into operation,' he told them. 'If there is no family, I understand the estate goes to the Crown.' Llewellyn paused and asked quietly, 'What about the business, sir? Presumably Mr Moon's half would go to his estate. That must be a worry for you.'

Astell's creased forehead confirmed it. 'As far as the income is concerned, yes. With Jasper gone, most of the income goes too, as he invariably brought in three-quarters or more of the profits. And, of course, his estate will retain rights in Jasper's part of profits already earned.' He forced a smile, but it was a little ragged. 'Though at least I have full rights to the leases of the business premises, though what good that will do me with Jasper gone . . .' His voice faltered for a moment, then he explained. 'When Jasper offered me a partnership, we agreed that, in the event of one of us dying, the business would become the sole property of the remaining partner.'

'You had a proper partnership agreement drawn up?'

'Yes. I managed to persuade Jasper that it was essential. The same solicitors who acted for us over the leases of the store and the offices above drew up the papers.'

'How was the profit divided?' Rafferty put in sharply.

Too sharply, it seemed, for Astell, as his answer was stiff. 'The agreement specified a fifty-fifty share of the profit, but it was drawn up before Jasper achieved any international fame and was hardly fair now. A few months ago I insisted he take his rightful share. In return, he paid the bulk of the business outgoings.'

'And his other income, sir? From his books, TV appearances and magazine work?'

Astell frowned, as if he was just beginning to appreciate the purpose of these questions. His voice became even more stilted. 'His income from that goes straight to his agent. It's never gone into the partnership account. Naturally, I'll be forwarding his share of the partnership income to the accountant as it comes in.'

'We'll need the name and address of this accountant, Mr Astell,' said Rafferty. 'And that of the agent. I meant to ask you before, but it slipped my mind.'

Astell flushed. 'I assure you I've never taken a penny from the business that wasn't rightfully mine. I resent your—'

Llewellyn broke in. 'I'm sure the Inspector didn't mean to imply that you had, Mr Astell,' he began.

Astell chose to ignore his assurances. 'Very well. Speak to the agent and the accountants if you must.' He named a local firm of accountants. The agent had an office in London. 'Check the books, too. You'll find everything in order. As I told you, I never even took the full share of profit to which our agreement entitled me. I certainly never helped myself to anything more.' He inclined his head. 'I'll say good day to you, gentlemen.'

Rafferty braced himself for the slamming door, but it closed quietly behind him. As they walked to the car, he commented ruefully, 'And I thought Librans were meant to be natural diplomats? At least according to Ma.' He sighed. 'Another talent that's passed me by.'

Chapter Five

Back at the station, Rafferty threw off his coat and shouted for tea, commenting, 'Though, diplomat or not, you must admit that Astell rather got on his high horse when I asked him for those names.' With a rueful grin, he added, 'For a moment there I sensed Bradley's PIMPmobile on my heels. Still, if Astell goes scurrying off to Bradley to complain, you'll be able to confirm that I was politeness itself. I even threw in plenty of "sirs". He had no call to get quite so sniffy.'

'Even an honest man is prone to anger when his honesty's questioned.'

Rafferty nodded absently. Probably Llewellyn was right and they'd find that Astell had been the soul of scrupulousness. But, he reflected, if he'd had his hands in the till up to his armpits, he was hardly likely to admit it. And even if Moon's other income didn't go into the partnership account, there would still be healthy enough amounts coming in to arouse temptation. Presumably, the clients made their cheques out to the business name rather than to either individual partner. It would have been easy enough for a man like Astell to help himself to parts of Moon's income and cover his tracks from any but the most rigorous scrutiny. But why *would* he? Rafferty reasoned. If what Astell had told them was true, he was entitled to a fifty per cent share of the profits anyway, yet didn't take it. Of course, Mrs Astell was reputed to be wealthy, so he could presumably afford it.

Still, Rafferty reminded himself, that wasn't *quite* the same thing as being wealthy yourself. It was possible Astell was too stiff-necked to be happy living on his wife's money and had only pretended to take less than his share to deflect Moon's suspicion. If this was what happened and Moon had caught him out, it could be a motive for murder. But, Rafferty frowned, as he realized the flaw in his theory, not for *this* murder. Even if Astell was helping himself to more of the profits than he was legally entitled to, he still couldn't picture him killing Moon so impetuously. It wasn't his style. Besides, he had been tied up most of that evening. Mrs Moreno hadn't finally left till shortly before 9 p.m., and then he had joined his wife. Though, he reminded himself, she probably extended her *little woman* syndrome to include lying for hubby.

Anyway, he decided, he could at least check up on the money angle. Flipping open the local phone book, he found the number of the accountants, picked up the handset and began to dial. He got the engaged tone, pressed the rest and tried again; and again. 'Come on, come on,' he growled. 'Get off the bloody phone.'

'Why don't you use the redial button?' Llewellyn asked mildly, as he pressed it. 'Then you can put the phone down.'

Rafferty replaced the receiver. 'Why didn't I think of that?' he asked disingenuously. He'd often wondered what that particular button was for. He'd pressed it once or twice, out of curiosity, but as nothing much seemed to happen he hadn't bothered again. Of course, the explanatory booklet had long since vanished – not that he'd got very far with it before his brain had given up, in any case. But as this was the age of technological tyranny, he would never be fool enough to admit his ignorance.

For some reason, Llewellyn had decided to connive in this concealment, passing on appropriate tips discreetly. Rafferty had never been sure whether compassion or condescension prompted him, but even though he half resented the help, he didn't refuse it. Modern policing demanded a wide range of skills, and if Bradley ever realized just how limited was his technological grasp he'd take great pleasure in writing it large in his record.

'Actually.' Llewellyn cleared his throat and Rafferty glanced up. 'Astell's wife interested me.'

'Wouldn't have thought she was your type,' Rafferty joked. 'Promise I won't tell Maureen.'

Llewellyn took a long-suffering breath. 'I meant that it struck me as odd that Astell should have popped in twice to check on her. Didn't you notice her prompt him? He looked puzzled for a second, before he agreed. Why was she so keen to mention the visits at all?'

'Now you mention it, twice does seem a bit excessive. Still, people are always anxious to cover themselves in such circumstances. I don't suppose it means anything. Even if she was totally alone from just after eight to eight-fifty I can't see her creeping out on such a night to kill Moon. She might have disliked the man, but that's hardly strong enough reason for murdering him. Besides, by the look of her, I'd have thought beating Moon around the head with his own crystal ball hard enough to kill him would be physically beyond her.'

Rafferty guessed what was about to come out of Llewellyn's open mouth and forestalled him. 'I know, I know. An open mind is a policeman's friend and conclusion-jumping his enemy. I haven't forgotten.' Not likely to get the chance, Rafferty added to himself, with you around. And even if I am guilty of jumping to conclusions, he mused, I still can't see her doing it.

After staring at the still silent phone with a frown, he said, 'I want you to get on to Moon's London agent. Check that Astell was telling the truth when he said he had nothing to do with Moon's profitable sidelines. Not that it's likely to make much difference one way or the other,' he muttered half to himself. 'It doesn't look as if he would have had the opportunity to kill him. But we'd better get it checked out.'

While Llewellyn busied himself with that, Rafferty glanced through the growing pile of reports, abandoning them with relief when Llewellyn put the phone down and told him that Moon's agent had confirmed that Astell had told them the truth.

Rafferty nodded. He had expected as much.

Half an hour later, he still hadn't got through to the accountant. So much for the benefits of modern technology, Rafferty thought. At least when you dialled a number yourself you had the satisfaction of slamming the receiver down when it was continually engaged. 'I reckon the bloody phone's redirected my call to a public phone box in the Outer Hebrides,' he complained to Llewellyn.

Llewellyn smiled his superior smile. 'It's always possible you dialled the wrong number,' he pointed out. 'It's easily done.'

Rafferty scowled. 'Might have known it would be my fault. Why don't you give them a ring, Mr Know-all?'

Of course, Llewellyn got through on the first attempt, obtained the information that Mr Spenny, the partnership accountant, was away on a late holiday and wouldn't be back till the following week, and made an appointment for Rafferty to see him as soon as he came back.

With great restraint, Rafferty merely nodded an acknowledgement when Llewellyn told him this. Sitting forward in his chair, he said, 'Let's see what we have to consider so far. Moon's office was broken into on the night of his murder. Could be a coincidence, could be someone trying to throw us off the scent. Of course, a thousand pounds is a large enough sum to kill for, especially when you consider how many people nowadays get murdered for the sake of a few pence. But whatever happened, and aside from the oddities I mentioned earlier, there are four other things we must consider about that break-in.' He began to mark them off on his fingers.

'One, if it happened *before* the murder, why did the intruder burgle an obviously occupied office? It *could* have been a drug addict, as I told Farley, but I doubt it. An addict would find easier pickings by mugging old ladies. Two, if Moon surprised him, why was the only injury to the *back* of his skull?'

'The intruder could have had a gun and forced Moon to turn around so he could hit him.'

'So why not hit him with the gun? Why bother to look around for another weapon?' Llewellyn's first objection satisfactorily disposed of, Rafferty went back to his counting. 'Three, if the burglar *didn't* attack him, if he left Moon still alive, why didn't Moon report the break-in? And four, if the break-in happened *after* the murder, why on earth would any self-respecting burglar break in at all and risk getting involved in what was obviously a violent death? Moon was slumped directly in front of the window.'

'Don't forget, the blinds were drawn. Any burglar might only have seen the body when he had actually climbed in.'

'OK, that's a fair point. But once he had, it strikes me he'd have climbed right out again, not gone rummaging through Moon's pockets and the desk for the key to the cashbox. If our burglar was that cool and hard-headed, he'd have gone for a more profitable line of work – armed bank robbery, for instance, rather than burgling an office on the off-chance of finding cash. No, I reckon we've got two separate people involved here. Two very different types.'

Rafferty twirled in his chair and gazed out at the rain. It was gusting sideways, as wind-whipped as the scurrying, forwards-leaning pedestrians. Depressed, he twirled back. 'I wondered if Moon might have invited a pick-up back for the evening. They could have had a lovers' tiff. It would explain the murder and the trashing of the office. A possible pick-up could have been hoping to throw us off the scent.'

'But why should he invite a boyfriend back to the office at all? He had a perfectly comfortable home. Farley was away, so he would have the flat to himself. Besides, even though Lilley said he had found no file for this Henderson, it doesn't mean he *wasn't* a new client. Moon may have made an exception. And don't forget that Mrs Hadleigh said that Moon had called Henderson a client.'

'Moon wouldn't be likely to flaunt any sexual dalliances in front of his cleaner. What would be the point? And even if Farley was spending a few nights away, Moon couldn't be certain he wouldn't return unexpectedly. Besides,' Rafferty, keen to test their new understanding, suggested with a grin, 'perhaps Moon liked his spare rumpy-pumpy under the stars? And with its star-spangled ceiling, that office of his would be perfect.' The summer heatwave endured with such reluctant stoicism by Rafferty who liked his weather comfortable was now becoming quite a fond memory, and he commented, 'You must admit, it's a bit parky for outside sexual shenanigans now.'

Llewellyn's light nod accepted both the argument and its presentation, and Rafferty was satisfied that Llewellyn was beginning to accept his black-tinged ways with humour. He didn't for a moment assume they had broken the back of their differing approaches, but at least they had made a start, and now he tapped the photofit picture that Mrs Hadleigh had worked on with their expert. 'Mind you, this Henderson bloke doesn't exactly look the ideal candidate for a bit of on-the-side naughties. A man as successful as Moon couldn't have been short of offers in that direction, so why settle for a down-at-heel near wrinkly?'

'I believe chronologically challenged is the term currently in vogue, sir,' Llewellyn dryly commented.

Rafferty, who'd had enough of having his prejudices criticized for one day, responded sharply. 'Don't start quoting the collected thoughts of the politically correct brigade at me, boyo. Your ancient Greeks are enough. Unlike the PC brigade, at least they understood that preaching at people is more likely to get their backs up than change their attitudes.'

'A little joke, sir, that's all,' said Llewellyn, his expression bland.

'Mm.' Rafferty, half suspecting that Llewellyn was now teasing *him*, deemed it wiser to say nothing more on the subject. 'Let's get this picture circulated. I want Henderson's likeness on the streets by this evening. I also want Moon's photographs circulated at the same time. It might throw something up. Send Hanks in on your way out. I want him to go and pay a visit to the partners' bank. If we can get the numbers of those stolen notes, we might be able to trace them. Come back when you've set things in motion, as I want us to go and see this Ginnie Campbell next and find out why she didn't come in to work this morning. We'll take a chance that she's at home.'

There was no answer at Ginnie Campbell's door. As they turned to walk back up the path, the door of the next terraced house opened and a neighbour stepped out in front of them.

'If you're looking for that Campbell woman, she's out.' Ginnie Campbell's neighbour was built on battle-tank lines and now she planted her solid, fluffy-pink-slippered feet more firmly on the shared path, blocking it as effectively as any armoured vehicle, and managing to look marginally more threatening as she crossed meaty arms over her flowered pinny. Eyes that looked as hard and dense as plum stones fixed avidly on them as she added, 'I can give her a message, if you like.'

'Thanks for the offer, but we'll come back.' Without success, Rafferty attempted to edge past her on the narrow path, but, as she didn't give an inch, he was forced to retreat.

'If you're looking for money, you'll be wasting your time,' she confided. 'She's got tally-men and debt collectors on her doorstep morning and night, but few of them manage to catch her.' Her eyes darted from one to the other, and she speculated artfully. 'You'll be the bailiffs, I suppose? They must be due about now.'

Rafferty took a quiet satisfaction in disappointing her. Still, with a thousand pounds missing from Moon's office, it was certainly interesting to discover that Virginia Campbell's circumstances were so straitened. 'We do need to see Mrs Campbell urgently,' he said. 'Have you any idea when she'll be back, Mrs . . . ?'

'Naseby. Mrs Naseby's my name. No, can't say I have.' She crossed her arms more firmly over her ample chest, dewlaps of mottled flesh on her upper arms wobbling, seemingly impervious to the chill wind that was steadily turning Llewellyn's ears bright red, and settled to gossip. 'Comes and goes at all hours. Heard her drive back from God knows where before eight o'clock this morning. Roared up in that car of hers with enough noise to wake the dead.' She sniffed. 'Might be able to pay her rent if she stayed home occasionally.'

'How do you know she's behind with her rent?' Rafferty asked.

'I've got a friend who works in the landlord's offices, that's how. Three months' she owes them.' As a car pulled up at the kerb her lips drew back in a spiteful smile and she told them, 'You're in luck. That's her now. Though I wouldn't count on getting any money.'

The car was a sports model and although its registration plate revealed that it was only a year old it had certainly been in the wars, as several large dents testified. Rafferty wondered how Ginnie Campbell could afford to pay for fancy cars when she couldn't afford the rent. But perhaps she couldn't, he mused, as the three of them watched her climb out of the car. Perhaps the car company featured among the debt collectors trying to catch up with her? No doubt Mrs Naseby would know.

Virginia Campbell was a statuesque redhead of about forty summers. Her carriage was proud and, as she approached, Mrs Naseby's lips thinned. The other woman's chin raised in response, her shoulders went back and her walk became more swayingly provocative. Dressed in a short, clinging and jewel-bright vermilion skirt, its satin sheen a defiant battle cry, Rafferty guessed, as the ample flesh of the crimplene chain-store-couturiered Mrs Naseby quivered with outrage, that she would have plenty of practice at out-facing the neighbours.

Sweeping them with a contemptuous glance, Ginnie Campbell asked, 'What's this? A welcoming committee? Come to ask me to join the neighbourhood watch?' Unthinkingly, Rafferty introduced himself and Llewellyn. Predictably, Mrs Naseby pounced.

'So, you've got the police on your tail as well now, have you?' she demanded with gratified spite. After looking Ginnie Campbell and her short skirt up and down she added, tartly, 'Can't say I'm surprised.'

Ginnie Campbell poked the other woman sharply in her ample bosom with a vermilion-painted forefinger and rounded fiercely on her. 'Just watch your tongue, you rancid old bat, or I'll put the evil eye on you.' She held up her left hand and made a darting motion towards the neighbour's face.

Mrs Naseby went pale, her aggressive manner crumbled. She backed towards her front door, chased by Ginnie Campbell's derisive laughter, and slammed the door behind her.

Rafferty was astonished to discover that the intimidating human tank should be as prone to superstitious fears as himself. As Ginnie Campbell's jeering laughter was abruptly cut off he reintroduced himself.

He'd barely finished when she snapped at him, 'Thanks a lot. Did you have to let her know you're from the police? She'll have the entire street convinced I'm on the game now.' Turning away, she stalked up the path to her door and disappeared. Exchanging bemused glances, Rafferty and Llewellyn followed her. She had left the door ajar and, after giving a cursory knock, they walked up the hall.

She was in the living room. As they entered, she removed her high heels and flung them in the far corner before she slumped in an armchair and said, 'Sit down, for God's sake. What do you want, anyway?'

After sitting on a shocking pink settee that was littered with discarded clothing, Rafferty told her the reason for their visit. Although her eyes widened and she stared at him open-mouthed, Rafferty got the impression that she had already known of Moon's death. There was no reason why she shouldn't, of course. His body had been discovered several hours ago; it was probable that, by now, news of his murder had spread like post-Christmas pine needles. But he wondered why – if she *had* already known about it – she should choose to pretend otherwise?

Gesturing for Llewellyn to take over the questioning, Rafferty studied her. Under the brave paint, her face had careworn lines that made her look every month of her forty-old years, and, as she bent her head, Rafferty noticed that the roots of her flame-red hair were liberally sprinkled with grey. He got the impression

68

that her aggressive dress and manner camouflaged a woman at the end of her tether. It wasn't altogether surprising, of course. Not only was she in debt, she was also a divorcee, with dyed red hair, a voluptuous figure and a too-proud manner; an ill-advised combination in a poor neighbourhood, where the men would eye her with hopeful lust and the women with fear and dislike. Now, he interrupted Llewellyn's slow but precise interviewing technique. 'You told Sergeant Llewellyn that you had today and yesterday off work. Could you tell us where you spent the time? I gather you didn't attend Mr and Mrs Astell's little anniversary evening?'

The question seemed to amuse her. 'God, no. I spent all day yesterday out with my boyfriend. We went to the races at Newmarket. Got back to his place in St Mark's Road about six, and stayed in all evening. I came straight back this morning. About eight.'

Rafferty nodded. Ginnie Campbell's home, like St Mark's Road, was in the southern part of Elmhurst, certainly well away from Moon's High Street premises. 'Not your cup of tea, I take it? This memorial do of the Astells'.'

'I wasn't invited, but I wouldn't have gone anyway. I believe in saving my admiration for *live* men, not dead ones. Jasper didn't get an invite either, but it's not as if he socialized with the Astells anyway. Sarah Astell didn't approve of him any more than she does me, so that's hardly surprising—'

Llewellyn broke in. 'Still, it seems odd that Mrs Moreno, an employee, should receive an invitation, when Mr Astell's business partner did not.'

'There's nothing odd about it,' she told him. 'Sarah Astell invited her because "Highly thought of" made it her business to fawn and flutter round her for some reason of her own.'

Llewellyn nodded. 'I see. It didn't cause an atmosphere at work because Mrs Moreno was the only one invited?'

'I told you. I didn't want to go anyway, and Jasper understood that Edwin could hardly invite him to his wife's ancestor-worshipping evening when his wife couldn't stand him.'

Rafferty was surprised that Mrs Astell's dislike of Moon should apparently be common knowledge. Though he wasn't particularly surprised that Astell should lie about it. His business partner had just been murdered. It was understandable that he should be at least as protective of his wife as he was of his clients. It would hardly be politic for the man to admit that his wife and his partner weren't exactly bosom buddies. Though by now Rafferty guessed he was already regretting his instinctive denial. 'Were you aware that Mr Moon had a client with him yesterday evening?' he continued. She shook her head and he pulled out one of the photofit pictures and showed it to her. 'A Mr Henderson. Do you know him?'

She glanced at the picture and shook her head again. 'I've neither seen nor heard of him before. Though I'm surprised Jasper should see a client on Thursday evenings. He liked to keep them free. His usual practice was to go out for an early meal before he got down to his latest book.'

'A meal?' Rafferty queried. He should have thought of that himself. 'Do you know what restaurant he went to?' If they found out what he'd eaten and at what time, it might help to narrow down the time of death.

'He usually went to that expensive French place in the High Street; the one a couple of doors away from our offices. Jasper fancied himself as something of a gourmet. Really he was more of a gourm*and*. Poor Jazz.' For the first time, she showed genuine regret. 'All his appetites were large, but then he loved life. The place'll be like a morgue without him.'

Plainly, Ginnie Campbell knew nothing about Henderson, and Rafferty put the matter from his mind. For now, he was more curious to learn her opinion of Jasper Moon and who might have killed him. 'I gather Mr Moon was homosexual,' he began.

'Jasper homosexual?' She laughed as if she found his diffident statement amusing. Once again, like a suddenly switched-off sound system, the laughter was abruptly cut off, disconcerting him. 'He was as queer as a piebald canary, Inspector. Not that I hold that against him,' she quickly added. 'Why? Do you think that might have something to do with his death? Do you think the boyfriend killed him?'

'Do you?' he countered.

She shrugged. 'How should I know? But Chris Farley was as jealous as hell, that much I do know. I often heard Jasper on the phone, placating him, when I passed his door.'

'Did he have any reason for this jealousy?'

'Again, how should I know? Chris might have been jealous,

70

might have had *reason* for jealousy for all I know, but I somehow can't see him having the guts to kill. Especially as he'd have lost the comfortable nest Jasper provided him with.'

That had been Rafferty's opinion. 'Tell me, Mrs Campbell—'

'Call me Ginnie. Everyone does. Mrs Campbell always makes me feel like a history teacher or something.'

' "Madam Ginnie," ' Rafferty quoted from one of the posters pinned up in Moon's office anteroom. ' "Palmist to the Stars".'

She smiled delightedly. 'You saw it? I'm surprised Edwin hasn't noticed it and made me take it down again. He told me it was too close to Jasper's publicity posters and wasn't even accurate, though that's not strictly true.' She gave another short laugh. 'It's two stars to be exact. And of the falling variety. Still' – she smiled, but beneath the smile her eyes were resentful – 'they can't get me under the Trades Descriptions Act. No one said my claimed stars had to be high in the sky.'

Rafferty guessed she minded very much that her skills were sidelined to the postal part of the business. Could it have any bearing on Moon's murder, Rafferty wondered, that both Mrs Moreno and Mrs Campbell harboured resentments against the partnership? Moon had been the most important partner and the natural target for any ill feeling. It could be significant, he decided. 'I'd like the name and address of your boyfriend, if I may.'

'Why?' She sat up straight, all amusement gone now, and demanded, 'Do you think I killed Jazzy?' She sounded angry, Rafferty noted. Angry and more than a little scared. Between the two emotions, she seemed edgy, and her beringed fingers clenched tightly in her lap.

'Did you have any reason to kill him?' he countered again.

She sat back. 'Hell, no. Oh, he could be infuriatingly pernickety sometimes. But, on the whole, he was an old love, generous to a fault. Why—' She broke off and then began again. 'Why, I know he used to go to old people's homes, do free readings and liven them up no end. Jasper was always a good turn. It was all done very privately. He always said that what he did was more of a vocation than a job. That's probably why he was so good at it. He had a great gift and he didn't believe it should be used purely for profit. He was kind, generous, superstitious, sentimental . . .'

'Sentimental? Why do you say that?'

She smiled. 'He adored mementoes of people and places. I remember he lost his keys a little while ago; he was always careless with them. He didn't mind so much about the keys, but he did mind about losing the keyring. Some old friend had given it to him years ago and he was terribly upset about it. And he carried around photos of friends and family, photos of star clients autographed with love and kisses. He kept them all in a wallet; first cousins, second cousins twice removed, great aunts. He dropped the wallet one day and they all fell out. He even had a photo of Sarah Astell as a baby; ugly little brat she was, too.'

'How do you know it was of her?' Llewellyn questioned.

'I asked him, of course. He seemed embarrassed to be caught with it, especially when we all knew how she snubbed him. I think he was hurt that she should dislike him. Jas could never bear anyone to dislike him, always tried to bring them round. And he loved kids, was always ready to act as a godparent if anyone asked him. I suppose, with no children of his own, he tried to make up for what he had missed with other people's. Of course Sarah Astell refused to let him near the little girl. Probably thought she'd catch Aids, or something. Sad, really.'

Rafferty found himself nodding. He was beginning to feel sorry for Moon, who, in spite of his wealth and fame, had been denied the family life others took for granted. With no siblings, he hadn't even had nephews or nieces with whom he could have played the benevolent uncle. The Astells' little girl was the nearest he got to the real thing, yet he hadn't been allowed near her.

Madam Ginnie pulled a face. 'He loved to buy presents for people. I knew he would have loved the opportunity to spoil the Astells' little girl, but he knew her mother would probably burn them, so he confined himself to buying for Edwin and his wife. I noticed he had a parcel for Sarah Astell on his desk. It looked like a video film as it was about the right size and shape. Imagine, having it bought *and* wrapped several days before her birthday. Wish I could be that organized.'

Strange that she should draw such a diametrically opposite picture of Moon to the one Mrs Astell had supplied, he mused; to one he seemed *organized*, to the other *careless*. Anyone would be forgiven for thinking they were speaking of two different men. Moon must have given his gift to Mercedes or Astell to deliver,

Rafferty guessed, and reminded himself to ask them about it. It was unlikely to be significant, but anything to do with the victim had to be investigated. Although surprised to discover that Moon went in for charitable work, Rafferty wasn't impressed by Ginnie Campbell's championing of him. It seemed like a clumsy attempt to deflect any suspicions they might have of her. After all, a large sum of money was missing and Madam Ginnie was apparently in straitened circumstances. She had also, so far, avoided giving him the name and address of her 'friend'. The fact that all the staff had keys meant that any one of them could have waited till they saw Mrs Hadleigh and Henderson leave and then slipped in and killed Moon. And that included his boyfriend. He had had access to Moon's office keys for five years. He could have had them copied on any occasion during that time, or even helped himself to the originals, letting Moon assume he had lost them. But, as Ginnie Campbell had said, Farley was the loser by Moon's death. And Rafferty did like a nice juicy motive before he seriously suspected someone. Even if only to save himself from Llewellyn's nagging reproaches.

'You were going to give us your boyfriend's details,' Llewellyn reminded her. With a casual confidence, she supplied it. 'And he'll vouch for the fact that you were with him all of yesterday evening?'

'Of course.'

Rafferty was thoughtful as they left, having instructed her to come in to the station to have her prints taken. The method of murder was just the sort of impulsive behaviour an irrational woman like Ginnie Campbell would go in for. He had already seen evidence that she had a temper to match her hair; had she begged Jasper for a loan and been refused? It was possible she had seen red and struck him with the ball before helping herself to the contents of the cashbox. And, although she hardly seemed the epitome of the conscientious employee, it was possible she had unthinkingly locked the box up afterwards. It would be interesting to see if her alibi checked out.

Chapter Six

Rafferty consulted his watch as they left Ginnie Campbell's. Unwilling for Llewellyn to discover another of his professional failings – his weak stomach – he managed to inject a brisk, businesslike note into his voice as he suggested they get along to the post-mortem. In the car, he handed the mike to Llewellyn before starting the engine. 'Get on to the station, Dafyd, and get them to check out this French restaurant. See what time Moon came in last night and what time he left, what he ate and if he ate alone.'

Llewellyn relayed the request. The answers came through just as they pulled into the mortuary car park. Moon had apparently arrived at the restaurant at 6.15 p.m. Although they didn't actually open for business till 7 p.m, Moon was a good customer and they always made an exception for him. He had dined alone and had left at 6.50 p.m.

'Thirty-five minutes.' Rafferty grimaced. 'Usually takes me that long just to get someone to take my order when I go to restaurants,' he complained. 'Go on. What did he have?'

'He always had only one course on Thursday evenings, I gather. This week it was prawns. And as he selected each week's meal the previous week, it was usually practically ready for him when he arrived. Of course, he had work waiting for him and didn't want to waste time. And, presumably, he was expecting this Henderson chap.'

'Let's hope it helps Sam narrow down the time of death.' He got out of the car and slammed the door. 'Come on, we're late.'

Sam Dally, pathologist, as well as part-time police surgeon, had already started the autopsy by the time they reached the mortuary. They entered with as little noise as possible.

'Jasper Moon, male, Caucasian, fifty-eight years of age,' Sam was intoning briskly to the tape. He raised his eyes from the cadaver, and, clicking off the microphone, told Rafferty, 'I got tired of waiting, lad, so I started without you. You'll be pleased to know you've got something in common other than your appalling taste in socks: you're both AB blood group. Maybe he supplied some of his rare claret when you put your fist through that window? Shame you won't get the chance to reciprocate.'

Rafferty gave Sam a taut smile. 'Isn't it, though?' The incident to which Sam referred had been during his marriage to Angie. And it hadn't been accidental. Stupid, yes, as his ma had told him, but accidental, no. It was the sort of thing you did when your marriage was lousy. His ma would have been deeply upset at the idea of divorce, which was why he had put all thought of it out of his mind for so long, but he had been seriously contemplating it again when Angie's illness had been diagnosed, and death rather than divorce had put an end to their mutual unhappiness.

The assorted odours of the room hit him then and he clenched his nostrils hard. The sights during the PM were bad enough, he always thought, but the *smells* were worse; urine and faeces overlaid with the scent of raw flesh slightly gone over. But at least they succeeded in removing all thought of the dead Angie from his mind.

He told Sam the time of Moon's last meal. Sam nodded, and made an incision from neck to pubis, detouring around the tough tissue surrounding the navel. Now, the odours became overpowering. Rafferty gazed at the ceiling, clenched his nose even harder, and began siphoning air through his teeth as he sensed Sam begin to remove the organs.

Unsurprised, he noted again that Llewellyn was as impervious to the stink of death as he had been to the high scents of the recent heatwave. Impassive, he stood beside Rafferty, barely blinking as the photographer's flash recorded each part of the procedure, taking the objective interest in the autopsy that Rafferty wished he could manage. And even though Rafferty aimed enough curses at his head to fill a Gaelic swearbox, they had no discernible effect.

'You were right about the prawns,' Sam commented, as he removed the contents of the stomach. 'It's a wonder he didn't choke to death, as he must have fair gobbled them down. Mind,

75

ye canna beat a good prawn. Doesn't look like the digestive process had got very far. Of course,' he added complacently, 'it varies widely, so that's not as much help as you might think.'

As Sam bent back to his work, Rafferty, still fighting a rearguard action with the contents of his own stomach – a particularly rebellious Irish Stew, which resented internment, one of the canteen's supposed specialities – attempted to retain both dignity and dinner by concentrating his attention on telling Sam about Mercedes Moreno's warning to Moon. Predictably, Sam was inclined to scoff.

'It wasn't the hand of fate that smashed that ball down on his skull,' he retorted. 'Silly woman was probably only trying to make herself look important. Didn't you say she was from South America? Those Latin types always like to dramatize themselves.'

A pragmatic Scot, Sam Dally rarely got excited about anything. As far as he was concerned, if you were a native of any country that boasted more regular sunshine than his own Highlands, you were prone to hysteria. He put it down to too much hot sun in impressionable youth and a continuing over-indulgence in spicy food, and neither reasoning nor argument could persuade him from his prejudices. He should try working with Llewellyn, thought Rafferty. That should shift 'em. Still, in Mercedes' case, Rafferty thought Sam's prejudices might be valid.

'Attacked from behind,' Sam went on. 'Most likely with the crystal ball, as it fitted the depression nicely. Unlike you, Rafferty, the victim had an unusually thin skull. If he hadn't and he'd been found earlier, he might have survived.'

'So it could have been a woman who attacked him?' Sam nodded. 'Any update on the time of death?' he added, hoping to squeeze some further information out of the cautious Scot.

Sam pursed his lips, frowned, and then committed himself. 'As I mentioned, the digestion process hadn't got very far, not that that's a very reliable indicator, but I'd say he'd eaten roughly two hours before death, which tallies with what you told me about the most likely time of his last meal. Rigor was virtually complete, temperature loss as expected, so I'd say he died between seven-thirty and nine-thirty in the evening, with the most likely time halfway between the two.'

Rafferty nodded. It tied in with what Astell had told them. He mentioned the marks Appleby had found on the wall, and asked, 'Could Moon have remained conscious for long enough to write anything on the wall? Or is it more likely someone else wrote it in an attempt to mislead us?'

'Head injuries are funny things. People with fractured skulls have been known to walk about for hours. So, yes, Moon could have either remained conscious or only blacked out for a while and then come to. Certainly for long enough to scrawl something on a wall. Mind, there's no saying whether he'd be capable of writing anything sensible. There was only the one blow and he died from it.'

The PM eventually finished and, thankfully, they left Sam still muttering into his tape recorder. Waiting for his stomach to settle, Rafferty was grateful for the concealing darkness of the autumn evening. Crowds of commuters would soon be pouring out of the station homewards, but Rafferty knew there was little chance of *them* going home yet. It was still only the first day of the investigation – though to Rafferty it already felt like he'd been on the case the best part of a week – and they had hours of work ahead of them. He breathed in sharply, and as the fresh air cleansed the stink of death from his nostrils, he felt sufficiently recovered to tease, 'Hope Maureen's got an electric blanket, Dafyd, as I can't see either of us being free to cuddle up to anything warmer than a pile of reports for hours.'

The flickering lights of the car park illuminated Llewellyn's heightened colour, and Rafferty guessed that Maureen, one of his innumerable cousins – intellectual, feminist and with decided opinions of her own – had overcome Llewellyn's old-fashioned scruples. She'd probably persuaded him up to see some superior etchings – Greek ones, most likely. About time somebody had, he thought. As they reached the car, Rafferty said, 'I want both Farley's and Ginnie Campbell's alibis checked out as soon as possible. Liz Green should have finished interviewing the TV and astrology groups by now, so put her on to it. I'd like her reports and those on the magazine interviews on my desk first thing in the morning. With luck, we should have some news on both Moon's previous identity and his phone calls by then; might give us a few useful pointers. Especially as neither Farley nor Astell were prepared to admit knowing Moon's real name, which I find unlikely. I have to wonder what he – and perhaps they – were trying to hide.

'While you're on the phone, you might get a few more answers from Astell, like how Mercedes and Ginnie Campbell got taken on. Whether it was through an advert or personal recommendation. I also need to get the address of his other guest, this what's her name – Clara Davies. Ring Farley as well. I don't want him to think I'm neglecting him. Ask him if he knows whether Moon wrote a will.'

When they reached the Constellation Consultants offices Llewellyn went into Astell's room and shut the door, while Rafferty went into Ginnie Campbell's office. He had set Lilley to checking through Moon's client files and pale blue folders were piled all round the floor, making the desk look like a raft in a sea of paper. 'How are you getting on?' he asked DC Lilley's bent blond head.

'I'm up to S.' Lilley's grey eyes were still clear and bright with enthusiasm, in spite of hours of poring over paperwork. Of course, it was his first murder case, Rafferty reminded himself, as he took the growing list of names and addresses of Moon's clients from Lilley. Had his own youth been so eager, so shining? he wondered. He couldn't remember. Too much experience – of life, death and everything in between – clouded his memory and separated him from the young man he had been. Quickly, he scanned the list and handed it back. 'Did Mr Astell check if any were missing?' Lilley confirmed it, and told Rafferty that Astell felt pretty sure they were all there. He also confirmed again what he'd rung and told them earlier, that there was definitely no file for any Henderson.

Rafferty nodded. 'You can make a start checking these names out first thing in the morning. I'll assign some more officers to help.' Llewellyn put his head round the door and Rafferty went out to the landing to talk to him.

'I spoke to Mr Astell,' Llewellyn reported. 'He told me Moon had taken both Virginia Campbell and Mercedes Moreno on; he knew Mrs Campbell through the Astrological Society. Mrs Moreno met Moon at the television studios. She simply turned up there and asked for a job. Moon took her on to run the shop, which was shortly due to open. I rang Farley, but he claims he doesn't know whether Moon left a will or not.'

Rafferty raised his eyebrows. 'How very incurious of him. Especially as he's lived with the man for five years and would seem to have a vested interest in how Moon disposed of his wealth. What about Clara Davies? Did you get her address?'

Llewellyn nodded. 'Do you want me to go and see her now?'

'No,' Rafferty decided. 'Leave it till the morning.' He opened the door to Virginia Campbell's office. 'Come on, let's give Lilley a hand. Young lad like him needs his beauty sleep and he's been wading through those damn files all day.'

Two hours later they'd finished going through the files and composing the list of the clients' names and addresses. It was 9.30 p.m, and Rafferty let Lilley go home.

'It's getting bloody cold in here,' Rafferty complained five minutes later when he and Llewellyn were alone. While he'd been wading through the remaining files he hadn't realized what a chill had settled on the room, but now he became conscious of it.

'I gather Mr Astell insisted on turning the heating off before he left,' said Llewellyn. 'Said he was sorry but with the future of the business so uncertain he had to start economizing somewhere. We could sit in the kitchen while we go through the list,' he suggested. 'It's an internal room, so it might be a bit warmer in there.'

'If it's not it soon will be,' Rafferty promised with a grin. 'I can't imagine that Astell thought of forbidding us the use of the gas stove. A gallon or two of hot, sweet tea should warm the cockles nicely.' Rafferty thought longingly of Sam Dally's hip flask and regretted not parting him from it while he'd had the chance.

Ten minutes later, they sat companionably in the small kitchen, hands wrapped round large, bone china cups they'd found in a cupboard. It was snug, as, ignoring Llewellyn's warning that it was a method of heating not approved by the Gas Board, Rafferty had lit the oven, opening the door wide so the heat blasted out at them. The kitchen was too small to accommodate the SOCOs, and they had elected to take their hot drinks to Astell's less cluttered office.

By the time they had read through the entire list of names, Rafferty was on to his second cup of tea. He tapped the list in front of him and grinned. 'Wouldn't mind analysing this Sian Silk's hand,' he remarked, with a sly eye on the Welshman. 'And the rest of her. Nice work if you can get it, hey? Wasted on Moon, of course.' Not to be drawn, Llewellyn simply sipped his tea. 'Let's run over the facts. Jasper Moon was a homosexual. He also occasionally bought stolen goods, both of which activities were likely to lead to him mixing with some pretty shady characters.' He waited to see if Llewellyn would be unkind enough to remind him that he had dismissed the criminal aspect earlier. When he didn't, he admitted, 'Maybe I was a bit quick to deny its possible importance. This criminal contact of his might have been small time and greedy. Let's face it, Moon's little thousand-pound spending splurges would be peanuts to a professional. Could be this crooked acquaintance of his bumped him off and went round the back and broke the window to set up the burglar scenario.'

'The method of murder certainly suggests he knew his killer,' Llewellyn agreed, before quietly reminding him, 'though Moon apparently wasn't expecting to see this friend of his till the next day. And, of course, again we come back to the unlikelihood of such a criminal relocking the cashbox and leaving the expensive knick-knacks.'

Rafferty nodded gloomily. Whichever way they looked at it, they kept coming back to that. It was beginning to get on his nerves. 'Anyway, we'll get the squad to check with their snouts. See if anyone has any clues to who this chap might be.' Sam Dally had said Moon had been attacked from behind – which, as Llewellyn had said, indicated he had known his killer, thus effectively eliminating any opportunistic burglar. The door beside the shop led directly to the first floor. It had an intercom system which would enable Moon to check the identity of any visitor before releasing the door. They hadn't yet found anything to indicate that Moon went in for blackmail, Rafferty recalled. At least, the contents of his office hadn't revealed any such proclivities. Of course, they had yet to thoroughly check his home and his bank account, though if he was sensible, any money extorted by such means would be stashed in a bank deposit box somewhere. Rafferty put his drained cup in the sink and turned off the oven. 'Better get back to the station. See how the house-to-house team is getting on and if there's anything on this Henderson man. His details should have been on the early evening news.'

But, in spite of television, radio and newspaper appeals, Moon's client, Henderson, had still not come forward by the next morning. Rafferty began to wonder if he might not have good reason for keeping his head down. They had found no file for him in Moon's cabinet. Of course, as no one else in the partnership seemed to have heard of him, it was possible that he was a new client for whom a file hadn't yet been made. But, whoever he had been, it seemed probable that, unless Moon had had another, later visitor, Henderson had been the last person to see Moon alive.

'Get on to the media again please, Dafyd,' Rafferty instructed. 'Get them to put out the Henderson appeal once more. *Someone* must know him. Unless we're very unlucky' – a possibility Rafferty felt he could never discount – 'he can't have vanished into thin air.'

Admittedly, Moon's consultancy wasn't confined to local or even national clients, extending across the Atlantic and beyond, but even so Rafferty had considered it worthwhile to check each Henderson in the local phone book; none of them had matched Mrs Hadleigh's description. They were lucky they at least had a description to give to the media.

Llewellyn nodded and went out. He returned an hour later, advised Rafferty that the Henderson appeal was going to be run again on that night's early evening news, and then added to a strangely distracted Rafferty, 'I've spoken to Clara Davies. She confirms what Mr Astell said. The party broke up early. She left in a taxi at five past eight. We've also got the answers from BT concerning the numbers that were called from Moon's phone.'

'And?'

'All innocuous, and, apart from a call to Astell shortly after, all were to office numbers rung before five-thirty p.m. and all the call recipients had unimpeachable alibis.'

'What did he call Astell about?'

'As you know, the day of the party was also Mrs Astell's birthday. Mrs Campbell told us Moon had a wrapped parcel for her on his desk, and Mr Astell said that Moon rang to find out whether she'd liked her present.'

'He didn't speak to her, then?'

'No. She was busy preparing that evening's snacks.' Llewellyn paused and went on to state the obvious, for which he had a remarkable propensity. 'At least now we know that Moon didn't call anybody much after six, it would seem to indicate that Moon's receiver *was* knocked off its rest during the murder, which narrows the time down.'

'Mm.' Rafferty lowered his gaze back to the papers on his desk.

'And this,' he slapped his hand down on the paperwork, 'which was placed in my grateful hand not five minutes ago, would seem to indicate someone with a possible motive. Seems Hedges *was* Moon's real name,' he told Llewellyn. 'And it wasn't wholly surprising that he changed it to the more mystic-sounding Jasper Moon. Because under his Hedges persona, Jasper Moon had a record. He was a teacher in his younger days, apparently, and had been convicted of sexually assaulting a young boy in his charge.' Rafferty's eyes were bright as he added, 'And guess what the name of the boy he assaulted was? Terry *Hadleigh*. And Hadleigh not only has a record for burglary, but I've just had Fingers Fraser on the phone. Turns out Hadleigh's fingerprints are all over Moon's office.'

Fraser had also dusted the cashbox and the video they had found in Moon's wardrobe. The cashbox had prints of the Consultancy's entire staff, but that wasn't surprising as they all handled it. If anyone else had touched it, they hadn't left prints behind. As for the video, the only prints they had found on it had been Rafferty's. Embarrassed by the last piece of information, and puzzled as to what it could mean, once he had mentioned it he moved swiftly on. Unfortunately, as he told Llewellyn, Hadleigh had left no prints on the crystal ball itself. That had been wiped clean, but in Rafferty's book that made him look more guilty rather than less, as most of the prints had a perfect right to be there. Astell had told him that most people seemed fascinated by Moon's crystal ball and couldn't help touching it. Maybe Hadleigh had been seeking the help of Moon in order to discover the likely success of his next petty criminal enterprise? thought Rafferty with a quirk of humour. Savouring Llewellyn's expected reaction, he paused before he added the *coup de grâce*. 'Not just any fingerprints, mind. He left those *bloody* ones on the windowsill.'

Llewellyn's reaction wasn't wholly gratifying. His lips pursed, his eyes narrowed and he complained, 'Seems a little bit too easy, don't you think?'

Rafferty sighed. 'I might have known you'd have some fault to find. That Methodist hard work ethic of yours has a lot to answer for. Why shouldn't we have something easy for a change? I'm certainly not going to turn up my nose at a nice open and shut case. That's just the way I like them. Could even tie up with your theory about Moon trying to scrawl his attacker's name on the wall. The scrawl wasn't that clear. Could be he tried to write a "T" rather than an "I". It's not as if you've had any luck finding any Ians, Isaacs, or Isaiahs known to Moon. Put out a call for Hadleigh pronto, Dafyd. Like yesterday.' He handed over the papers before adding, 'And get yourself in front of a mirror and practise smiling. The way you look at the moment, you'll frighten our good fortune away.'

Llewellyn made for the door and opened it. Constable Beard stood on the other side, carefully balancing a tray with two mugs of tea. He was keeping it well away from his uniform jacket, with its gleaming buttons, in case of spills. Before Llewellyn disappeared, Rafferty added, 'Hadleigh's last known address and his usual haunts are in the file. Though if he is our killer, he's unlikely to be at any one of them. Probably gone to ground.' Llewellyn nodded and departed.

'Hadleigh, did you say?' Constable Beard carefully placed one mug on each of the desks and straightened up, his lined face wincing slightly, as if his rheumatics were troubling him. 'Would that be Terry Hadleigh you're talking about, sir, son of Mrs Ellen Hadleigh?'

Rafferty nodded. 'That's right. Why? Do you know them?'

'Lord love you, yes.'

Rafferty managed to keep a straight face at this unusual mode of addressing a senior officer. Some of his colleagues objected to Beard's familiarity, but it didn't worry Rafferty; he certainly preferred such up-front behaviour to the devious office politics that others went in for. Besides, Beard was something of an institution at the station and, in Rafferty's opinion, had more than earned the right to consider himself the equal of anyone there. 'Go on,' he now encouraged. 'Tell me about them.'

'Mrs Hadleigh herself is a very respectable, hard-working woman. Believes in keeping herself to herself. But that son of hers used to be one of our more regular customers as a lad. Before your time, I imagine. Spends most of his time in London now, I hear. You've obviously read his file, so you'll know he was into petty theft, burglary; even, er, soliciting. The times we live in, hey?' Beard sighed and shook his head sorrowfully. 'I was eighteen before I knew there was such a thing as a *female* prostitute, never mind any other sort. I wouldn't have learned that much but for having to do national service.'

'Yes, it's a man's life in the army,' said Rafferty. 'Learn how to kill, learn how to strip a gun, learn how to put your condoms on. Seems like Hadleigh may have moved up several leagues. Into murder, no less.'

'Doesn't sound like Terry Hadleigh's cup of tea,' Beard objected. 'He's never been into violence. In his game, he's too likely to be on the receiving end.'

'That's as maybe, but the evidence indicates otherwise. And a fine mess he's made of it. Dabs all over the place. Do you reckon Ellen Hadleigh might know where he's to be found?'

Beard nodded. 'Possible. He usually comes running home to Mum when he's in trouble, when he's short of cash and wants to scrounge. If anyone knows where he is it'll be her. You might try that pub by the river at Northgate as well, the Troubadour. Last I heard, that's his favourite haunt when he's here. Where he goes for a drink and a pick-up. Maybe some of the other customers might have an idea of his whereabouts, too.'

Rafferty nodded. He knew the place. It was a gay bar. Henry, the landlord, had been running the place for about five years, since returning from up north; he'd been born and brought up in Elmhurst. His parents had run an up-market bar and restaurant, the George Inn, in the south of the town for years. They'd only retired when their son had returned to Elmhurst.

'Tell Llewellyn to get copies of Hadleigh's mug-shots circulated, will you, Bill? And tell him to come back when he's done that and we'll pay a visit to this pub. I'd like to learn as much as possible about Sonny Jim before we see his mother, and his favourite gay haunt sounds the best place to start.'

Contentedly, Rafferty picked up his tea and sipped, determined to savour his unusual good fortune. An open and shut case wasn't something that fell into *his* lap every day. But, as Llewellyn's comment took insidious hold, doubts began to fill him, and he put the cup down again and stared pensively into space.

Although he knew Henry, the landlord, by sight, Rafferty had never needed to go into the Troubadour's bar. Henry was a big chap and could handle himself. He ran a well-ordered pub and there was rarely any trouble there.

Rafferty realized that Henry must have inherited his parents' photo gallery of their famous and not so famous patrons when they retired. Many pubs made a feature of such things, though Rafferty had reason to doubt the stars had patronized the George as frequently as the collection of pictures implied. He'd taken Angie there once or twice. She'd been keen to rub shoulders with TV personalities, and, anything for a quiet life, Rafferty had given in and taken her. The meal had cost an arm and a leg, but to Rafferty's relief and Angie's annoyance, the nights they'd gone they'd not seen so much as a weather girl. She hadn't asked to be taken a third time.

He was amused to see Henry even had a photo of the Queen, taken during her Jubilee year, as the large silver 1977 sign made clear. It had a centralized place of honour amongst the famous faces who had also supposedly patronized his parents' restaurant that year. Though Rafferty doubted that even Henry's parents expected to convince many that the Queen had *really* popped into their place for a leisurely prawn and steak dinner.

The Troubadour was busy, but the conversation died and the crowd parted as he and Llewellyn made their way to the bar. Conscious of the assessing stares, Rafferty wasn't sure whether to be amused or insulted to find the glances dismissed him almost immediately before moving on to his immaculately groomed sergeant. But maybe he was wrongly assessing either of their supposed attractions, he told himself. Perhaps it was simply that the Troubadour's customers all had reason to recognize a policeman when they saw one, and that their more obvious interest in Llewellyn was simply because he was the most elegantly turned out copper they'd seen in a long while.

There was the expected quota of willowy queens and butch, leather types that frequent any homosexual haunt, but nothing too overt. After all this was Elmhurst, not Soho.

'Henry.' Shuffling his feet and trying to ignore the whispered comments behind them, Rafferty greeted the landlord and introduced Llewellyn.

In front of the customers, Henry always pretended he didn't know any of the local police. Now, with an arch smile, he ignored

Rafferty's greeting and went into a well-worn routine for the benefit of his customers. 'What'll it be, dears? I do a nice line in Old Fashioneds. Or else there's a Long Sloe Screw Against the Wall.'

Rafferty smiled thinly. 'Too rich for my blood. I'll have a half of Elgood's bitter, and my friend' – this produced a titter from behind them – 'my friend will have an orange juice. I imagine you've heard about Jasper Moon's murder,' he murmured when the landlord had brought the drinks.

Henry immediately dropped his comic turn and nodded soberly. 'We're all pretty cut up about it. You in charge of the case, then?' Rafferty nodded. 'I hope you get the bastard who did it.'

Rafferty sipped his bitter, savouring its delicate hop aroma. He was surprised that Henry should be so amenable. In front of his customers, too. It was far from usual amongst homosexuals, even in a murder case. 'He must have been well known around here,' he commented, 'with his morning television spot and so on.'

'Quite a regular was Jasper, when he was at home. He liked to sit on that stool there in the corner of the bar.'

'Known him long? Like before he needed to change his name?'

Henry studied him for a moment, nodded, then told him quietly, 'Wondered how quickly you'd find out about that. I knew him slightly years ago, long before he began calling himself Moon, though as he seemed unwilling to talk about those days, or the court case, I never pushed it. Used to go to my parents' restaurant when he worked for that photographer chap Alan Carstairs.'

Rafferty raised his head. 'Hold on. I didn't know Moon had worked for Alan Carstairs. How long ago was this?'

'Oh, years and years ago.' Henry rubbed his chin thoughtfully. 'Must be knocking on for forty years ago now. He only worked for him for a year or two, though. Must have decided working for such a prima donna wasn't all it was cracked up to be. Never showed his face in the George again, that much I do know. Didn't set eyes on him again myself till I opened this place.'

Rafferty nodded. It explained why Sarah Astell hadn't known Moon. He'd have been long gone before she was born.

Henry went on. 'Carstairs could be demanding, I know, because years later my parents held his daughter's twenty-first birthday bash in their function room. Queen's Jubilee year, it was. It was the only function he ever booked at the George, though you'd swear he entertained there all the time and contributed to half the profits from the way he threw his weight around. I wouldn't mind, but he didn't exactly push the boat out when it came to spending his money. Had the cheapest set menu. With a man like that, you'd have thought he'd have had marquees on the lawn and an orchestra, but not a bit of it. Still, even if he wasn't Mum's favourite customer, he was very well known.' Henry grinned and nodded towards the wall of famous faces and Rafferty followed his gaze to the family group around the birthday cake. 'She made sure she got him on film during the birthday bash. She was determined to get *something* other than complaints and a stingy cut-price cheque out of him for being such a pain.'

'You were telling us about Moon,' Rafferty reminded him when Henry dried up.

'So I was. Anyway, when he left Carstairs he decided to take up art again, only this time as a teacher. But obviously you know all about that.'

Rafferty nodded. 'What about Terry Hadleigh? We understood he came in here sometimes. Have you seen him recently?'

The landlord shook his head. 'Can't say I have. Rarely comes in now. I heard he spends most of his time in London. Why?' Henry's gaze narrowed shrewdly. 'Think he did it?'

'Just routine enquiries,' Rafferty answered quickly. Even though the landlord seemed anxious for Moon's killer to be caught, he might just clam up if he thought they suspected another homosexual of killing him, even a low-life like Hadleigh. 'Did you ever see them together in here?'

'No. But then I'm not here every night. Got another pub ten miles away now. I spend half the week there.'

Rafferty nodded and said, 'It would help if we could eliminate Hadleigh from our investigation. Did he have any particular friends here? Someone who might be able to tell us where we could find him?'

The landlord shook his head. It seemed Beard's information had been stale, as Henry added, 'I don't encourage my place to be used as a pick-up joint. Got my licence to think of. Not that Terry Hadleigh was ever too popular, anyway. Reckon he'd have trouble giving it away now, last I saw of him.'

'What about Jasper Moon? Did he have any particular friends?' Llewellyn asked. 'Anyone he was close to?'

'Apart from his live-in boyfriend, you mean? No. Jasper was friendly with everyone, but he didn't play away from home if that's what you mean. At least, he *hadn't*.' The landlord frowned. 'But now you mention it, there had been rumours recently that he was seeing someone else. Jasper was very close-mouthed about it, but rumour has it he had a regular thing with someone in his office on Thursday evenings. It's probably why Jazz refused to give Farley a key to the building. It was the only place he could get away from him.'

'Did he want to get away from him?'

'I would if I'd been him. Farley is the jealous type. Wanted to keep Jazz to himself. I think he was scared stiff he'd lose him. Jasper was a bit of a soft touch, to tell you the truth. He even gave that red-headed termagant Ginnie Campbell a job when she was on her uppers, though we all told him he'd regret it. Jazz just said that providing she didn't dip her fingers in the till she could have a job with him for as long as she needed it. Dishonesty amongst friends was his pet hate, you see. Thought it showed the worst sort of disloyalty. Funny, really, as I gather he wasn't above buying things off the back of a lorry when it suited him. Still, takes all sorts.'

Interested to discover that Henry knew of Moon's little hobby, Rafferty questioned him further, but it was apparent that the landlord had no idea of the identity of Moon's supplier.

'Farley didn't like him doing favours for other people,' the landlord confided, returning to his earlier point. 'If he wasn't sulking about that, he made scenes when Jasper bought a round of drinks; anyone would think it was *his* money. Jasper was an open-handed guy; he earned a lot and he spent a lot. We all liked him. But as for that Farley . . . We all wondered what Jazz saw in him.'

'You can say that again. Chris Farley is a prize bitch.'

Rafferty turned to find himself face to face with a slender youth in pale blue, with blond hair curling becomingly around his collar. The landlord excused himself to serve a customer at the other end of the bar, and the youth enlarged on his previous comment.

'Farley upset most of the people in this bar at one time or

another. Used to come in here wearing that showy black cape of Jasper's, the little hair he's got swept back, just like he was Count Dracula or something. He could certainly bite. Draw blood, too, sometimes. We're all sorry that Jasper's gone, but you won't find many in here offering Christian Farley a shoulder to cry on.' He leant forward conspiratorially. 'Actually, I got the impression that Jasper was tiring of him. Not surprising, of course, because as Jasper became more well known, started appearing on television and so on, Farley became even more jealous. He's thrown a few tantrums in here, I can tell you. All over nothing. Jasper wasn't into playing around. At least, if he was, he'd been reasonably discreet about it. Until these recent rumours, that is.' Rafferty got the impression the youth had hoped to step into Farley's shoes.

'I did wonder if he'd met up again with someone from his past, the great love of his life. He only talked about it when he had one over the eight and got maudlin and then he let slip that there was one ruined relationship he would always regret.' The blond sighed. 'That was some torch he was carrying. No wonder Farley was prone to jealousy. There's nothing as difficult to compete with as the ghost of a past love.' His expression as blue as the dregs of his cocktail, he brightened when Rafferty offered to buy him another.

As soon as it was served, he resumed his story. 'Jazz was popular, always willing to do a reading for nothing. He liked to flirt, but it was no more than that. He put up with a lot from Farley. I'm amazed Jasper hadn't thrown him out months ago.'

Rafferty concluded from this that Moon had received more than enough encouragement to do so. He wondered if Moon *had* been carrying on a secret affair? But whether he had or not, Rafferty felt he'd certainly learned sufficient to turn Farley into one of the chief suspects, and he trawled his net a little wider to see what else he could pick up. 'I hear Terry Hadleigh comes in here too, sometimes. Do you know him? Is he a friend of yours?'

The blond looked piqued. 'Do you mind? Me, friends with that little tart? There's no need to be insulting.'

Rafferty sighed. Telling himself he should have got the tactful Llewellyn to do the questioning, he tried again. 'Do you know if he was a particular friend of Jasper Moon?'

'I'm sure I couldn't say. I'm not a dating agency, dear. I don't keep tabs on every little sexual divertissement that goes on around here. And it's not as if Jasper came in here that often. He was always flying off somewhere.'

Rafferty had another word with the landlord. But as he told him that no one else in the pub had known Terry Hadleigh well, or would be likely to know where to find him, they finished their drinks and left.

'Interesting that Moon worked for Alan Carstairs,' Llewellyn commented.

'It would be more interesting if it wasn't so long ago,' Rafferty replied. 'Sarah Astell didn't mention it, though I doubt she knew. Alan Carstairs seems the type to have got through employees at a great rate of knots. I imagine Moon was one in a very long line. Remind me to ask her about it, though. Just to clear the matter up.' They got in the car and Rafferty started the engine. 'Next stop Ellen Hadleigh. Let's hope she has some idea where Terry is and that she's willing to tell us.' He jerked his head back towards the pub. 'Even though Carstairs doesn't appear to have been one of his successes, it seems Moon was a past master at winning friends and influencing people.'

'When you're successful, everyone wants to be your friend,' Llewellyn commented succinctly.

Smiling sourly, Rafferty asked, 'Where'd you get that little homily from? Another of your know-all Greek chums, I suppose?'

Llewellyn nodded. 'Ovid, as it happens. From his Tris—'

'I've got another one for you: a murder victim becomes everyone's best buddy even quicker. *That's* from *Rafferty's Ruminations*. And even if Moon's turned into some kind of plaster saint now he's dead, the boyfriend hasn't. *And* he's the jealous type. I wonder if *he* suspected that Moon was seeing someone else? Perhaps, when we've seen Ellen Hadleigh, we ought to go and visit Farley again? As far as possible suspects go, he seems to be fast coming up on Terry Hadleigh's heels. It might be worth checking out his alibi again.'

Chapter Seven

Ellen Hadleigh lived near the railway station, in a flat on a Council estate. Rafferty knew from the frequent police call-outs that this was where the Council housed their more troublesome tenants, though he doubted Mrs Hadleigh came into that category. Her respectability would be used as a barrier against her neighbours; having heard what Beard had said about her son, he realized why she should need to. They would know all about Terry's arrests for soliciting; he had featured in the local paper on several occasions, even if, as Beard had said, it had been some time ago. She'd lived alone since her son had moved out.

The Council seemed to have spared every expense in maintaining the estate. Most of the shed doors had been pulled off their hinges, the bricks enclosing the weed- and litter-filled flowerbeds were tumbling down, and, from the roof, a steady cascade of rainwater splashed noisily on the cracked paving.

Rafferty checked his notebook as another train clattered past. Ellen Hadleigh lived at number thirty-nine, on the third floor. Glad to get out of the relentless downpour, which had continued with barely a break for the best part of a week, they walked through to the lift. Predictably, it smelled of stale urine. Rafferty wrinkled his nose and, while Llewellyn tried to get the lift to work, he studied the graffiti adorning its walls.

'Sharon loves Tracey,' confided one epistle. Another declared, 'Tracey loves Shane'. A third said, 'Get out of this lift, you ugly bastards'. The rest, mercifully, were in an unreadable, semi-literate scrawl. Rafferty's spirits drooped. He was glad to get out of the stinking little grey box when Llewellyn told him the lift seemed to be out of order.

They trudged up stairs littered with discarded contraceptives and dried pools of vomit. A young girl of about eighteen passed them as they reached the third flight of stairs. She was pale faced and dull eyed, as though robbed of her spirit by her soulless environment. She carried a fat, grizzling toddler under one arm and a fold-up pushchair under the other. Llewellyn, ever the gentleman, offered to carry the heavy child down for her and was rewarded with a suspicious look from under spiky blonde hair. Clutching the baby more tightly, she hurried past them. The little boy, presumably frightened by the sudden acceleration of their descent, screamed and his cries echoed and re-echoed painfully round the concrete stairwell.

'That'll teach you to accost strange young women,' Rafferty remarked. 'Surely your mother told you it wasn't a good idea?'

Llewellyn's long face grew morose, his expression that of a misunderstood Victorian gentleman whose hobby of saving fallen women was being wilfully misinterpreted. 'I only wanted to help her. Surely she didn't think I was . . .?'

'For God's sake, Dafyd, of course she did.' It was a constant source of amused amazement to Rafferty that, for all Llewellyn's superior university education, he could still be surprisingly naive about some things. Of course, he had spent a large part of his youth living the unworldly country life of a Welsh minister's dutiful son. Showed what too much religion could do to a man, thought Rafferty. Thank God he'd never taken to it.

'Listen, Einstein. Her fellow tenants don't live in your particular intellectual ivory tower, unfortunately for her. More like Sodom and Gomorrah. For all she knew, we could have been rapists operating in tandem. Wouldn't *you* be scared to meet two "ugly bastards" like us if you were on your own? The poor bitch probably gets accosted on these stairs several times a week.' He punched Llewellyn lightly on the arm. 'Never mind, *I* know your intentions were strictly honourable. Come on. It's up here.'

Number thirty-nine was at the end of the balcony. As Llewellyn knocked on the door, Rafferty studied the exterior of the flat. Although the door, in common with the rest of the block, needed a coat of paint, the knocker gleamed from a regular and vigorous application of polish.

The door opened a mere four inches, restricted by the cheap security chain, and Ellen Hadleigh's face peered suspiciously out at them. 'Oh.' Her expression stiffened as she recognized them. 'It's you. What do you want? I've told you all I know.'

Llewellyn, presumably still put out by the incident on the stairs, and unwilling to conduct the interview on the landing, had lost some of the shine from his usually impeccable manners. 'So, you're saying you had no idea that Jasper Moon used to be known as Peter Hedges and that he assaulted your son as a boy?'

She quickly denied it. 'Of course I didn't.' As usual, with unpractised liars, she tried too hard to justify her lies and forgot to voice shock, dismay, horror at what was supposedly unwelcome news. 'How could I know such a thing when I never saw the man but the once? He was away in America when I started there and even when he returned shortly before his death, he never arrived till after I'd finished my work and gone. It was only the night of his death that I set eyes on him and that was for a matter of seconds.'

Far from satisfied with her answers, Rafferty persuaded her to let them in. Her face withdrew and the door closed. It opened again a moment later, with a noisy rattle as the chain was released. About to remove his coat when she invited them to sit down, Rafferty kept it on instead, as he realized the room was like an ice box. He wondered how she managed? Presumably the only income she had was a small state pension and whatever she could pick up through various cleaning jobs. How often did she sit alone and in pain, unable to afford to heat the freezing room adequately? He guessed that her poverty was of that proud variety that would spurn any offers of charity, though he rather doubted any would be likely to be offered, anyway. With charity, as with everything else in life, those who shouted loudest got the most.

As though she had read his mind, she leaned forward in her chair and turned the gas fire on. Her manner defensive, she explained, 'I'm sorry it's so cold in here. I've been doing my housework, so I didn't bother to put it on.'

Rafferty nodded, happy to collude in the lie that the chill of the room was from choice rather than necessity. But how likely was it, he asked himself, that she would do her housework in what looked like her best dress? A long-sleeved, high-necked navy affair that gave the appearance of semi-mourning. 'You were saying you had seen Jasper Moon once only, for a period of seconds, and had no idea that he was Peter Hedges,' he began, taking over where

Llewellyn had left off. 'Yet Jasper Moon was well known. He was the astrologer on several glossy women's magazines, with his photograph prominent at the top of the page. He appeared on morning television. You had many opportunities to see his face and recognize him. Surely—'

'I can't afford to buy glossy magazines,' she told him scornfully. 'A pound and more most of them are. Do you think my pension stretches to such extravagances? I buy essentials and that's all. And when I get up I prefer to listen to the radio. It's easy to see you don't suffer from arthritis, Inspector. If I sat slumped in front of the television first thing, my legs would just stiffen up and I'd never be able to get to my work.'

What she said seemed reasonable. And what she said about watching morning television seemed eminently logical, too. Yet from what Beard had told them, it sounded as if Terry made a habit of running home to Mum when he was in trouble. It was improbable, after the biggest trouble of his life, that he wouldn't follow his usual practice. And even if Ellen Hadleigh hadn't realized Moon's true identity before his murder, her son would be sure to blurt it out along with the news of his death. 'Do you know where your son is, Mrs Hadleigh?' he asked.

'No. I've no idea.'

'It's very important we find him. Jasper Moon was murdered, and your son's fingerprints have been found in his office. Seems likely he could be in serious trouble. Very serious. I'm sure I don't have to tell you that this matter goes way beyond his usual petty offences. Now, perhaps we can try again? Can you tell me what possible reason he could have for going to Moon's office?'

After staring assessingly at him for some seconds, she must have realized that, if she was to help her son, she had to tell them the truth, for she said, 'All right, I'll tell you what I know. I don't want you thinking the worst of him. But,' she fixed him with a firm gaze, 'my son didn't go there to murder him, as you seem to think. Unlikely as it seems, they'd become friendly.' She frowned and looked down at her red, work-worn hands where they gripped each other in her lap. 'I had no idea *who* Jasper Moon was, no idea of what had been going on till my son told me he was dead.

'Terence was in a terrible state when he got here that night. I thought at first he must have been attacked. But then it all came out. He'd found Moon lying dead in his office – murdered. He said Moon would have been expecting him, that he used to go there the same day every week. It was a regular thing, and I gather it had been going on for a month or two.' She sounded bitter at the deceit.

'Why did he go there?' asked Llewellyn. 'Were they – having an affair?'

'No!' Vehemently, she denied it. 'Moon was helping him to get together a portfolio for entry to art college.'

Rafferty raised his eyebrows. '*Moon* was?'

'Seeing as you know what that man did to my son, you'll also know that Moon was trained as an artist. Anyway,' she went on, 'after knocking and ringing for a while, he went round the back and climbed on to the flat roof. He only broke in because he could see Moon's feet through the chink in the curtains and thought he'd been taken bad. Do you think he'd have broken in if he'd known he'd been murdered? With *his* record?'

Rafferty thought it kinder not to mention the possibility that her son had killed Moon for the contents of the cashbox. He could have watched Moon through a chink in the curtains, counting the money, and decided he'd rather have the money than the art lessons – if they had even happened and weren't just a product of Terry Hadleigh's artful imagination, which seemed likely.

'I can see what you're thinking,' she told him again. 'But my boy's not stupid. If he'd gone there to steal, he'd have worn gloves. He wouldn't have left his fingerprints for you to find. My son isn't stupid,' she repeated. 'He knew that much.'

Rafferty didn't contradict her. Admittedly, nowadays, even the most moronic of burglars had heard of fingerprints. But, surprisingly, a lot of criminals still didn't bother to wear gloves. He didn't think Terry Hadleigh would have been any different from the rest of his breed. Even if he had exercised more caution than most, if he had gone there for the reason she said and had robbed Moon on an impulse, he presumably wouldn't have had gloves with him anyway.

'What time is all this supposed to have happened?' Rafferty asked.

Her chin went up again. 'Not supposed,' she insisted. '*Did* happen. About eight-thirty. That's when Terence found him. But he'd been ringing on the intercom at the front for several minutes before that. He could see a light on in the hallway and when he went round the back Moon's office light was on. He said it all seemed as usual, except that Moon didn't answer the intercom.'

'Did your son happen to mention how he met Moon again?'

'They met in some pub. Terence said he recognized him straight away.' Her eyes looked searchingly into Rafferty's, as if anxious to discover if they would think her son had been on the make.

He probably had been, Rafferty guessed. He'd probably made a beeline for the well-known Moon, confident of an evening's supply of free drinks – and other benefits – for keeping his mouth shut about the assault. 'Moon would have recognized Terry, Rafferty told her. He nodded at a teenage photograph of Terry Hadleigh on the mantelpiece and recalled the latest mug-shots they had of him. 'He hasn't changed so much. As soon as he saw him, Moon would have been out the door like a shot. The last thing he would be likely to do was to befriend him, to chat about old times.' Although Rafferty suspected he knew the real answer, he asked the question anyway. 'So why would Moon offer to give Terry art tuition?'

'I don't know.' She met his eyes without flinching. 'I really don't know. Terence said he'd only mentioned his artistic ambitions to Moon in passing. He didn't expect him to offer to teach him.'

Rafferty was sceptical. Moon had too much to lose to take a chance on Hadleigh's forgiveness or discretion. If Moon's past became known, would the morning television people be willing to keep him on as resident astrologer? Would the magazine editors continue to offer him work? Their readership was predominantly female, and unlikely to take kindly to the continued employment of a known child molester. Fearing for their circulation in a tough, competitive world, the magazines would be likely to drop him as quickly as the television station. Of course, if Hadleigh had recognized and threatened him before he had been able to get away, Moon might well have decided that art tuition would be the lesser of two evils.

Ellen Hadleigh must suspect that her son would have threatened Moon with exposure, as she struggled to supply a reason for his benevolence. 'Seems Moon had a bit of good in him somewhere, after all,' she eventually offered. 'Must have realized he owed my boy something for what he'd done to him. He ruined his life, ruined both our lives. The endless gossip and sniggers meant we had to move from Wakestead.' She named a town about eight miles away. 'We couldn't move too far, as I had to be able to get to my jobs. My health wasn't too good even then,' she explained. 'And I knew, if I gave them up all at once, I might have trouble getting other work. Had to give up our lovely Council flat and all we could get at short notice was a swap into this sewer.' She glanced at them, then away. 'I suppose my Terence thought a bit of tuition wasn't much to ask by way of compensation. Terence always used to be so good at art at school, until—' She broke off, as though she couldn't bear to speak of the actual assault. Gathering herself together, she recommenced. 'Anyway, Moon offered to give him some coaching, bring him up to the necessary standard for college. That's why he went there. Not to steal, as you seem to think.'

'Why didn't you tell me this before, Mrs Hadleigh?'

She raised her gaze from the tightly clenched hands in her lap. 'I hoped you wouldn't find out anything about it. Stupid of me. I should have guessed that Terence's fingerprints would be all over the office. But,' she added sharply, 'would you have believed me, if I had told you voluntarily?' Rafferty said nothing, but his expression gave him away. 'I thought not. I know what you're thinking. My son didn't kill him. He was never violent, not my Terence, you must know that. It was always petty things he got in trouble for.'

Her story sounded so improbable it might even be true, and, uneasily, Rafferty began to wonder if his open and shut case might not be getting away from him? Certainly, what she had said tied in with both the PM and Astell's evidence. If Hadleigh's story to his mother was true, and *he* hadn't killed Moon, then he must have missed the real murderer by only a matter of minutes. 'He didn't see anyone, I suppose?' he asked hopefully. She shook her head.

'You said he looked through the window,' Llewellyn broke in. 'Didn't he notice that Moon's office was a shambles, with files all over the floor?'

'I told you, he only had a limited view through the chink in the curtains. He could see Moon's feet and the area just in front of

97

the window, but nothing else. Not till he was over the sill.'

Rafferty nodded gloomily. Moon's office had two solid desks at right angles to one another in front of the window and the files had come from the filing cabinet at the far end of the room. There had been one or two papers near Moon's feet, but if he had noticed them, Hadleigh might have assumed Moon had dropped them as he fell. With his limited view of the room and the angle of Moon's body, Hadleigh would have been unable to see either the shambles or Moon's smashed-in skull.

The front door hadn't been forced. And, apart from Hadleigh's broken window, none of the entry points at the back had been forced either. Which, once again, indicated that if Hadleigh hadn't killed him then the murderer had either had access to a key or had been admitted by Moon himself.

'I'd like you to tell me exactly what happened to your son when he was a boy, Mrs Hadleigh,' he told her. 'Please forgive me for asking it of you, but I want to hear it in your own words.'

Her eyes suddenly damp, she dabbed at them with a large, practical white handkerchief. It had been ironed, Rafferty noticed. He could see the stiff creases where the iron had criss-crossed the folds. She sniffed, put her handkerchief away, and sat up straighter in her chair. 'He was only fourteen. Just a lad. And small for his age. Nice looking, too. Moon – Hedges – was Terence's art teacher. He persuaded my boy to stay after school to help him sort out the art store. At least, that was the excuse he gave, but once he got him alone in the storeroom, he assaulted him. It was lucky that one of the cleaners heard his cries and discovered them or else . . .' She couldn't keep the bitterness out of her voice as she added, 'How that court came to let that wicked man off with a suspended sentence I'll never understand. I suppose I should be grateful the cleaners interrupted his-his—' Apparently unable to find an adequate substitute for the word buggery, she fell silent for a few moments before continuing.

'The attack and then the court case afterwards had a bad effect on my Terence, but he refused to talk to anyone about it. He just clammed up in the court and could barely be brought to say anything.' Her expression hardened again. 'I'm convinced Hedges threatened him in some way. Anyway, he got off very lightly. My lad began to go to the bad soon after. At first it was just little things, money missing from my purse and such like. My husband left us shortly after. Not that he was much of a loss. Tom Hadleigh was always a waster. Too keen on the good things of life but unwilling to work to pay for them. He ran off with a wealthy widow fifteen years older than him.'

With an abrupt gesture, she dismissed her ex-husband. 'We were better off without him. My mother was right. I wish I'd listened to her.' She sighed. 'I suppose I took to Tom because he was something of a dandy and as different a man from my fist-handy father as I was likely to find. More fool me. He took to drink and gambling a few years after we married. I even found out he'd been visiting some kind of brothel in Soho.' She pursed her lips. 'Funny, that, because he'd never been much of a one for the physical side of marriage. Terence wasn't able to kid himself that his dad was such a saint after that, I can tell you, I made sure of that. My son was a perfectly normal lad before that attack, very loving and thoughtful. That evil man, Moon, had a lot to answer for.'

She looked Rafferty firmly in the eye as if daring him to dispute it and told him, 'He's not a bad boy. I don't care what anyone says. He's never hurt anybody. He was more sinned against than sinning.' Her face began to crumple, but after a fierce inner struggle she fought off this display of weakness with the only thing she had left: pride, fierce and undefeated by all that life had thrown at her. 'The only person he ever hurt was himself. He wouldn't deliberately hurt anyone, I know that. He was always such a gentle boy. That's why . . .' She stopped and flushed guiltily.

'Why you lied for him?' Rafferty said softly, guessing the rest. He felt sorry for her and wished he didn't have to make her admit to the other lies. But Superintendent Bradley's heart was made of pure granite and compassion a word not in his vocabulary, so he forced himself to go on. 'There was no Mr Henderson, was there, love?' Surprisingly, he wasn't angry. He managed to forget the hours, the money and manpower wasted in search of the non-existent Henderson. But he wanted the matter cleared up. 'Jasper Moon had no client the night he died, did he? You invented him so we would have another possible suspect to concentrate our energies on.'

Ellen Hadleigh seemed to shrink in her respectable dress, as if part of her had seeped out into the faded upholstery of her arm-chair. Her work-red hand retrieved the dampened handkerchief from a sleeve, as, from lips bloodless and tightly compressed, she whispered, 'How did you find out?'

'I just remembered the name of the tobacconist's shop across the road from Moon's consulting room. That's where you got the name from, isn't it? I must admit, it seemed strange that Moon should see a client that night. Everyone told me he rarely saw clients on Thursday evenings; he liked to keep them free for other pursuits. Of course you didn't know that. How could you? You'd only worked there for a few weeks and Moon hadn't even been in the country till a few days before his death.'

Her head nodded in acknowledgement, and, as Rafferty stood up to go, she asked anxiously, 'Are you going to arrest me for wasting police time?'

He reassured her, and she sank back in her chair in relief. After thanking him, she asked, 'You'll-you'll let me know if-when you find Terence?'

Rafferty nodded. 'Please don't get up,' he added, as she began to struggle to her feet. 'We'll see ourselves out.' As he opened the front door, he heard the pop of the gas fire being turned off.

Rafferty glanced back at the rain-soaked flats as they reached the car. 'What a dump. She's not had much of a life, has she, poor cow? Precious few happy memories, I shouldn't wonder, and even less to look forward to.'

Llewellyn waxed philosophical as he climbed into the passenger seat; the prospect of suffering Rafferty's driving tended to bring on such moods. ' "The mass of men – and women – lead lives of quiet desperation." '

'More wise words from your ancient Greeks?'

Llewellyn shook his head. 'Thoreau.'

'French, hey. I always thought the French were too busy with cooking and cuckolding to bother with philosophizing.'

'Actually, he was American.'

Rafferty sighed. 'Mind, he's got a point. I'll be feeling a bit quietly desperate myself if we don't shake something loose from all this. Get on to the station, Dafyd, and ask them to notify the media that this Henderson chap doesn't exist. I'll speak to them myself later this afternoon, but I'll be more popular if they have the news before they put their papers to bed or have to alter the running order of their programmes.' When Llewellyn had got through to the station and relayed the message, Rafferty asked, 'What do you reckon to this story about Terry Hadleigh and the art lessons, anyway?'

'Could be true.'

'Could also be a pack of lies.' Rafferty rammed the gear lever into reverse and Llewellyn winced. 'Hadleigh and his mum had all night to concoct it.'

'In that case, I'd have thought they would have managed something rather better than a tale about art lessons. Ellen Hadleigh might be an unfortunate woman, but she didn't strike me as a stupid one.'

Rafferty nodded gloomily. But he clung desperately to his hopes of an early conclusion to the case. 'It could also be a clever double-bluff, though I doubt either of them are that smart. Still.' Rafferty executed a nifty turn that had Llewellyn sucking in a quick breath as he just missed hitting the pavement, and headed back the way they had come. 'When we pick him up we can ask him to produce his etchings, and I'll want something a bit more impressive than a copy of that sunflower picture you rave about. Looks as if it was dashed off in a spare half-hour by a backward ten-year-old. And it's bloody ugly. I might be willing to believe Terry Hadleigh's turned artistic if he can produce some decent evidence. I'll even buy one for Ma.'

Rafferty heard his telephone ringing before he reached his office. He thrust the door open and snatched up the receiver.

'Appleby here, Joe.'

'Glad to find it's not only us poor detectives who work on weekends.'

'You know me, keen as mustard. I rang about those threads of fabric you found on the victim's desk. I thought I ought to let you know that they were from an expensive material. Cashmere, no less.'

'How long do you reckon they'd been there?'

'Not long, I'd guess. Whatever they came from was new fabric; it had never been washed or dry-cleaned. They were caught on the lower part of the desk, so presumably came from a skirt or a pair of trousers. The black material was woven through with silver metal threads.'

'The glittery bits.' Rafferty nodded. 'They'd be some fancy pants, and no mistake.'

'It takes all sorts. Anyway, we've subjected the fibres to a battery of tests: cross sectioning, micro-spectrophotometry – you name it, we've done it. We've got the fibre type, the dye composition and chemical behaviour. If you manage to find the material these threads come from, we'll be able to match them. Could be your murderer, Joe.'

Rafferty snorted. 'And I'm the Queen of the May. They're probably just from the day-wear of one of Moon's more conservative rock star clients and nothing to do with the case at all.'

'Quite likely, as it's obviously a very up-market fabric. If it's a help, there was no blood on them. We'll be giving them a few more tests, anyway. But I thought I'd update you on what we've got so far.'

'Thanks AA. You'll let me know if you come up with anything further?'

'You bet.'

They had an early night. They deserved it, Rafferty decided, especially as they would be spending all of Sunday absorbing the mass of reports. Whatever else went on during a major investigation, the reports never stopped. Whenever they returned to the station, there they were waiting, as demanding as a wife and as impossible to ignore. Llewellyn rang Maureen and arranged to meet her. Unexpectedly, he asked Rafferty to join them. 'We're going to the Red Lion in the High Street,' he told him.

'What?' Rafferty grinned. 'The original teetotal Taffy in a pub? Don't tell me Maureen's finally persuaded you to abandon your youthful vow?'

'No.' Llewellyn's lips moved a fraction closer to his ears, so Rafferty knew he was smiling. 'They serve coffee – cappuccino. Maureen introduced me to it.'

'Very nice, too. So what are we waiting for? Lead me on to this up-market oasis, MacDaff. With my open and shut case looking decidedly iffy, I'm in need of some consolation.'

When he got to the pub, Rafferty's earlier mood of high optimism slid even further away. Although Llewellyn and Maureen made strenuous efforts to include him in their conversation, keeping the discussion suitably low-brow for Rafferty's benefit, every so often it would veer off back to their more intellectual interests and he would feel out of it.

He offered to buy the next round and escaped to the bar. While he waited at the counter, he glanced back at the intimate corner booth. Llewellyn's and Maureen's heads were bent close together over the table, probably taking the opportunity for a quick enthuse about some Greek or Latin know-all while he was at the bar, thought Rafferty morosely. Whatever they were discussing, they were so completely absorbed in it and each other, so natural, so right together and so obviously a twosome, that *any* third party trying to share their intimacy was bound to feel like the biggest, greenest and hairiest gooseberry on the bush. Or so Rafferty told himself. Only trouble was, it didn't stop the sudden and totally unexpected tidal wave of jealousy that swamped him, leaving him empty of everything but a deep melancholic well of loneliness as the jealousy drained away.

Angry with himself, he tried to shrug the feeling off. So he was lonely. So what? he demanded, as he tried to catch the eye of the snail-paced barman. So were countless other people and they got by. Tonight, though, Llewellyn and Maureen's closeness had brought him face to face with his own loneliness, and the feeling refused to be shrugged off. Forced to face it and himself – the first serious confrontation since his wife's death had ended their disastrous marriage, nearly three years ago – he realized he had *never* experienced the closeness that Llewellyn and Maureen seemed to share. Not with anyone; not with his wife, or with any of the women with whom he had had a series of short relationships both before his marriage and since Angie's death. They had been little more than bodies that he had taken to ease a physical need.

He knew he was gaining a reputation at the station as something of a Jack the Lad. Mr Love 'em and Leave 'em, Mr Screw 'em and Scarper. This sudden, unexpected insight made him realize that he no longer liked himself very much.

I must be getting old, he thought, his face setting in grim lines as he admitted that he was tired of shallow relationships. What he wanted was some easy loving domesticity.

The admission momentarily unnerved him. Because, if his ma

discovered his change of heart she was capable of renewing her matchmaking campaign. And that was the last thing he needed. His ma's idea of what constituted a good wife didn't match his own requirements; childbearing hips were definitely not amongst them. It was only his continuing lack of response that had convinced her she might as well stop parading nubile nuptial prospects for his selection like a madam at a brothel. No, he certainly didn't want her starting *that* up again. Rafferty was very fond of his ma, but she was a strong-willed woman and had as much staying power as a whalebone corset. If she were ever to guess he had done a volte-face . . .

No, he had every intention of finding his own wife. Only, he realized, as he caught the barman's eye and finally got served, he'd better make a wiser selection of soulmate than he'd managed last time. *One* unhappy marriage was bad enough, two didn't bear thinking about. He paid for the drinks and headed for the booth.

Soon after, Rafferty made his excuses and left. He wasn't good company tonight, he told them, when they protested. And an old man of nearly thirty-eight needed his beauty sleep. They hardly noticed he'd gone.

Chapter Eight

Rafferty entered the station on Monday morning still shell-shocked from the quantity of reports he had absorbed the day before, oblivious to the blur of faces clustered round the drinks machine until one of them hailed him.

'Too proud to talk to an old man, Joe?'

'Hawkeye. Sorry. I'm a bit preoccupied.' Harry 'Hawkeye' Harrison had been Rafferty's immediate superior when he had joined the force; he had taught Rafferty a lot, and he had some fond memories of him. Now retired from the police force, Hawkeye worked as a security guard in a tailor's in the shopping centre at Great Mannleigh, ten miles to the north. But he missed the camaraderie of the force and often popped in for a chat. 'How's tricks?'

'So-so. Mind, I reckon you'll have to start calling me "Bateye" soon. That damn security video screen plays havoc with the eyesight.' Whether it did or not, they were still bright with mischief as he asked, 'Still single, Joe?'

Rafferty nodded, waiting, warily, for the usual teasing. But, for once, it didn't come. Instead, Hawkeye's next words highlighted a previously unconsidered advantage to his single state.

'Lucky bugger. At least you can call your wardrobe your own. Only last week my missus gave away my favourite tweed jacket to Oxfam. Then, she insisted on dragging me round the shops at Great Mannleigh for an hour and a half to get a new one before I started my shift. Saw that astrology chap, Astell, hunting through the rails. You'd think he'd be able to foretell when his wife's about to pull a similar stunt and give away his old penguin suit. Women! Stocking up their own wardrobes should be enough for them without poking about in ours.' With the ease of long practice,

Hawkeye glided from small talk to the real reason for the visit. He gave Rafferty a shrewd glance, before asking, 'So, how's the murder investigation going?'

Rafferty scowled. 'You know that saying "Slowly, slowly catchee monkey"?' Harrison nodded. 'That's how I'm playing it.'

'That bad, huh? Never mind.' Harrison sympathized. 'If Long Pockets complains, you can always tell him you're not only saving the force's face and fortune by avoiding a court case for wrongful arrest, but you're also preventing the unravelling of the woollen veil he's knitted over the public's eyes with his politeness programme. What more does he want?' Hawkeye grinned. 'He's not twigged the PIMP aspect yet, I take it?'

Rafferty shook his head. 'If he had, you'd have heard his bellow all the way to Great Mannleigh.'

'True.' They both paused reflectively. Then Hawkeye said, 'Shame about Jasper Moon. I rather liked him. He might have put his pecker in peculiar places, but his heart was in the right spot. Ever since I caught those young tearaways who'd been vandalizing his street door he always gave a good Christmas bung to the Widows and Orphans fund.'

Rafferty frowned as yet another witness depicted Moon as aspiring to sainthood. What was it about the man? Their child-abuser seemed to be turning into a veritable *Father* Teresa. Liz Green's reports had been the same. According to her, Moon had been a favourite at the TV studios, he'd sorted out the love-life of the editor at one of the magazines he wrote for and steered the editor of another to a more suitable line of work. He'd even managed to avoid serious jealousy at the Astrological Society, which, given that it was apparently composed in the main of assorted old queens, must have been a major achievement. Rafferty had to admit that this case was giving his prejudices a severe hammering. Llewellyn would be pleased.

After further reminiscences, Hawkeye headed for the canteen to renew other old friendships. Rafferty went up to his office on the much less enjoyable exercise of continuing the murder investigation. He found Llewellyn already there, reading through the latest reports. 'Hadleigh not turned up yet?'

Llewellyn shook his head, and Rafferty sighed. Until they found him he felt stymied. A major suspect in the investigation and the combined strength of the Met and Essex forces couldn't lay their hands on him. 'I want you to ring Moon and Astell's partnership solicitor,' he told Llewellyn. 'Ask him about the intestacy rules. We might as well investigate other avenues while we're waiting for the artistic Terry Hadleigh to turn up.'

Their investigations had revealed that, not only had none of the town's solicitors drawn up a will for Moon, but neither had any of the solicitors working within a ten-mile radius of Soho. Rafferty was beginning to agree with Astell – that Moon must have written his own will. Although he had little knowledge of the law on such matters, he knew enough to realize that writing your own will was a chancy business. Put one word out of place, or neglect to put another word in, and your estate could be distributed in a way you had never intended. Moon had been foolhardy if he *had* written his own will, especially as, if it had ever existed, it now seemed to have disappeared. But if it *had* existed, Moon would surely have needed two witnesses to sign it, and Rafferty made a mental note to ask amongst Moon's friends and acquaintances to see if any of them had witnessed such a document.

At last, Llewellyn hung up the phone. And two minutes later Rafferty learned that he had been wrong about the need for witnesses. It seemed that if Moon had written his will in his own hand – a holograph will, as the solicitor had termed it – it would still be legally valid with just Moon's signature. Rafferty consoled himself for this latest disappointment with the thought that, as they were having no more luck in finding the will than they were in finding Terry Hadleigh, it hardly mattered. 'Let's have the rest,' he said.

'There are strictly applied rules as to who can inherit and in which order when there is no will. These are a bit complicated, but, roughly, where there's no spouse, the estate passes to the surviving relatives in the following order: descendants such as children and grandchildren – legitimate and illegitimate – then parents, brothers, sisters and their descendants, then grandparents, uncles, aunts and their descendants, then great-uncles and great-aunts and their descendants, namely second cousins, second cousins once removed—'

'All right, all right, I think I've got the gist of it,' Rafferty broke in. 'Moon had no relatives closer than second cousins. Presumably they get the lot?'

'They would have done, yes.'

'*Would* have done?'

'They may well still get it. Probably will. However, the Inheritance Act of 1975 widened the scope of those who can make a claim on an estate. That's what I meant when I said it was complicated. It would be up to the Courts.'

Rafferty smothered a sigh as Llewellyn continued, his voice now taking on the dry, precise tones of Moon's solicitor. ' "Any person – and this includes friends or relations – who immediately before the death of the deceased was being maintained either wholly or partly by the deceased may apply to the Court. The Court can then make an order for a lump sum or periodical payments. And can also make a wide variety of other orders, for example for the transfer of the deceased's house to the applicant." '

Rafferty stared at him as the implication of Llewellyn's words sank in. 'Let me get this straight. Are you saying that if there *was* no will, or if no will is found, *Farley* could apply for a lump sum under the Inheritance Act?'

Llewellyn nodded.

'But what are his chances of getting anything?'

Llewellyn shrugged. 'The solicitor wasn't prepared to commit himself on that.'

'Typical,' Rafferty muttered.

'But the key word, apparently, is whether the applicant was *maintained* by the deceased. And Farley was. Of course, the Court might still turn him down, but it would be worth his while to try. He didn't work, he had no income other than what Moon provided. I spoke to the local DSS earlier and he had never even applied for unemployment benefit or social security.'

'Why should he put himself to the bother of filling in all their wretched forms when he was living the life of Reilly at Moon's expense?' was Rafferty's terse comment. 'If Moon left him nothing, it certainly makes it more likely that he should have destroyed any home-made will. At least with the Courts he had some hope of getting *something*. They'd been together for five years and he hadn't worked for a good chunk of that time.' Rafferty tugged thoughtfully at his chin. 'But it all seems a bit too iffy for murder. Farley would surely want a more rock-solid guarantee that he'd get his hands on the loot before he killed

Moon, jealousy or no jealousy. Friend Farley strikes me as having a definite eye for the main chance.'

He began to rummage through the latest reports on his desk, stiffening as he found one that had something positive to say. 'Listen to this,' he said. 'Witness rang in – anonymously, of course, aren't they always? – to say they'd seen someone with a remarkable similarity to Farley on several occasions hanging around outside Moon's consulting rooms on the last couple of Thursday evenings before they flew to the States. Wonder if our anonymous informant is the blond bombshell in the Troubadour? Seems the sort of thing he'd try. Worth looking into, anyway,' he concluded. 'I shall have another little word with the emotional Mr Farley.' He glanced despairingly down at the pile of reports still awaiting his attention and sighed. In spite of the previous day's Herculean efforts, the paperwork was once more mounting up. 'But not just yet. I'd better plough through these first. You know what the Super's like. If a man's not on top of the paperwork, he thinks he's not on top of the case. And if I don't get this lot digested, he's bound to ask about them. Besides' – he grinned weakly – 'one of the station crawlers is bound to let him in on the joke soon. With an imminent eruption from Bradley on the cards, it's not a good idea to supply him with more fuel.' The phone rang, and, muttering 'Hope this isn't Vesuvius,' he reached for the receiver. 'Inspector Rafferty.'

'Inspector, my name's Rachel Hetherington.' Rafferty breathed a grateful sigh at the reprieve. 'I work for Life and Leisure Insurance Company.' Rafferty was just about to say that, as a single man, he hardly had need of life insurance, when she continued. 'I've read about the murder of Jasper Moon and I wondered if you might be interested to learn that we hold an insurance policy on his life. It's for a very large sum.'

Rafferty's heart skipped a beat. They had found no insurance policies at Moon's flat. Farley was the only person in a position to remove such a document from Moon's papers. Unless it had been quite innocently lost, a possibility Rafferty couldn't discount, only the murderer would have had the prior knowledge necessary to remove it. And only the beneficiary, guilty of murder for gain, would need to. 'Who's the beneficiary?'

'A chap called Christian Farley. Lives at the same address as the policyholder. Do you know him?'

'Oh yes. I know Mr Farley.' It was the answer Rafferty had expected. 'Could you let us have a copy of that policy?'

'Certainly. I'll drop it round to the station. I only work round the corner.'

'That's very good of you. Many thanks.'

He hung up. 'Did you get all that?' Llewellyn nodded and issued the expected word of caution. 'I know,' said Rafferty. 'It doesn't prove anything. But even you must admit it's damn suspicious.'

'Is that the policy?' Llewellyn asked half an hour later.

Rafferty nodded. 'Yes. And it's here in big dark letters that Hadleigh wasn't the only one with a motive for killing Moon. Christian Farley had several hundred thousand of them, all in sterling. So, with what we've learned about Moon's insurance policy, Farley's jealousy and his possible spying activities, he's suddenly become even more interesting. The thing is, will he admit that he knew he stood to gain a large sum in the event of Moon's death?' He paused. 'Is Farley's friend still singing the same song?'

'Yes. For what it's worth he still insists Farley was with him all evening. But WPC Green said he seemed high on something when she spoke to him again this morning. She had a much more revealing conversation than before. Said he seemed to have a grudge against the police. She got the impression he'd say anything to the force, as long as it wasn't the truth. Not a terribly reliable witness.'

'So, if Farley's little friend tells lies to the police on principle, it's possible that he'd tell lies about Farley's whereabouts. Motive *and* a weak alibi. Better and better.' Rafferty digested this, then asked, 'What about Mrs Campbell? Did Lizzie Green turn up anything more on her?' Liz Green had already spoken to the boyfriend, and he had confirmed what Ginnie Campbell had said.

Llewellyn nodded. 'When WPC Green went back this morning and spoke to his neighbours, they said she could easily have slipped out the back way without the boyfriend or themselves being any the wiser. The boyfriend is a drinker – drinks himself insensible regularly, apparently. They also told her that Mrs Campbell's car must have been parked elsewhere, as it wasn't outside the house.'

'So Ginnie Campbell's another one who could have slipped out without too much trouble. Has WPC Green typed up her latest reports?'

Llewellyn nodded. 'She was finishing when I spoke to her.'

'Get her to bring them in to me, will you? I want to read them before I speak to Ginnie Campbell and Farley again.' He never minded reading the pretty WPC's reports. They were always pleasantly brief.

Told that the police had a witness who had seen him hanging about outside Moon's offices on Thursday evenings just before their US trip, Christian Farley reacted with a self-pitying rage.

'Don't you understand I *had* to find out if anything was going on?' he demanded. 'Jasper, even before he became rich and famous, could have had anyone. Do you think I didn't realize that? Ever since we've been together I've felt insecure, scared of losing him. And, as I became older and my looks faded, I became more and more frightened. How could I help it? I was jealous of all those beautiful people he mixes with. How could I expect to compete?'

Farley flung himself down on the black leather settee. 'He'd started coming home late every Thursday evening. He told me he was working on his latest book, wanted to get it well along before the trip to the States, but he could do that just as easily on the computer here. Of course, he wasn't working on his book at all, as I discovered.' Farley's green eyes glittered with a peculiar malevolence. 'He had that little tart Terry Hadleigh up there with him. I saw them. Jasper was . . . Jasper was naked. I saw him through the curtains.' Farley's pink and white complexion took on a mottled hue, as if several strong emotions were battling within him. Self-pity won. 'To think that after all this time, and all the beautiful people, it should be that cut-price whore who took Jasper away from me.'

Rafferty forbore from reminding him that, as Jasper Moon was dead, Hadleigh had gained nothing, whereas Farley himself was now a rich man. 'Were you aware that Mr Moon had taken out a large insurance policy on his life, with you as the beneficiary?'

Farley paused before answering, as though debating whether lies or truth would best serve him. Then, his voice harsh, he admitted, 'Yes, I knew. But I didn't kill Jasper to get my hands on it, if that's what you're implying.' He denied removing the policy from among Moon's papers, insisting that Moon himself had lost it. 'Surely you've learned by now that Jasper was notoriously slack with any sort of paperwork? I know he said he'd contact the insurance company and get a replacement, but obviously he never did so. And, for the record, I wasn't anywhere near his office last Thursday. You just try to prove otherwise. I loved him, I tell you. The last thing I wanted to do was lose him. Without him, my life is empty.'

Empty, apart from all the lovely money that would now fill it, thought Rafferty cynically. If he'd already lost Moon's love he had nothing to lose by killing him and everything to gain – as long as he was confident of getting away with it.

They left him then, with the warning that they would want to see him again.

'Right.' Rafferty consulted his watch. 'I'm off to the accountants. I don't know what time I'll be back.'

Mr Spenny, the accountant who dealt with the partnership books, was a thin, stooped man with a ruff of white hair, but his eyes were as sharp as those of any of Zurich's gnomes. He seemed to take as a personal slur on his professional abilities the suggestion that there might be something untoward in the accounts. He had already explained at length in his slow, rather prissy voice that he had gone through the appointments book that Rafferty had dropped in for him, matching the appointments up with the invoices. Now, he proceeded to go through it all a second time, just in case Rafferty should have any doubts, explaining that the invoices all tallied with the appointments and the payments into the bank account tallied with the invoices. Ginnie Campbell was responsible for opening the post and entering the details of incoming payments and while the idea of collusion between her and Astell was a possibility, Rafferty considered it unlikely.

'What about withdrawals?' Rafferty asked when Mr Spenny finally paused for breath. 'Have there been any unexplained amounts taken from the account?'

Mr Spenny drew his thin lips together. 'No indeed. I've been through the bank statements as you requested. Nothing has gone out of the account other than the usual amounts for petty cash, the wages and the partners' own monthly drawings. I can assure you, you're quite mistaken if you suspect any financial improprieties.'

After thanking Mr Spenny for his time and trouble, Rafferty walked slowly back to the station. He had a lot to think about.

'Seems Edwin Astell hasn't had his hand in the till,' Rafferty told Llewellyn when he returned to the station. 'So that's one of my theories gone the way of the dodo.' Gloomily, he wondered how many more would have a similar fate before he finally found Moon's murderer.

His hours at the accountants and the resultant fog in his brain had tired Rafferty out, and he decided to call it a day. Llewellyn was going to some late art gallery showing with Maureen. With a grimace, Rafferty recalled that he, too, had a date – with his ma and the clairvoyant, Madame Crystal.

The doorbell gave a stentorian clamour. Startled, Rafferty dropped the hairdryer, and its hot blast scattered the paper he had been doodling on earlier in the week. He glanced at the clock as he rushed to answer the door; he might have known his ma wouldn't wait for him to collect her. Any excuse for a nose into his love-life would do.

'Hello, son.' Kitty Rafferty's gaze wandered from his half-dried hair, past his shortie Chinese dragon dressing gown, to his large bare feet. 'Can I come in?' she asked. 'Or do you plan on entertaining the neighbours to a kung-foowi demonstration?'

'You're early,' he told her, as she shut the door. 'I said I'd collect you.'

'I got her next door to drop me off on her way to her eldest girl's. I thought it best. You know how difficult you find it to get anywhere on time, and I didn't want to be late. Now we've time for a cup of tea. I hope you've got proper tea-leaves as I told you, not your usual dustbags,' she called as she made for the kitchen, 'and then I can read your fortune.'

Rafferty, aware that his ma was capable of making use of his own groceries to poke about in his love-life had made sure that any tea-leaves had been consigned to the bin. He congratulated

113

himself on his foresight and wondered how he would be able to prevent her bringing her own next time.

After he had finished drying his hair, he realized that neither the promised tea nor his ma had appeared, and concluded that she was taking the opportunity to have a snoop. Tying the knot of his belt tighter, he made for the door, only to meet his ma on her return. As he had suspected, she had a glow of satisfaction but no cups.

'What's the matter, Ma?' he enquired sarcastically. 'Couldn't you find the kettle? It's not like you.'

'Mind your tongue, Joseph Aloysius. You're not too big for a slap on the legs.'

He grinned. 'So where's the tea, then?'

'Sure and I've left it to brew,' she explained. 'I know how strong you like it and those awful bags you buy take for ever.' Deprived of a roundabout snooping route by the dearth of tea-leaves, she was forced to make a frontal assault. 'Done any entertaining lately, son?'

'When do I get the time to entertain, Ma?' he prevaricated. 'You know I'm in the middle of a murder investigation.'

She sighed. 'Dafyd doesn't seem to let his work interfere with his love-life.'

'That's because you've got his love-life under your personal supervision, Ma,' he reminded her dryly. 'He doesn't get a chance to neglect it.'

'Sure and you could do a lot worse yourself than let me find a nice little girlfriend for you,' she told him tartly. 'But no, not you—'

They'd had this conversation too many times for Rafferty to want to hear it again. 'Anyway,' he told her firmly, 'Dafyd's not in charge. The case is my responsibility and it has to take priority over anything else.' Even your quest for grandchildren from your eldest son, Rafferty silently added.

Bested for now, his ma made a moue of annoyance. But it didn't stop her scrutinizing the letters that Rafferty had stuck behind the clock. Obviously, his being there was cramping her style, for she suggested he get some clothes on.

Rafferty left her to continue her snooping. When he returned, the tea was poured and she had collected his scattered doodles from the carpet. He stood in the doorway watching her as she quickly perused them. 'Hoping for love-letters, Ma?'

'Do you have to come creeping up on a body?' she demanded. 'And it's only tidying up, I am. What was all this rubbish doing round the floor, anyway?' she asked as she glanced down at the sheets. 'Doodling, is it?' Her eyes twinkled wickedly. 'Did you know a man reveals a lot in his doodles. Take yours, for instance—'

Rafferty plucked the sheets out of her hands. 'They're *not* doodles,' he told her firmly. 'If you must know, that's what Jasper Moon scrawled on his office wall just before he died. I copied it last week at the scene of his murder and have been trying to see what else I can make out of it ever since. Dafyd thinks it's a toss-up between attempts to write an "I" and "T". Someone's initial, you see. I reckon he's right.'

'God bless us and save us,' she muttered. 'Sure and anyone with a brain in his head could see it's nothing of the kind,' she told him. 'I'd have thought Dafyd, at least, would—'

'All right, Miss Marple,' he broke in irritably. 'Tell the thick detective what *you* reckon it is.'

'If you'll give me a minute, I'll not only tell you, I'll *show* you.' She began to hunt through her capacious handbag. 'I know what you think of my little hobby, so I don't suppose you'll believe me till you've seen the evidence with your own eyes. Wait now till I find it.'

Rafferty folded his arms as pale blue knitting wool for the latest grandchild, her worn tobacco pouch, several spectacle cases and packets of extra-strong mints were all emptied on to the carpet before she found what she was looking for. 'There, Mr Detective.' She opened a magazine and triumphantly thrust it at him. 'Take a look at that.'

Rafferty took the magazine. He looked. He flushed.

'Well might you blush. Now will you be telling me I don't know what I'm talking about?'

With mock humility he shook his head and told her, 'Not me, Ma. Not ever again.' With a grin, he gave her a smacker on the cheek, picked her up and swung her round. 'You're a wonder, that's what you are.'

'And so are you – a wonder to me I ever gave birth to you. Now, put me down and drink your tea.'

He did so and held up the magazine. 'Can I keep this?'

She nodded. 'But I'll want it back, mind. I haven't read it yet.' She returned her belongings to her bag, stood up and gulped down the rest of her tea. 'And now that I've solved your murder for you, is there any chance we can make tracks for Madame Crystal's and get a few answers from your daddy?'

Rafferty breezed into his office the next morning, told a startled Llewellyn that the case was as good as solved, and handed him his ma's astrology magazine. 'Take a look at that.'

Llewellyn glanced briefly at the page indicated, before he turned to the front of the magazine, raised his eyebrows, and asked perceptively, 'Do I detect the assistance of the indomitable Mrs Rafferty in the matter?'

'You do,' Rafferty told him sheepishly. 'We now know what that symbol means. It wasn't an attempt at an initial, at all, but the astrologer's way of writing the sign for Gemini. Jasper Moon was a professional astrologer. What was more natural than for him to scrawl the identity of his murderer in the astrological language he used every day? Which is what Ma kept repeating all the way to that damn clairvoyant's last night. As I told her, perhaps if he'd written it more clearly we'd have got there quicker and without her assistance. Still.' He rubbed his hands gleefully. 'All we have to do now is find out which of our suspects is a Gemini and we've cracked it.'

'Gemini.' Llewellyn frowned as he studied the page. 'But this says that the sign covers the end of May and most of June.'

'That's right,' Rafferty agreed. He felt a moment's anxiety at Llewellyn's doubtful expression, but even Llewellyn couldn't argue with accepted astrological fact, he reminded himself.

'No, it's wrong,' Llewellyn contradicted. 'Because none of our suspects was born during those weeks. I've got all their details in here.' He patted his breast pocket where he kept his notebook with its neatly recorded information.

Rafferty stared at him. 'One of them must have been,' he insisted. 'Obviously, whoever killed him recognized the significance of Moon's clue and lied to you. You're too trusting, man. You shouldn't believe everything you're told.'

Llewellyn's lips thinned. 'No one lied to me. I checked their details. You know I always check everything.'

That was true, Rafferty knew. Llewellyn might frequently be a pain in the behind, but he was a painstaking pain.

'Virginia Campbell subtracted a few years from her age but she didn't worry about the month. The others didn't even bother to lie about the year.' It was Llewellyn's turn to look smug. 'Not one of our suspects was born during the dates given here. None of them is a Gemini.' Llewellyn took out his notebook, found the appropriate page and handed it to Rafferty with a flourish. '*Ecce signum*. Look at the proof.'

Rafferty snatched the notebook and studied it, before throwing himself into a chair, all his jovial bonhomie sunk to his boots. He'd been so *sure* he was on the right track at last. He lost his temper and scowled at Llewellyn. 'You needn't look so bloody cocky. How many bright ideas have *you* come up with?' he demanded. 'All I get from you is smart-arse quotes. Why don't you try this one for size? *Dūn an doras mās é do thoil é.*' His pronunciation was shaky; luckily Llewellyn wouldn't know that.

Llewellyn raised his eyebrows in that superior way he had. 'Irish?' Rafferty nodded. 'Would you care to translate?'

'You're damn right I would. It means, put a lump of wood in the hole.'

'Pardon?'

'Shut the bloody door, man,' Rafferty translated again. 'And make sure you're the other side of it!'

His expression injured, Llewellyn retreated to the doorway, from where he fired a parting salvo. 'At the risk of getting my head bitten off, I was going to tell you that I finally got an answer from those Memory Lane video people. They said Moon ordered four copies of the video and paid by credit card. The videos were posted to his office the week before his murder. Makes you wonder what happened to the other copies.'

No it doesn't, Rafferty muttered to himself. Between clients that don't exist and blood-red clues that make no sense, I'd rather have a rest from wondering.

As the door shut softly behind his sergeant, Rafferty slumped. He already regretted his outburst, but sometimes Llewellyn got right up his nose. Angry with himself, Rafferty took his temper out on the other departed; it was the only way he could be sure of having the last word. 'Not up to much, were you, Jasper, old love?' he taunted the glossy photograph of Moon which he had pinned to the noticeboard at the start of the case. 'Not only did you fail to predict your own death, you couldn't even manage to give us a halfway decent clue.'

Chapter Nine

Demoralized after receiving such a knock-back, Rafferty gave himself a pep-talk. You're a copper, he reminded himself. And coppers 'cop', not cop-out. You've still got a case to investigate; still got suspects with shaky alibis, so get on with it. You can start by having another word with Ginnie Campbell.

As Rafferty opened the door of the Psychic Store, he snatched a glance at Llewellyn's face. The Welshman, still put out over Rafferty's angry outburst that morning, was barely talking to him. Even an apology had done little to thaw the air. But instead of throwing him deeper into the glooms, Llewellyn's 'nasty smell under the nose' expression filled Rafferty with a new determination to catch Moon's killer. It was just going to take longer than he'd thought, that was all.

There was music playing in the background. Strangely soothing, it sounded like a rushing wind interspersed with the cries of sea birds and the calls of whales and dolphins.

'Do you like it, gentlemen?' Mercedes Moreno materialized beside them and fixed Rafferty with her great dark eyes.

'It's – unusual.'

'It's designed to relax the stressed mind,' she told him. 'Would you like a copy? It's a very reasonable price.' She paused and added softly, 'I'm sure even Edwin would be happy to offer a discount in your case, especially if it calms your mind sufficiently to enable you to catch Jasper's murderer.'

Rafferty smiled. 'Very good of him. But I think it will take more than my listening to the dolphins' greatest hits to secure a conviction.'

'I see you are a sceptic, Inspector. Perhaps our stones and crystals would be more to your taste?'

Rafferty, remembering the claims for these trinkets painted on the shop window, shook his head. 'I don't think so. I don't believe in such things.'

Mrs Moreno stared at him as if he'd just uttered the psychic equivalent of blasphemy, before commenting, 'Even a sceptic can't totally deny the wonderful properties of crystals. Their use in radios and watches; their ability to 'oscillate' at specific vibratory rates. Surely you're aware of this?'

Rafferty was forced to admit that he was.

'Then why are you so ready to reject their powers in other areas of life? It is not logical.'

Llewellyn could have told her that logic had never been one of his strong points, but as this would have forced him out of his standoffish mood, he said nothing, and merely twitched his lips downwards in a way that more than adequately expressed his thoughts on the subject. Rafferty ignored him.

'You must at least let me try to convince you of their qualities before you reject them,' Mrs Moreno insisted. Her voice filled with the fanatical conviction of the true believer. 'Tell me what areas of your life are causing you anguish, and I will tell you which of our gems and crystals has the power to help you. If you have money problems, you should wear Jade as it promotes a long and prosperous life; if you have love problems,' she gestured at a stone with a pale, pearly sheen, 'a moonstone exchanged with your lover will ensure your passion is returned; if you have health problems,' she pointed at another stone, 'a bloodstone will stimulate physical strength.'

From childhood, Rafferty had resented the Catholic Church's automatic assumption that they owned his mind, his soul, and any other bits they fancied. Now, as a matter of bloody-minded principle, he always firmly resisted the arrogant insistence from any other empirical quarter that he should do *this*, think *that*, believe *the other*. To reinforce his stance, he brought out his sharp cynic's pin and applied it. 'I've got a murder to solve,' he reminded her bluntly. 'I don't think trinkets will help me with that.'

It seemed he'd only succeeded in pricking her professional pride, for her voice rose on a triumphant note, as she told him, 'That is where you are wrong. I shall prove it to you.' She looked down at the selection of gems and crystals displayed on the counter. 'I will prescribe for you a suitable stone.' After a few moments, she placed a violet-pink stone in his hand and commented, 'Most people, at first, do not believe in the power of the stones. I simply tell them to wait and let the stones convince them.'

A likely story, thought Rafferty. And if they needed further convincing, no doubt she bashed them over the head with the biggest stone in the shop. The threat of physical violence was the greatest persuader of all, as most of the world's religions had discovered centuries ago.

She glanced down. 'This is sugalite. It aids in the development of the Third Eye seeing or inner vision. It unclogs the mind and enables it to get to the heart of things. You will find it beneficial, of this I am certain.' She closed Rafferty's fist over the stone and moved his hand close to his head. After a few moments she asked, 'Do you get any sensation from it?'

Rafferty was about to deny it, but then he became aware that his heart had begun to flutter and that the hairs on his arms were standing on end. The stone seemed to generate a warmth on his palm and now he realized that the headache that had been nagging at him earlier had faded. Irritated, and feeling slightly foolish at the admission, he told her what he felt.

Half expecting a triumphant 'Hallelujah', Rafferty was surprised that she restricted herself to a more restrained response.

'That is good,' she told him. 'It indicates there is a rapport between you.' He went to give the stone back to her, but she closed his hand over it and told him, 'Keep it. Carry it with you always. Call it my contribution to your investigation.'

Rafferty simply nodded. Apart from any other consideration, he sensed it would be foolhardy to offend the intense South American woman. She reminded him of an iceberg, nine-tenths hidden, and he wondered what lay concealed beneath that cool white exterior.

'Actually we came to see Mrs Campbell,' he told her. The forensic team had finished their work now and the offices as well as the shop were again in use. 'I imagine she's upstairs working?' Mrs Moreno's face tightened and Rafferty realized just how little love there was between the two women.

'Yes. She has just returned from seeing a client. A very important man who was one of Jaspair's regulars. She hopes that if she retains his custom she will keep her job.' She smiled again, but this time her smile was one of cool gratification. 'Once she had hopes for a partnership, now she just hopes to stay in employment. Is sad, no?'

Rafferty pretended innocence. 'Is Mr Astell thinking of winding up the business?'

'No.' Her forehead creased as she considered his remark. 'At least, I do not think so. What I meant was that her services may no longer be required here. Edwin never took to her, though Jaspair liked her a lot. I think this was because he found her outrageous, like himself. But I think even he was beginning to find her tiresome. She was *too* like him and made him aware of traits in his character that he preferred to ignore. She was also very impetuous and demanding. She wanted to prove to him that she could be good with the clients, but she got little more chance to do that than I. Edwin told me he had wanted to look into her background before Jaspair took her on, but Jaspair said he already knew as much about her as he needed. Besides, he felt fate had decided it for him. He wanted help with the natal charts; she wanted a job. Fate he felt had decreed that the two should come together. It was the same with me. Six months ago I have no home, no job, no money. Then, from nowhere I meet Jaspair and before you know it, I have all these things. It was fate, you see, Inspector. Fate, Kismet, Nemesis. Call it what you will. You cannot deny its power.'

She was right there, at any rate, thought Rafferty. But he wished his experience of fate had been as kind as Mercedes Moreno's had apparently been. When he had once complained to Llewellyn on this very subject, solemn-faced, the Welshman had told him that by his rise to Inspector, he had put himself under the sway of Nemesis, the Greek goddess of retribution and vengeance.

Uneasily, Rafferty remembered what Llewellyn had told him, that Nemesis illustrated a basic concept in Greek thought: that people who rise above their condition expose themselves to reprisals from the gods. At the time he had assumed that Llewellyn's tongue had been firmly in his cheek. But now, as Llewellyn's dark eyes met his, their very expressionlessness made him uneasy. Did Llewellyn know something he didn't? Had Nemesis, or Superintendent Bradley, her current earthly form, dis-

122

covered his little joke? Worse: was he about to issue reprisals?

Seemingly unaware of this by-play going on under her nose, Mercedes Moreno confided, 'La Señora Campbell has much ambition. She wanted to impress Jaspair with her skills, and she felt that Edwin was deliberately thwarting her. She accused him of sabotaging her hopes for a partnership. Was not true. She knew that her work would be on the postal side before she started here.' Her narrow shoulders executed a tiny shrug. 'She is foolish woman. Is it likely that Jaspair would allow such a one near the more valued clients? She has no subtlety, no discretion. The postal clients were generally – How you say? – one-offs, or at the most, they would want a twelve-month, once-a-year forecast. She could do little damage there. But the personal clients were repeat business. Some came every week.' She paused to light several joss sticks and a delicious fragrance wafted under Rafferty's nostrils.

'Is sandalwood.' She threw the remark over her shoulder as she placed the sticks in jars dotted around the shop before returning behind the counter. 'Señora Campbell could not become a partner in any case,' she told him. 'She has no money. I believe she is in much debt and is being pressed for payment.'

Mrs Moreno presumably had no money either, Rafferty reflected. Yet she too seemed to harbour ambitions beyond her ability to pay for them. If it wasn't for the fact that her alibi checked out, he would think she was trying to cast suspicion on Ginnie Campbell in order to remove any suspicion from herself. Yet her alibi had stood up to scrutiny. She had told them she had gone straight on to the Astells' that evening. Originally leaving at 8 p.m., she had returned just before 8.10 to collect her forgotten gloves and had stayed chatting with Astell in the kitchen till getting on for 9 p.m. If Sam Dally and Ellen Hadleigh were to be believed, Moon had certainly been dead by then.

On the other hand, they already knew that Ginnie Campbell had an erratic personality. Sufficiently thwarted she would be capable of violence. She only had her 'friend's' evidence to back her up; yet if the friend's neighbours were to be believed, it was hardly a solid alibi. She could have returned to the office that night to speak privately with Moon. If Moon had brought one of her eruptions on himself by denying her hopes for a partnership, she might easily have physically attacked him. Rafferty doubted that Moon would have agreed to such a tempestuous person having a share in the business. He had an emotional partner at home; he surely wouldn't want one at work as well. From what Mrs Moreno said he had begun to regret taking her on at all. Yet he hadn't got rid of her. Why?

Rafferty recalled what the landlord of the Troubadour had said. Moon had guaranteed her a job as long as she didn't contravene his esoteric moral code. Was it possible he had caught her with her hand in the till? If he had, she would find not only her over-optimistic hopes for a partnership crushed, but her job would be likely to go, too. He looked up to catch Mercedes Moreno's smoky gaze fixed intently on him. It made him uneasy and he headed for the stairs at the back of the shop. 'Thanks for your help,' he said. Remembering his manners, he hefted the stone. 'And for this. I hope it does the trick.'

'There are no tricks involved,' she coolly reproved. 'I am not a conjuror, Inspector. But I do have a certain professional pride. If you carry the stone with you always, you will discover its properties for yourself.'

'Right. Well, thanks again.' Perhaps, he mused, while he was here, he should take the precaution of obtaining a stone to charm away Bradley's wrath? It would be no use, though, he realized. *Nothing* could be that potent. Besides, the woman gave him the creeps. He wanted to get out of reach of her mesmeric eyes. He had a superstitious suspicion she would set some hex on him if he turned his back on her.

As they climbed the stairs to the offices, he wondered if she was hoping that Edwin Astell would offer *her* a partnership? He would certainly need someone and she was there, on the spot. Maybe she was hoping that Astell would be so desperate for someone reliable to help get the business back on its feet that he wouldn't expect her to put any money in? He shook his head. Too many *maybes*, Rafferty, he told himself. He found he was still clutching the sugalite that Mercedes Moreno had forced on him and, with a scowl, he thrust it in his pocket and promptly forgot about it.

Ginnie Campbell didn't appear to be working very hard. Her

124

computer screen was blank and the pile of post on her desk had yet to be opened. If she was set on keeping her job, it was hardly the way to impress Astell, thought Rafferty.

'Inspector.' Her violet eyes were watchful. 'What is it this time?'

'Just one or two little queries. You told us you were at your friend's house the entire night when Jasper Moon was murdered. Trouble is, none of his neighbours saw your car outside. Perhaps you can explain why?'

Her hasty temper flared. 'Are you saying you don't believe me?'

'No. What I'm saying is we have to check such statements, which is what I'm doing. I suggest you calm down and answer the question.'

Her violet eyes deepened to a stormy purple. Rafferty felt waves of barely controlled rage. It shook him and briefly he wondered if she was quite sane. He felt relieved that Llewellyn was there and that there were no blunt instruments handy.

'My boyfriend's neighbours are as unfriendly as mine,' she finally told them. 'They enjoy causing trouble. I don't suppose any of them mentioned that the people across the way held a party that evening? My boyfriend and I had been out for the day, as I told you. When we returned we had to park in the next street because the neighbours' guests had taken the nearer spaces.'

'I see. Thank you. We'll check it out.'

'Do that,' she told him, with a toss of her bright hair. Her rage had passed as quickly as it had come; now she was merely sullen. 'You can check as much as you like. Maybe this time the neighbours will tell you the rest.'

He nodded. But, as he told the still aloof Llewellyn as they made their way back to the station, she could have slipped out the back way. There was an alley running along the rear of those houses, and it would be dark well before 8 p.m. It could be no more than a five-minute drive to Moon's office from St Mark's Road; time enough to argue with Moon, kill him and return without the neighbours being any the wiser.

From what the neighbours *had* told them, the boyfriend was a drinker who had a habit of passing out for hours. If it had suited her plans, Rafferty doubted it would have taken much effort on her part to render him totally insensible. He was still convinced she was hiding *something*. But whether it was her own guilt, or information concerning one of the other suspects, they had yet to discover.

Terry Hadleigh still hadn't turned up. They'd already been searching for him for several days; he'd obviously gone to ground. He would have to surface sometime, Rafferty reminded himself, and when he did, they'd nab him. Hadleigh could be the key to this case, he realized. But until Rafferty had heard his story from his own lips, he wouldn't know whether to believe it or not, and, until they *did* find him, the investigation had to continue.

There were still several avenues they had yet to check. The squad had already worked their way through the greater part of Moon's client list. Most of the names on it lived very public lives and – to Rafferty's chagrin, as he still had faint hopes in that direction – even the Geminis amongst them were easily eliminated. So much for his ma's bright idea. It seemed now that his first thoughts had been right after all, and that Moon, like those on hallucinogenic drugs convinced they had found and lost the very secret of the Universe, had felt he was scrawling something important when all he had written had been meaningless gibberish. He was already dying, confused and disorientated. How likely was it, he now asked himself, that in such a state he had been able to write a lucid message?

To add to his other disappointments, Rafferty discovered that Sian Silk, the film actress and one of Moon's more luscious star clients, had been in America at the time of the murder. In spite of his suddenly discovered desire for a partner in life, he could still appreciate the film star's charms and he had been looking forward to interviewing her. Thoughts of her sultry attractions would have warmed the long winter nights . . .

Llewellyn was luckier, as another of Moon's clients, and – as Rafferty discovered – one of the Welshman's idols, Nat Kingston, the prominent local writer and critic, had not only had an appointment with Moon on the day of his murder but had been unable to produce a solid alibi. When he had mentioned Kingston's name, Llewellyn's standoffish air had faded to wistful, and Rafferty, grateful to find a way to render Llewellyn as close to sweetness and light as he ever got, had decided there was no need for *both* of them to be disappointed. They were on their way to see Kingston now.

Nat Kingston had written only four books, each one taking about five years in the writing, but, according to a now almost chatty Llewellyn, they were much admired by the literati amongst whom he had a reputation not far short of genius. Reclusive almost to a Howard Hughes degree, Kingston was nowadays reputed to rarely leave his home. He lived alone – apart from a male secretary-companion, Jocelyn Eckersley, to whom Rafferty had spoken – in a detached house that overlooked the sea a little further along the coast from Elmhurst. His literary-buff sergeant told him that Kingston had never married, never been known to have any involvement with women and – given Moon's homosexuality – Rafferty's brain immediately leapt into suspicion mode.

They approached the closed wooden gates of Kingston's isolated house, and Rafferty pressed the bell set into the wall. A few seconds later a voice squawked from the grille beside the gate post. Rafferty explained their business and the gates swung silently apart. For once, the morning was balmy, and they had driven down with the windows open. Now, as the gates slid smoothly shut behind them, Rafferty could hear the sound of the ocean beyond the house. Kingston's home, a gaunt, grey-stone mansion, was perched near the cliff edge.

As they got out of the car the front door opened and a youngish man came down the steps to greet them. 'He must be the secretary,' Rafferty murmured. 'When we get to see Kingston himself, you can do the talking. Soften him up by praising his books. Lie if you have to. All writers are supposed to be vain.'

'I won't need to lie,' Llewellyn replied softly. 'Kingston's a great man. It's a rare privilege to meet him.'

Rafferty thought of other so-called 'great' men, whose towering reputations time and truth had tumbled, and he muttered warningly under his breath, 'Just remember, you're here as a policeman, interviewing a possible suspect in a murder case, not as some sort of literary groupie looking to mark another notch on your bookcase.' Luckily, before Llewellyn's reproachful expression found utterance the secretary had reached them.

'Inspector Rafferty?' He was older than Rafferty had thought. In his mid-thirties at least, but with skin so smooth he looked as if he had just come out of a trouser press. 'I'm Jocelyn Eckersley, Nathaniel Kingston's secretary.' He spoke Kingston's name with reverence, as if, to him, the writer had the status of a god.

Rafferty nodded. 'Mr Eckersley. I explained on the phone that I need to speak to Mr Kingston in connection with the death of Jasper Moon and—'

'You explained that, certainly.' Eckersley's smoothness was of the steely variety, as his voice attested. 'But you didn't really explain *why*. I told you that my employer rarely leaves the house. He certainly hasn't been visiting and murdering prominent astrologers. It's too bad that he should be disturbed like this, especially as I really can't believe he can help you with your investigation.'

Another of Rafferty's collection of prejudices – this time against smooth types – gave an edge to his voice. 'Perhaps you'll allow me to be the judge of that, Mr Eckersley. Could we see Mr Kingston now, please?'

Eckersley stared at him for several seconds, his expression hostile, before acknowledging by an inclination of his head that Rafferty had the upper hand. He turned without another word. They followed, and as they rounded the corner of the building Rafferty could see the great man himself. He was sitting alone on the terrace, gazing out over the grey North Sea.

'Mr Kingston spends a great deal of time there when the weather's fine,' Eckersley murmured distantly. 'It's one of the few pleasures he has left.'

As Rafferty drew closer, he began to understand why Eckersley had been so protective of his boss. Kingston's body was shrunken as if he had some wasting disease; if so, it explained why he rarely left his home. His face was in profile, his fleshless cheeks fell away sharply, leaving his high-bridged nose prominent, like that of an emaciated eagle. He turned at their approaching footsteps. His eyes were a piercing cornflower blue, and looked astonishingly youthful in a face owning more skull than flesh. Rafferty's earlier suspicions fell away as it became apparent that, even with the walking stick that rested against his chair, Kingston would have enough trouble hobbling around his own home, never mind climbing the long flight of stairs to Moon's consulting rooms and murdering him.

'Inspector?' In spite of his physical degeneration, Kingston's voice was surprisingly strong and rich, each syllable given its full weight in a voice that could have been made for the stage. 'My

128

secretary told me you would be calling. Come, sit down by me and keep an old man company for a while.'

Rafferty sat. 'I didn't think you liked company much, Mr Kingston.'

'It depends on the company, Inspector. But I think I'll risk it.' He might be old, sick – dying, even – but Kingston had a definite presence. Rafferty glanced at Llewellyn. The Welshman's pale face had a slight flush at the cheekbones, his eyes drank Kingston in as though he was determined to commit every detail of the meeting to memory. 'I hear a tiny hint of blarney in your voice,' Kingston continued. 'And the Irish generally have a refreshing candour and lack of pomposity. As one gets older, one finds most people wearisome. Now I have neither the stamina nor the time for clacking tongues that say little and minds that peck over the banal as if it were Holy Writ.' He paused and gave them a gentle, self-mocking smile. 'I'm being tiresome. A self-indulgence of the aged that I've always deplored. You wanted to speak to me about Jasper Moon's murder?'

'Yes.' The secretary hovered protectively over his employer, as if he suspected Rafferty would lurch across the table and drag a confession out of him, and Rafferty felt increasingly conscious that they were here on a fool's errand. 'I believe you were one of Jasper Moon's clients?'

'Hardly a client,' Eckersley broke in. 'Mr Kingston consulted Moon just once, some months ago. I really don't see—'

'Thank you, Jocelyn.' Kingston turned his head the barest fraction as if the least exertion tired him. 'Perhaps you would be good enough to bring some refreshments for our guests?'

'But . . .'

'Is coffee all right?' Kingston glanced at the two policemen, who nodded. 'Good coffee is one of the pleasures forbidden to me, but I think, just this once . . . Oh, and Jocelyn,' he added, as the secretary still hovered, 'I think our guests might enjoy some of that fruitcake Teddy sent.' Though he spoke softly, his voice was firm, and Jocelyn retreated.

'I must apologize for my young friend.' Kingston's gentle smile embraced them both. 'He means well, but he can be a little over zealous. Still, what he said is correct. I consulted Jasper once, about three months ago. Perhaps I should explain that I had already met Moon several times at literary functions; we have the same publisher. He impressed me, even more so as a good friend of mine had consulted him and Moon warned him he should consult a doctor as his palms showed the beginnings of a health problem. Moon was right, as my friend's doctor confirmed. My friend suggested I see Moon when I complained of feeling unwell; he even made the appointment for me. Anyway, I kept the appointment.'

'You didn't think of consulting a doctor?' Rafferty asked.

Kingston smiled ruefully. 'Even so-called literary lions can be squeamish kittens when it comes to their health. Ignorance is bliss and all that. You know how one puts these things off. My own doctor had retired, I didn't find his successor very congenial, and I simply hadn't got round to making alternative arrangements. So, as a compromise, I saw Jasper Moon.'

'Did Moon come here for the consultation?'

'No. I went to his office. I was stronger then. My secretary drove me. Anyway, at first Moon would say little more about my health than that I should consult a doctor as soon as possible. I insisted that he tell me more. I imagine he thought he was breaching some code of ethics to which he adhered, but finally he did me the courtesy of accepting that I knew my own mind and admitted that my hands showed all the signs of an extremely serious disease. He was right, I'm afraid, as the doctors confirmed when I finally saw them. I haven't long to live. That was the only occasion I saw him.'

'I see.' After glancing at Llewellyn's stunned face, Rafferty shuffled in his seat, uncomfortable with Kingston's serene acceptance of his own imminent death.

'Please don't be embarrassed.' Kingston's death's head smile embraced them both. 'I have had a good life, a rich life, more than most people have. I am not afraid to die. Ask whatever questions you feel necessary.' Still Rafferty hesitated and Kingston's eyes crinkled as if Rafferty's discomfiture provided him with a secret amusement. 'Come now, Inspector. I'm sure you haven't come down here just to admire the view. Ask away. Before Jocelyn returns. Preferably *before* I die.'

Rafferty smiled. He liked this old man. On the way down, he had imagined himself being squashed by the writer's superior brain, but he wasn't the intellectual ogre he had assumed. He was beginning to enjoy Nat Kingston's company and he fell in with his suggestion, forgetting that he had told Llewellyn to ask the questions. Anyway, Llewellyn still looked stunned at the news of his idol's imminent death. 'Moon's appointments diary had your name entered several times, the first three months ago as you said, and the last on the day he died. Can you explain that?'

'I'm afraid I was humouring him, Inspector. He seemed to think I would need counselling once I had the doctors investigate his warning. So he made further appointments which I had no intention of keeping. It seemed kinder to let him do so. I didn't meet him again. I read that he died last Thursday, but I can assure you I didn't kill him. I was here all that day, as I am every day. Violence is anathema to me. It always has been. Words have always been my strength, my sword.' The eyes were gently mocking. 'Seeing me now, the physical wreck I have become, you probably won't believe me when I say I can be a veritable terror for the truth. But Moon believed it and so he told me what I needed to know.'

He held out his hands. They were as pale, as wasted as the rest of him; the lines on his palms were broken up, and all but the head line were weak, islanded as they crossed the palm. 'I was still fairly robust when I saw him, but Moon knew. Although he urged me to see a doctor, I think we both knew it was too late for that; my health worsened swiftly soon after I had seen him. I could see the pity in his eyes. That's what made me so insistent.'

He put his hands back in his lap. 'I've always believed a man has the right to make decisions about his own life and to do that he needs to know if his death is imminent. The doctors told me I would die without treatment, but I would also die *with* treatment. There seemed little point in putting my poor body through torturous regimes to gain a few more weeks of life, so I came home. I wanted to arrange my affairs.' His gaze returned to the ocean, and he smiled his gentle smile, as if he saw something out there that more earth-bound mortals couldn't see. 'I have now done so and I can die in peace.'

They sat in a curiously companionable silence after that, broken only when Jocelyn Eckersley brought deliciously fragrant coffee in giant cups. He had forgotten the fruitcake. Llewellyn, his face even more mournful than usual, chatted quietly to Kingston about his life and work. The old man answered him politely enough, but

131

Rafferty got the impression the subject bored him. That part of his life was past, done with, his manner implied. All that remained to Kingston was eternity and whatever place in the annals of the great the literati decided to award him. They left soon after, Llewellyn so subdued that he didn't even point out that he had been supposed to ask the questions.

'That's one suspect out of the running,' Rafferty ventured to comment, when they were halfway back to the station.

Llewellyn turned his head. 'You didn't seriously suspect him, did you? A man like that wouldn't descend to murder. Only the highest, most honourable motives would prompt a man like that to kill.'

'I liked the old man myself,' Rafferty told him. 'But he still had to be questioned. You know that. It's called policework, Dafyd,' Rafferty gently reminded him. 'Remember that quaint old word?'

They had now worked their way through all of Moon's client list with no result. They had all checked out. Astell would be pleased, Rafferty thought. He's been itching to get them all off my suspect list. His thoughts were interrupted as a call came through on the radio. The elusive Terry Hadleigh had finally turned up, the need for food and money having brought him out of hiding. Harry McGrath, one of Rafferty's contacts in the Met, had spotted him draped on the euphemistically named 'meat rack' in Piccadilly Circus, among the rest of the bodies for sale. He was expected back at Elmhurst at any time.

Rafferty put down the radio mike. Sitting back in the passenger seat, he instructed Llewellyn to put his foot down; a pointless request with Llewellyn, of course, who was caution itself behind the wheel. However, Rafferty made no comment. He merely sat, running over in his head the best way to conduct the coming interview. At the least, he hoped they would get to the bottom of the business of the art lessons.

Chapter Ten

'So, the Prodigal Son has returned,' was Rafferty's comment, as he stepped into the interview room. Hadleigh was slouched in his chair and, apart from scowling in Rafferty's general direction, he didn't look up. 'I'm afraid the canteen's right out of fatted calves. But we've plenty of juicy questions. I'm sure I don't need to tell you what about.'

The only response this brought from Hadleigh was a sneer and an even lower slouching. His thin face looked gaunt beneath his bleached blond hair. He seemed to suffer from an acute case of arrested development. Not only was he short – he could be no more than 5'5" – at first glance he could easily be mistaken for a teenager, an anorexic teenager dressed in the universal youth uniform of skintight blue jeans and sleeveless black tee shirt. The tee shirt was too big for him and looked as if it had been borrowed from a larger friend. The armholes were designed for more muscular limbs, and Hadleigh's thin, white goosebump-blemished arms, hanging from the depths of the black cotton, gave him a curiously defenceless, childlike air which was not only disconcerting but at odds with his attempted hard man of the streets, couldn't-careless manner.

Rafferty reminded himself that Hadleigh was forty-one, long past the age of innocence, and, notwithstanding the early homosexual assault, would appear to have embarked on his later dissolute lifestyle with enthusiasm. At any rate, he'd never made any strenuous efforts to break away and find a legal way of earning a living. He'd rarely held down any job for more than a few weeks, never shown any inclination to self-improvement. Yet now, if his mother was to be believed, he had developed artistic aspirations. Rafferty's lip curled and he sat down on the other side of the table, picked up Hadleigh's bum-freezer leather jacket and threw it at him. 'You look cold. Better put this on.' He didn't want any crusading brief making accusations of ill-treatment.

Rafferty signalled to Llewellyn to turn on the tape recorder, cautioned Hadleigh and fed the relevant details into the microphone. 'Right, Mr Hadleigh, as I'm sure you're aware, Jasper Moon, the well-known astrologer, was found murdered in his consulting rooms on Friday the ninth of October. I want to know what you can tell me about it.'

Hadleigh ignored the thrown jacket, which had fallen to the floor. He denied any knowledge of Moon's death and tried to assume a cocky pose. But whether guilt or fear had damaged his acting skills, his heart didn't seem to be altogether in it.

'Come on, Hadleigh. You left your fingerprints behind; bloody prints. We know you broke into Moon's consulting rooms on the night of his murder, so you needn't bother to deny it. Looking for something to steal, were you?' Rafferty made no mention of what Mrs Hadleigh had told them about that night. If Terry wanted to tell them the same tale he had the chance.

Sullenly, he told them, 'I don't know what you mean. I didn't steal anything.'

'Oh, I see. It's a coincidence that a thousand quid went missing that night, I suppose?'

Hadleigh stared at him. 'A thousand quid? But—' He broke off, and resumed his sullen expression. 'All right,' he admitted bluntly. 'So I was there that night. But I didn't steal anything,' he insisted, then more quietly he added, 'Jasper was my friend.'

'You must have a forgiving nature, seeing as Moon or Hedges as he was then assaulted you as a boy.' Hadleigh flushed and shuffled on his chair, as if the hard surface hurt his thin buttocks. 'Now that we've managed to establish that you *were* there, perhaps you'd like to tell me why? Into reminiscences, were you? Or was it something else you were after? Like money to keep your mouth shut?'

Hadleigh's lips tightened as if to stop himself responding to Rafferty's taunt. 'If you must know,' he said thinly, 'Jasper was giving me art lessons.'

Rafferty smiled. 'What a coincidence. That's what your mother told us. And when did this interest in art develop? At Pentonville, was it?'

134

'No. At school.' Hadleigh had apparently decided to open up a little, for now he went on, 'I've always been interested in art. And I was good at it, too. Jasper knew that. I want to go to art college and that's why he offered to give me some training. He said he'd finance it, too.' His lips pouted like those of a spoilt child. 'He was my last hope. Now he's dead and I'll never get there.'

'Your mother mentioned something about building up your portfolio. Where are these alleged masterpieces of yours? I'd love to see them.'

Hadleigh's openness hadn't lasted long. Now his voice was sullen again. 'They're in a lock-up garage belonging to a friend of mine.'

'I'll have this friend's address, if I may.'

Half expecting there to be no friend, Rafferty was taken aback when Hadleigh supplied the address with no difficulty. 'Now perhaps you'll believe me.'

'As to that, we'll wait till we've checked with this friend of yours.' Rafferty got up. 'That shouldn't take long. We'll be back before you know it. In the meantime, I suggest you remember exactly what happened that night. Because I shall want to hear all of it.'

Rafferty glanced at his watch as the interview room door closed behind them. 'We'd better get a move on,' he said to Llewellyn, 'or we'll be late for the inquest. But first I'll get Lilley to look into this portfolio business. Before I speak to Hadleigh again I want to know, one way or the other, if he's telling the truth about these art lessons. If he is, I reckon it could throw this case wide open.'

As expected, the inquest was adjourned. Sam Dally caught up with them as they headed for the exit.

'Can't stop, Sam,' Rafferty told him. 'Got urgent business.'

'So had I, with a woman,' Sam told them, as by a neat sleight-of-foot, he manoeuvred himself in front of them and succeeded in slowing them down. 'But I missed her. Tall redhead in peacock blue. Did you notice her at the inquest?'

'You could hardly miss her, Sam.' Rafferty lengthened his stride, skirted Dally and lunged ahead. Dally was forced to break into a trot. 'That's Ginnie Campbell, one of the suspects in our murder case. Why?' Rafferty threw a grin over his shoulder. 'I must say you look a bit gobsmacked. Case of lust at first sight, is it?'

'Lust be blowed,' the practical Scot panted his reply. 'That woman's cost me money, which is far more important.' He grabbed Rafferty's arm and forced him to stop. 'For God's sake, man, can't you stand still when I'm talking to you?' With a sigh, Rafferty obliged. 'That's the feckless female who caused my accident. Turns out she hasn't got any insurance. Means I'm going to lose my no-claims bonus,' he grumbled. 'She must have recognized me, too, as she made herself scarce pretty damn quick.'

Rafferty's earlier eagerness to get back to the car vanished. He turned and stared at Sam's indignant face. 'Wait a minute. Let me get this clear. Are you saying that Ginnie Campbell was in the vicinity of Moon's consulting rooms early on the morning that his body was discovered?'

'Haven't I just said so? She bashed into me round the corner from the High Street. Got her number, too, though fat lot of good it did me. And if the way yon woman drives is any indication of character, which to me it is, you won't have far to look for your murderer. She fair murders the Queen's highway, at least, and its poor, unsuspecting, law-abiding users.'

Rafferty and Llewellyn exchanged glances. Ginnie Campbell had told them she had gone straight home from her boyfriend's house on Friday morning. Yet now they discovered she had made a detour via the High Street, which was a rather circuitous route for her to have taken. On its own, the lie seemed insignificant. But taken with the fact that she had ample opportunity to return to the office on the evening of Moon's murder, it became much more interesting. If she had killed Moon on the spur of the moment and rushed from the scene in panic, she couldn't be certain she hadn't left some incriminating evidence behind. Hence the necessity for an early visit the next morning.

Rafferty sighed. If Hadleigh turned out to be telling the truth, this latest discovery meant the case was so wide open he hardly knew which of the crop of suspects to interview first. So far, the only one amongst Moon's close associates who had no possible motive or opportunity was Mercedes Moreno. But there was still time for something to turn up, he reflected. Moon's death had so far unearthed several juicy titbits. He couldn't help but wonder if there would be more.

Rafferty didn't have long to wait to find out. When they returned to the station it was to find that the bank notes stolen from Moon's office had turned up; or rather most of them had. They had been paid into the bank account of Robb and Trim, a local firm of money-lenders. When Rafferty and Llewellyn had questioned them as to how they had come by the money, they hadn't been able to pass the buck fast enough. One of their customers had used a wad of new notes to settle her debts, they told Rafferty. A Mrs Campbell. A Mrs Virginia Campbell. Rafferty, who had intended to speak to her very soon, was forced to put her name at the top of a growing list.

'Damn.' Ginnie Campbell flung herself into her chair. 'Thought you'd be round when I saw you with that fat doctor. Knew he'd recognized me. I suppose you want to know why I lied when I said I'd not been near the consulting rooms on Friday morning?'

'That's the general idea,' said Rafferty mildly, as he looked round for somewhere to sit. The living room was as untidy as it had been on their previous visit. Rafferty even thought he recognized the same clothes scattered on the furniture. 'You might also explain how you came by the money stolen from Moon's cashbox.'

Her eyes first widened, then narrowed. Rafferty could imagine the furious thought going on behind her technicolour eyeshadow. He wasn't altogether surprised when she immediately went on the attack.

'I hope you don't think you're going to pin this murder on *me*. And, for your information, I didn't *steal* it. Jasper lent it to me. I was desperate for money; you know that already, thanks to that old bag next door, and Jasper promised to lend me a grand. He knew I had planned to spend Thursday with my boyfriend. He gave me the Friday off as well, so I could get my financial problems sorted. He knew Del – Derek, my boyfriend – was very jealous – he was very sympathetic about that – and that I wouldn't be able to get away on the Thursday without a lot of explanations. My boyfriend doesn't know about my debts,' she added.

'OK,' Rafferty said. 'For the moment I'll forget that your boyfriend has the convenient habit of drinking himself unconscious, and accept that you couldn't get away.' Forget it but not believe it, Rafferty muttered to himself. 'So tell us about Friday,' he invited. 'I assume the boyfriend wasn't a problem that day too?'

'No. He had to go back to work on Friday, so I was able to leave early. Jasper had promised that the money would be there for me as early as I liked on Friday morning. He said he'd leave it in the cashbox and I was to help myself when I was passing. I was just to make sure that I locked the box up afterwards, otherwise Edwin would nag him. I knew where in his desk he kept the key, of course. Only trouble was, he got himself murdered before I could collect. Just my luck.'

'So what happened?'

'Well, I got to the office early, just after seven o'clock.' Rafferty nodded. Although it didn't prove anything, it at least fitted with what they already knew. Astell hadn't arrived till 7.30 a.m. 'I found the place turned upside down, Jasper dead and the window in his office broken. As you can imagine, I was horrified. But, as the debt collectors would be even more horrifyingly unpleasant if I didn't pay them as I'd promised, I looked to see if my money was still there. To my astonishment it was. I took it and left. After that it just seemed easier all round to pretend I'd never been there at all.'

It had all come out very pat, thought Rafferty. But then she'd had plenty of time to concoct her story. He stared at her. She stared back, bold as you please, and without a hint of shame at her callous actions. God, he thought, in unwilling admiration, the wretched woman had more front than Brighton. She had lied about her whereabouts on the morning Moon's body was found, lied again about the money, yet still she seemed to think they should believe her now.

According to Mercedes Moreno, Moon had begun to regret employing Ginnie Campbell. If that was true, how likely was it that he would be willing to lend her a thousand pounds? It seemed far more likely that she'd asked, been refused and vented her frustration in the time-honoured way before helping herself to the cash. From what they knew of the boyfriend, his alibi wasn't worth the oxygen he had used up talking about it. How could it be, when the betting was that he had spent half the evening passed out on the settee?

Ginnie Campbell was in debt up to her ears and beyond, being pressed by loan sharks; in such a situation that grand would have been very tempting. Rafferty debated what to charge her with; interfering with the course of justice; leaving the scene of a crime; robbery; brass-faced cheek or just plain murder? However, he confined himself to warning her not to even think of attempting a flit and then they left.

'It'll be interesting to find out if Lilley's turned up Hadleigh's portfolio,' said Rafferty as they walked back up the path to the car, 'especially now we know he didn't take the money. I also think a little digging into his friendship with Jasper Moon might prove rewarding. Art lessons or no, there's something there that doesn't jell. Hadleigh's hiding something, and I don't think it's murder. He seems – I don't know – *ashamed*, and I doubt turning the screws on Moon would cause such an emotion. I want to find out what has.'

Rafferty opened the cell door. 'Come along, Mr Hadleigh. We'd like another little chat.'

This time, he proceeded more cautiously. Part of Hadleigh's story checked out, and, although that didn't mean that Hadleigh couldn't still have murdered Moon, it made his story that bit more believable.

'You'll be glad to know that we've found your portfolio,' he told him. 'Including several paintings of Jasper Moon. They were even signed.' Rafferty produced paper and pen. 'Maybe you'd like to reproduce the signature for me?' Hadleigh snatched the pen and signed, as requested. Rafferty got Llewellyn to take them to Lilley to check against those on the paintings. But Hadleigh's eagerness to give his signature indicated they would match, Rafferty realized gloomily, as he felt the last hopes of his open-and-shut case sliding away. 'You've got quite a collection,' he remarked. 'Some of it's pretty good, not that I'm an expert, of course.'

He expected a sneer from Hadleigh at that. Instead, Hadleigh said simply, 'Jasper was a good teacher. He always was. I didn't kill him. I had no reason to. You don't understand. I . . .'

Rafferty was tired. It had been a long day and he wasn't in the mood to listen to any more lies. 'Suppose you help me to understand?' he bluntly demanded. 'From where I'm sitting you

139

still had a very good reason for killing him . . . That assault on you when you were a boy.'

'I didn't kill him, I tell you.' His glance evasive, Hadleigh mumbled, 'And that business happened a long time ago. If I'd wanted to kill him I could have done it before now. I've known who he was for ages.'

'OK, so if you didn't kill him, why did you run away? If you were such great friends, why didn't you phone the police when you found his body?'

Hadleigh began to twist an initialled signet ring round and round on his little finger. 'I needed time to think. Can't you imagine what a shock it was to me to find him like that? I could see he was dead, and I just panicked, I suppose. I knew my prints must be all over the place. I thought it was only a matter of time before you found out about the court case years ago and put two and two together to make five. I didn't kill him,' he repeated. 'That's the last thing I'd be likely to do. Especially as . . .'

There was definitely something odd here, Rafferty decided. He rubbed his tired eyes and wished his overburdened brain would be more co-operative. It was as if Hadleigh was trying to convince them that he had no grudge against Moon–Hedges. Yet how could that be? 'Especially as?' Rafferty repeated. 'Especially as he was making it worth your while to keep quiet and throwing art lessons in as a bonus? Is that what you were going to say? It must . . .' He paused as Terry Hadleigh broke into a harsh laugh that held no trace of humour. 'Perhaps you'd like to share the joke?' Rafferty invited.

The laughter stopped as quickly as it had begun. He no longer attempted to put on the earlier tough guy act, but glanced indecisively from Rafferty to Llewellyn and back again, bit his lip, and then blurted out, 'He never touched me when I was a boy! I lied about what happened all those years ago.' He raised large, pale blue eyes. They had a fixed, staring quality that would have been intimidating in a larger man. Rafferty supposed that cool stare had helped him survive in a dangerous profession, had given an impression that steel existed within the emaciated frame.

'I lied and went on lying. It seemed easier that way. But how could I admit it? How could I admit it was a case of "like father like son", after all the unhappiness my father had caused Mum?'

140

'Are you saying your father was homosexual?'

Slowly, at first, as if he spoke of something that had been kept in the dark cellar of his mind and was unused to daylight, Hadleigh began to explain. But as he continued, his words began to tumble over one another, as if he was relieved to be able to unburden himself. 'I think my father was terrified by his own feelings and went overboard in the opposite direction to deny they existed. He managed to build himself up quite a reputation as a ladies' man, but it never quite rang true to me. My mother must have suspected. I know she came to despise him. She used to call him a poor excuse for a man. I didn't want her to think the same about me. That's why, when they found Hedges – Moon – and me together, I lied about what had really happened.'

Hadleigh looked sorry for himself as he met their appalled expressions, as if the world had unaccountably ganged up on him. 'It wasn't my fault,' he insisted. 'I didn't *want* it to happen like that. I had no choice. She-she put words in my mouth, didn't she? I suppose she couldn't bear to face the truth, so, of course, I had to be innocent. I didn't want them to press charges, but she insisted. How could I have told her she'd got it all wrong? That I'd been the one who had made advances and been rejected.'

The old-fashioned terms gave a comical, music-hall aura to Hadleigh's story. Rafferty tried to imagine Moon as some innocent Victorian miss compromised by an unwanted suitor, but found it impossible. He'd been a grown man, an experienced teacher, surely fully capable of repelling a young lad's impetuous experimentations?

Hadleigh must have read what was in his eyes. 'You don't understand,' he told him. 'I deliberately set up an opportunity to be alone with him. I stayed behind at school that night as I'd managed to persuade him to let me help sort out the art storeroom. Of course, at school he kept his inclinations quiet, but I knew. He was about thirty then, yet he'd never married. I followed him home once and watched through the windows. There was another man there. They were kissing. But even if I hadn't seen that I'd have known he was gay. There was something about him I recognized because my father and I had it too. He'd always been my favourite teacher. I-I wanted to experiment and he seemed the perfect one to experiment with.'

141

He paused for a moment before going on. He was careful not to meet Rafferty's eyes again and kept his gaze glued to the table. Hadleigh swallowed hard, his prominent Adam's apple bobbing up and down like a toy yacht on a pond, his voice now reduced to little more than a whisper. 'But he was appalled when I tried to kiss him. I felt dirty, perverted, angry. I wanted to hurt him in return. Until then I'd been so set on my plans that I didn't give the cleaners a thought. But I've always had good hearing and when I heard them come into the art room I decided to make him sorry for throwing my feelings back in my face. I began shouting and crying and loosened my clothing. Jasper tried to restrain me, that's how I got the bruises on my arms.'

His voice turned pleading now, as if desperate to have them understand. 'If I'd given a moment's thought to the consequences, I'd never have done it. I just acted on impulse; one I've regretted ever since. But I loved him, you see, and he'd hurt me. I couldn't help myself. I came to love him even more, lately.' Him or his money? Rafferty wondered. 'I hoped he might come to love me, too. Sometimes I thought he did, but he never once . . .' His voice trailed away and he sighed. 'I was never able to bring myself to tell him I loved him. I was scared he'd reject me again. Each time I tried, I'd see again the horrified look in his eyes as I tried to kiss him all those years ago; how appalled he looked when that storeroom door opened.

'I'd locked it behind me, of course, as a precaution, and put the key in my pocket, but the cleaners had a key, as they kept some of their cleaning stuff in there.' His head hung dejectedly between his coathanger-thin shoulders. 'Anyway, when my mother was called to the school, I had to go on lying. How could I tell her the truth? Only, after it all happened, the court case and everything, I felt differently. I wanted to hurt her. So I started to thieve.

'Afterwards, I felt sorry for him. I wanted time to go backwards, as if it had never happened. Only it didn't. The case had been in all the papers and even though my name hadn't been published, enough people knew I had been involved for word to get round. And then, of course, my mother attacked him after the court case.' That was the first Rafferty had heard about it. He presumed it had been kept quiet. That would be something else that might be worth looking into. 'How could I have said it was all untrue after that?

'The headmaster was all for hushing it up. It only came to court because Mum over-reacted. She had hysterics when the headmaster seemed to believe that Jasper might be telling the truth when he said he had done nothing, that I was the one who ... I think Mum wanted to punish someone for the way my father had treated her, for all those years of humiliation. Any man would have done from her point of view. It's my fault that it happened to be Moon on the receiving end.'

'It doesn't explain why Moon agreed to give you tuition in art,' Rafferty objected. 'It doesn't explain it at all.'

Hadleigh seemed surprised at Rafferty's comment. 'Surely you can see that when I bumped into him in Elmhurst and discovered he lived here, enough years had gone by for him to forgive me. He even understood my feelings, why I'd done what I did. He told me he'd found his homosexuality difficult to come to terms with when he was young, had even tried to deny it by having one or two affairs with women, but it was no good. Anyway, by the time I met him again, he was rich, successful. And he felt everyone deserved a second chance to make good. He decided to give me that chance.'

Hadleigh smiled, adopting again the cocky pose he had assumed when first interviewed, but now, his breast-beating over, with far more success. His smile revealed small, neat teeth, their prettiness spoiled by the marks of decay between them. 'You could say I'd done him a favour. If it hadn't been for me he'd have still been teaching in some crummy school and would probably have been heading for his first nervous breakdown.'

As Hadleigh seemed to have forgotten the little matter of Moon's murder in his bout of self-justification, Rafferty bluntly reminded him of it. 'Instead of which, he's dead. Some favour. He must be grateful.'

'It's not my fault he's dead,' Hadleigh snapped. The bright blue eyes were resentful. 'I didn't kill him. Why should I? I had no reason to.'

'So you say. Still, it's convenient, isn't it, that you're willing to "confess" to telling lies *now* about Moon's supposed assault? Why should I believe you?'

143

Hadleigh stared at him. 'Christ, do you think this is easy for me? Can't you see that I wouldn't be telling you macho bastards all this now if there was any other way to convince you I had nothing to do with his death?'

Rafferty stared back, unwilling to believe him. But Hadleigh's indignant aggression had the ring of truth. 'Your mother said you found his body about eight-thirty. Is that true?' Hadleigh nodded. 'How many people knew about these art lessons?'

'Only Jasper and me. He preferred it like that. His lover was inclined to be jealous and would only cause a scene if he knew. The last thing I wanted was to give him more problems.'

'Did Moon ever tell you why he opened his consultancy so close to his old haunts? After the court case, I'd have thought he would have wanted to stay as far away as possible.'

Hadleigh nodded. 'Jasper used to have his business in London, but when Astell became a partner and worked longer hours, his wife started complaining. She's a sickly sort,' he quickly explained, 'and too attached to her old home to move. She didn't like Astell commuting and returning home late in the evening, so when Jasper learned of her complaints he told Astell to look for premises in Elmhurst. The court case had happened years ago. He'd altered a lot physically, put on weight, dyed his hair, grown a beard. He'd even changed his name, so he thought he'd be safe. And he was. Apart from you, no one ever connected Jasper Moon and Peter Hedges.' He paused. 'Unless you count whoever sent Astell's wife those cuttings about the case.'

'Cuttings?' Rafferty repeated. 'What cuttings?'

'The ones my mother found lying around their house. If it hadn't been for them and Sarah Astell she might never have realized that Peter Hedges and Jasper Moon were one and the same.' He frowned. 'Funny, that.'

Rafferty was sorry to discover that Ellen Hadleigh had told them more lies. 'You're saying that your mother knew who Moon was *before* he was killed?'

'Yes. Why?' Hadleigh's mouth twisted. 'Did she say something different?'

'Never mind. When did she see these cuttings? Was it recently?'

'I've no idea. I hadn't seen her for weeks before I turned up at her place on Thursday night, and she started on me like a crazy woman. It was only when I told her that Moon was dead and I looked like being in the frame for his murder that she stopped.' He grinned. 'That shut her up right enough.'

'Did you ever tell your mother the truth about the assault?'

'Of course not.' A note of self-pity was evident in Hadleigh's voice as he went on. 'She wouldn't have believed me, anyway. Don't you know I'm mother's blue-eyed boy who can do no wrong?' He gave another humourless laugh. 'There was no point. I knew that well enough.'

Lilley popped his head round the door. Rafferty halted the interview and went into the corridor. 'Well?'

'As far as I can tell, the signatures on the paintings and that slip of paper are the same. Do you want me to get them checked out further?'

Rafferty shook his head. 'No. Leave it. For once in Hadleigh's life, I think he's telling the truth.' He dismissed Lilley and returned to the interview room.

'I don't suppose you have any idea who might have sent these cuttings to Mrs Astell? And why?'

Hadleigh shook his head. He seemed genuinely bewildered that an attempt had been made to rake up a scandal that was nearly thirty years old. What on earth was the point of it? Rafferty wondered. And why send them to Mrs Astell of all people? Surely Ellen Hadleigh was a more obvious recipient? On a sudden impulse, as he walked to the door, he asked, 'By the way, I suppose you know who Moon used to buy his bent gewgaws from?'

Without pausing to think, Hadleigh nodded. 'It was Danny Lewis.' It seemed his soul-bearing had given him a taste for telling the truth. Rafferty didn't expect it to last. 'Jasper told me he always bought from Danny.' Hadleigh gave a taut grin. 'Said us fags should stick together.'

Rafferty supposed he should be grateful that the news ended one line of enquiry. Because Danny Lewis had been residing at Her Majesty's pleasure in Elmhurst Station cells from Thursday afternoon till the following morning. On a charge of receiving. A doubly apt charge, it now appeared. Danny Lewis had kept his homosexuality very quiet, as it was the first Rafferty had heard of it. But even his earthy humour failed to find much cause for amusement in the double-entendre.

145

Llewellyn had remained pretty much a silent observer during the interview. He sometimes preferred that and Rafferty had thought little of it. But as they closed the door and walked away, he discovered that his sergeant had been occupied in working up yet another theory.

'Did you know that there's a body of opinion amongst psychologists that a boy who is brought up by a mother embittered against men may try to compensate by fostering the more feminine side of his character?'

Rafferty, after a few moments absorbing this and translating it into plain English, asked, 'Are you saying he may turn out bent?'

Llewellyn's lips thinned. 'I wouldn't put it quite so bluntly, but yes, that's what it amounts to. I wondered if, deep down, Ellen Hadleigh suspected her attitude influenced her son's developing sexual identity? By continually telling the boy what rotters men were, she could have caused him to reject his own masculinity.'

'Freud would love you,' Rafferty scoffed. 'Are you trying, in that long-winded, intellectual way of yours, to say you think Ellen Hadleigh blames herself as much as Moon for the way her son turned out?'

Llewellyn drew in an irritated breath. 'Maybe she did, at one time. But I think it's more likely that, as time went by, she managed to transfer any guilty feelings on to Hedges–Moon. That would be one way to blot out her own feelings of guilt. Hadleigh implied as much. *She* couldn't face up to her own guilty feelings, so she put a double load on Moon. It could be that, as the years went by, she succeeded in convincing herself that Moon bore sole responsibility for her son's degenerate lifestyle.'

'Am I to take it from your convoluted arguments that you now think Ellen Hadleigh murdered Moon? I know she lied to us about knowing who he was, but—'

'I'm merely examining the *psychological* angles,' Llewellyn retorted. 'And Ellen Hadleigh is a strong possibility from the psychological standpoint.'

In the interests of investigative harmony, Rafferty made no further digs. For himself, though, he wasn't sure that Llewellyn was on the right track. His own mother had had plenty of derogatory things to say about men in general and his father in particular during his formative years, yet he had never felt homosexual inclinations.

146

No, he thought, if Ellen Hadleigh had killed Moon, he didn't believe suppressed feelings of guilt had pushed her into it. Unlike her son, she still felt she had every reason to hate Moon. Hadleigh had admitted he'd never told her the truth about the attack. She had years of anger and bitterness stored up. And when the initial shock had worn off after she had discovered Moon's real identity, she would have been likely to think of little else but what Moon had done to her son, to both of them. That anger would have been increased by the thought that she had been skivvying for her son's molester, the man who had, she believed, ruined both their lives. She must have thought he had been laughing at her, laughing at her and her son, because she would know that when Astell told Moon her name, he would have recognized it immediately.

Hadleigh surely realized that he had incriminated his own mother? But perhaps that was what he wanted? Rafferty reasoned in a sudden burst of insight. By forcing him to give evidence against Moon, he had had to lie and lie again when all he must have wanted was to go off into a corner and hide his shame. Instead of being able to put the matter quickly behind him with little damage to anyone, by her insistence on the prosecution she had ensured that shame had lasted years, had made it impossible for him ever to hope that Moon would return his love. Because of all that had gone before, when they finally met up again he had felt unable to meet Moon on equal, adult, terms.

'I want a look at those cuttings,' Rafferty decided. 'I also want to find out exactly when Ellen Hadleigh saw them. He consulted his watch. It's too late to do any more tonight, but first thing tomorrow I want you to get Hanks to look into Hadleigh's assertion that his mother really did attack Moon after the court case. As for us, I think another visit to Sarah Astell might be a good idea.'

Chapter Eleven

Ellen Hadleigh opened the door to their knock when they visited the Astells' home the next morning. Her eyes widened apprehensively when she saw them, but she stood back, gesturing for them to enter the hall, when Rafferty told her they had come to see Mrs Astell.

'Mrs Astell didn't say she was expecting you.'

'Probably because she isn't,' Rafferty replied. 'We couldn't get an answer on the phone.'

'She unplugs it when she's resting.'

Rafferty nodded. He often felt like doing the same. He remembered he'd made her a promise. 'We found your son,' he told her. 'He's at the police station now.'

'And?' Ellen Hadleigh's eyes searched his face. 'Do you believe he didn't do it?'

'Let's just say that what he's told us checks out.'

Ellen Hadleigh let out a sigh of relief. Rafferty wondered if she'd be quite so pleased if she knew her precious son had dropped her in it? Still, now that she had heard some good news on the son front, she appeared happier. She must be confident that her lies wouldn't be discovered. For now, Rafferty didn't attempt to question her on the subject. He wanted corroboration from Sarah Astell first.

As usual, Sarah Astell was in her sitting room. She looked as though she'd been crying, as there were hastily wiped marks of recent tears on her face. Astell was there too, going over some figures. Rafferty explained why they had come.

Sarah Astell frowned. 'How did you find out about those cuttings? Surely Mrs Hadleigh didn't—?'

'She didn't mention them.' Rafferty paused, but didn't tell her who had. 'You know you should have told us about them yourself?'

She nodded. 'I would have, of course, but I felt I owed it to Mrs Hadleigh to keep her confidence. Besides, I hardly think they could have any bearing on his murder. It was all many years ago.' Her face twisted. 'I felt it likely that, if the burglar didn't kill Moon, one of his perverted friends must have done it.'

Rafferty merely nodded. 'If I could see those cuttings?'

She threw off the rug and, getting up, walked with a slow, unsteady gait to a little side table and pulled open a drawer. She handed him a batch of clippings.

Rafferty quickly scanned them. The stories added nothing they didn't already know. The clippings contained various shots of Hedges, as he then was. But if he hadn't already known Moon and Hedges to be one and the same, he would have been hard pushed to recognize him. The scar on his face was the only real giveaway. 'I'm surprised you recognized him from these,' he remarked. 'He's changed a great deal.'

'He worked for my father ten years before these pictures were taken.'

'But surely,' Llewellyn interjected, 'you could have been no more than a toddler when Moon worked for your father. How did you even remember him at all?'

'I wasn't even a toddler, Sergeant,' she told him. 'I wasn't born till the autumn, months after he left, so, of course, you're right. I had no personal memory of him, but only the morning the cuttings arrived my daughter had been asking me for some dressing-up clothes – she's getting to that age – and I immediately thought of the evening dresses my mother used to wear when she was young. They're too good a quality to throw away and are stored in a trunk in my parents' old room. That's where I found the albums featuring Moon. I'd never seen them before. I had no idea who he was until that day. I rang my mother and asked her a few questions. She remembered that time very clearly. She told me that Moon, or Hedges as she knew him, left my father's employ in the February or March of that year. My mother didn't actually say so, she seemed unwilling to say much about that time, but I got the impression that my parents had put the albums away out of disgust when they heard about the court case. Quite understand-

149

able, of course. Mother told me they'd been very fond of him. Treated him like one of the family, almost.'

'Strange they kept them at all,' Rafferty remarked. 'If they felt so badly about him.'

'I never asked my mother that. I imagine they just wanted them out of sight and out of mind, then forgot about them. They led very busy lives. My father was often away, and although my mother rarely went with him she spent a lot of time entertaining his wide circle of friends and business colleagues.'

Rafferty nodded. He'd meant to ask her to confirm what Henry at the Troubadour had already told them and had forgotten. Now she'd saved him the trouble. 'Moon seems to have had a variety of jobs,' he commented. 'I understand he originally trained as an artist.'

'So I gather. But earning a living as an artist has never been easy. According to my mother, when he was offered a job with my father he jumped at it.' Scornfully, she added, 'I suppose he hoped the association would help him make his name as an artist. But he was only some kind of jumped-up office boy for my father, held the fort for him when he was abroad and helped arrange his social and business diary. Of course, as you say, he's changed a great deal in the intervening years, and if it hadn't been for the scar under his eye I mightn't have known him. That was what made me make the connection.'

She pulled several worn albums from where they had been placed on the shelf. As she did so she dislodged some other books. 'My father's old journals,' she commented, as, reverently, she tidied them back. 'He used to keep a record of all his travels.' Handing the albums to Llewellyn, she told them, 'That's Moon, the one between my parents.'

Llewellyn studied the picture for some moments before he handed it to Rafferty. Moon would have been about twenty, he guessed. Apart from the scar, he bore so little resemblance to the older Moon that it could have been a different person. Moon had an arm flung round each of the Carstairs' shoulders in a manner over-familiar for an employee of those times. Rafferty wasn't altogether surprised that the young Moon should be so presumptuous. He had been an extraordinarily good-looking youth. He handed the albums back and picked up the cuttings again. 'I'll hang on to these, if I may.' She nodded.

'The cuttings say nothing here about the name of the boy. How did you know it was Mrs Hadleigh's son?'

'I didn't. I left the cuttings lying on the table in here. Mrs Hadleigh found them.' She bit her lip. 'It was most unfortunate. When I returned shortly afterwards, she was in tears and it all came out how it had been *her* boy whom Hedges had assaulted. Unthinkingly, I blurted out his current identity, assuming she must have recognized him too, but, of course, it immediately became obvious that she hadn't. Until I told her, she had no idea Hedges and Moon were one and the same. Naturally, she was terribly upset. Of course, she has only been working at the offices for a few weeks and Moon had been in America for nearly all that time. It was my husband who employed her, my husband who dealt with the administration side of the business, wages and so on. Even if he'd been there the whole time, owing to his television commitments Moon rarely arrived before ten o'clock, a good hour after poor Mrs Hadleigh would have finished her cleaning. So she had little or no chance to recognize him.

'I felt awful to be the one to tell her she had been working for the very man who had assaulted her son. But, once the words were out, there was little I could do to soften the blow. I was angry, too, that even now his wickedness should cause them more pain.' She sighed. 'Old sins tend to have long shadows, Inspector.'

Rafferty nodded. He didn't tell her that the sins hadn't been Moon's. It was up to Terry Hadleigh, not him, to put the record straight. The trouble was, by doing so he was likely to cause even more pain than he had already. Long shadows indeed. He felt a stab of pity for Moon. As far as he could see, Moon had – apart from his harmless fancy for bent merchandise – led a blameless life; had even forgiven the man who had caused him to be branded a child-molester. He might now be dead, but he deserved to have that brand removed from his memory, at least among the people who had known him well, and he resolved to have another little word with Terry Hadleigh when the case was over, to see if something couldn't be quietly salvaged from the mess caused by that long-ago deceit.

Rafferty turned to Edwin Astell, who had been quiet all this time. 'Did you mention to Mr Moon that your wife had received these cuttings, sir?' Rafferty asked him.

Astell shook his head. 'I saw little point in upsetting him.

Besides, although I know my wife believed what was in the cuttings, I wasn't convinced. And, even if he did assault that boy, it was all years ago. People change.'

'Have you any idea who sent you these clippings?' Rafferty asked Mrs Astell.

She shook her head. 'None. They simply arrived in the post last week, with nothing to indicate who had sent them.'

'What day last week? Do you remember?'

Her mouth turned down. 'It's not something I'm likely to forget, Inspector. It was last Wednesday. In the morning post.'

'And when did Mrs Hadleigh find them?'

'That same morning.'

The day before Moon's murder. Was it coincidence? he wondered. Or cause and effect?

They made their goodbyes and left shortly after. Ellen Hadleigh had, apparently, finished at the Astells' for the day, as when Rafferty asked to question her, they discovered she had gone. They would have to catch up with her at home.

As their car approached the gate, a middle-aged woman and a young child turned into the drive. 'That must be the Astells' little girl,' said Rafferty, as he stopped the car and wound the window down to say hello.

The child's manners were as old-fashioned as her father's. When Rafferty introduced himself and Llewellyn, she held out her hand and shook theirs as if it was the most natural thing in the world for a five-year-old to behave like a deal-overdosed tycoon. Rafferty just managed to restrain a chuckle as her solemn little face gazed earnestly back at him. With a struggle, he recalled the child's name. Not surprisingly, it was as old-fashioned as the rest of her.

'We've just been to see your mummy and daddy, Victoria,' he told her. As he remembered the signs of recent tears on Sarah Astell's face, he added, 'Your mummy looked a bit down in the dumps. I think she'd be glad if you went and cheered her up.'

Victoria nodded. 'Mummy is often sad. Sometimes she cries.' She shook her head and tutted, just like an over-anxious parent, before adding, 'She says she has no friends, that nobody really likes her.' Rafferty reflected that her words could have found their echo in any home in the country, even if their subject was usually a teenager rather than a parent. 'I tell her *I* like her, that the foreign lady at Daddy's office likes her. But she still cries.' Her thin little chest heaved an enormous sigh. 'Does *your* Mummy get sad like that?' she asked Rafferty.

Rafferty smiled. 'No. Not often. When she does she either goes to the bingo or round to one of my sisters' houses. She soon cheers up playing with her grandchildren.'

'I'd like a brother or sister to play with,' Victoria confided, in the wistful voice of the only child. Out of the corner of his eye, Rafferty saw Llewellyn, another only child, nod his involuntary agreement. 'But when I ask Mummy if I can have one, she goes all sad again.' She pulled back the sleeve of her coat and stared hard at her watch. Suddenly, she was a child again as, with her tongue curled firmly around her upper lip, and the fingers of her right hand slowly counting off the hours, she worked out what the little hand was doing. 'It's getting late,' she told them. 'I'd better go now, or else Mummy will worry. Bye.'

Rafferty watched as she toddled up the drive. The nanny or whoever she was got up from the bench where she had been waiting and joined her. What a serious little girl, he thought. But that was hardly surprising, he realized. With a mother permanently ailing, she wouldn't have a lot of amusing company, and, perhaps, with the self-sufficient Astell for a father, she didn't need it. There certainly seemed to be a lot of him in her; she even shared his eczema. Rafferty had noticed just a little bit on her hands.

'Right.' He opened the car door. 'The next priority, now we've had the business of the cuttings confirmed, is to see Ellen Hadleigh again. See if she's prepared to tell us the whole truth now.'

'What is it this time?' Ellen Hadleigh sank into her worn armchair after she had let them in.

'We know that you lied to us, Mrs Hadleigh,' said Rafferty. 'You might as well admit it. You knew who Moon was the day before he was murdered.' He took the borrowed clippings out of his pocket and laid them in her lap. 'I believe you've already seen these. Do you want to tell me about it?'

She drew in a ragged, distressed breath and stared at the yellowing clippings as if she had never seen them before, but she didn't attempt to deny the truth of what Rafferty had told her. 'I thought . . .' she began and then stopped.

'You thought Mrs Astell wouldn't say anything?'

She nodded. 'I'd been up in the attic that morning, sorting out a load of old films that had belonged to her father. They were that dusty, so I came down to her sitting room where I'd left my rags and polish. That's when I found those cuttings. I was so shocked I cried out, and Mrs Astell came running in. She was almost as upset as me when she realized the cuttings were about my boy. She made me a cup of tea. Even gave me one of her fancy embroidered handkerchiefs.' A faint smile momentarily lightened her heavy features. 'Mind, it was a silly little thing. About as much use as a tissue to a hippo with a head cold. Still, she was very kind. That's what made me think . . .' The smile faded. 'Silly of me to have just assumed it would be our secret, that she wouldn't tell anyone.'

'I don't think she would have done,' Rafferty said gently. 'Only I found out about them from someone else and asked her.' He noted that she didn't ask who had told them. Perhaps she guessed? 'I'm surprised Mr Moon didn't speak to you about the court case,' he said. 'He must have recognized your name.'

She shook her head. 'I doubt he ever knew it. I doubt he even knew I was working there, as the previous cleaner left while he was in America. It wouldn't have occurred to Mr Astell to mention it and introduce us. He can be a bit of a snob, you know. I don't think Moon even saw me that evening, as he went out right after the Moreno woman left and I was in the kitchen then as well as when I heard him return. I left a few minutes later.' Rafferty nodded, but resolved to check with Astell whether or not he had mentioned her name to Moon.

Ellen Hadleigh stared bleakly at the cuttings, her expression puzzled. 'You know, it's odd, but under her sympathy, I got the impression she was pleased to discover something really bad about Moon, yet since his death she seems to have gone to pieces. Mr Astell's had to call the doctor out to her several times.' She raised her head, her forehead puckered. Then she looked down at the cuttings again and her expression hardened, her voice filled with a surprising vigour, as she added, 'Sarah Astell doesn't know her own mind. But I won't be wailing over his coffin. I'm glad he's

154

dead. Very glad.' The strength of her emotion seemed to sap her remaining strength. For, seconds later, she was struggling for breath. Alarmed by her colour, Rafferty told Llewellyn to fetch her a glass of water.

She recovered surprisingly quickly, and sat quietly sipping her water, rallying enough to give them a tiny smile. 'Don't worry, Inspector. I've had these attacks before. I'm not going to die on you. It'll take more than this to see me off.'

She still looked drained, in spite of her brave words, and slumped back into the chair. Her skin looked grey, her lips bloodless, but, somehow, she had rediscovered her air of defiance. She might be poor, her expression suggested, but she still had a few shreds of pride. Individually, pride or revenge were good enough reasons for murder, Rafferty realized suddenly. But together . . . ?

He stood up. Her skin still had a pale and clammy look and he was worried about leaving her on her own. 'Is there anyone who can stay with you?'

She shook her head. 'I'll be all right.' She stared at him from eyes that were stubbornly independent. 'Just leave my boy alone. He's not your murderer. He doesn't have it in him.' She closed her eyes again.

Rafferty knew he should bring her down to the station and question her further. Somehow, he couldn't do it. He suspected that, in spite of her defiant air, she was very near the end of her strength and the stress might be too much for her. He was only a policeman, not some form of heavenly avenger, and he didn't want her death on his conscience. Besides, he didn't think she'd be going very far. He told her he would send a WPC out to stay with her. She just nodded, without opening her eyes. Maybe by the time the WPC arrived, she would have decided to talk some more.

'Maybe Moon's last message *did* mean something after all,' Rafferty commented as they walked down the stairs to the car. 'That sign could have been a roughly scrawled "H" for Hadleigh, rather than a "T" or an "I" or the sign for Gemini. Moon was dying; suppose he made two attempts at writing the cross stroke and missed with both of them?'

Slowly, Llewellyn nodded.

Gratified that the Welshman agreed with him for once, Rafferty, carefully forgetting that Llewellyn had already mentioned the matter, added, 'After all, if it meant nothing, why should anybody bother washing it off the wall?'

'Why indeed?' Llewellyn murmured *sotto voce* as they got in the car and headed back to the station. However, he didn't bother to remind Rafferty that he had already made that very point right at the beginning of the case.

Hanks had been quick. As they walked through the door, he called after them and told them the results of his digging into Mrs Hadleigh's alleged attack on Moon. After praising his efficiency, Rafferty dismissed him and led the way up to his office. 'So Terry Hadleigh was telling the truth about that as well,' said Rafferty as he settled behind his desk. 'Interesting that although he must have known Moon's true identity for some time, his mother had only learned of it the day before. Especially now we know that although Terry Hadleigh might never have shown a tendency to violence, his *mother* had.'

Hanks had spoken to the brief who had represented Moon at the time of the case. He had confirmed that Ellen Hadleigh *had* attacked Moon after the court case and that he had taken an umbrella with a stout wooden handle away from her; but not before she had cracked a bone in his wrist, which was why he remembered the incident so well. Fortunately for her, not only had no reporters got hold of the story – which explained why the cuttings had made no mention of it – but Moon, surprisingly, had refused to press charges, even though he had suffered concussion. Moon had been lucky. But for the speedy intervention of his brief, it might have been a lot worse, especially given his thin skull. Instead, he had gone on to live another twenty-eight years, only to meet his end in a very similar way.

The two attacks on Moon showed a worrying similarity and Rafferty asked himself if that similarity was merely a coincidence, or an indication of something more? Ellen Hadleigh had been a much younger and fitter woman then, but even though she was now aged and crippled, the intervening years had done nothing to diminish her hatred. Such hatred could fuel even the weakest body to acts of violence.

'We assumed she was covering up for her son when she made up this Henderson character, and she may well have been,' Rafferty commented. 'But she could just as easily have been covering up for herself. Perhaps it's time we investigated Ellen Hadleigh's movements a little more closely?'

'What about the other suspects? Ginnie Campbell, for instance, and Farley and . . .'

Rafferty smiled. 'Me – I've not got many psychological theories, but the one I do hold firm to is that emotional types are their own worst enemies. If we leave them to stew for a little longer, we'll get more out of them – if there's more to be got. For now, let's just concentrate on Ellen Hadleigh. Check what time the taxi dropped her off home that evening,' Rafferty instructed. 'I want the times narrowed down as much as possible.'

When Llewellyn had gone, Rafferty simply sat for a few moments, staring blindly at the reports that were still piling up. Ellen Hadleigh had suffered badly at the hands of men all her life; abusive father, cheating husband, weak and deceitful son. It would be too ironic if, in a moment's deviation from a painfully honest life, she had killed the one man who had never done her any harm.

Chapter Twelve

'I checked with the taxi firm,' Llewellyn told Rafferty later that morning. 'They confirm they dropped Ellen Hadleigh at her flats at about five past eight on the night of the murder. They were delayed for a few minutes at the level crossing,' he explained briefly. 'I've asked Lilley to ring every taxi firm in a ten-mile radius to check that she didn't order another taxi to take her to Moon's, when she paid off the original one. He's getting on with it now, but he'll be some little while, I imagine.'

Rafferty nodded approval. 'Good work, Dafyd, it's a point worth checking. But even if she didn't get another cab, she should still be in the running. Her flat is no distance from the High Street. There are two entrances to those flats. She could have walked through the internal corridor towards the lifts as if she intended going up to her flat and left by the pedestrian entrance. It would have saved her five minutes. Moon's phone was off the hook at eight-twenty and back on five minutes later – which indicates he died around then. He was certainly dead at eight-thirty or a little earlier if we accept that Terry Hadleigh spent five minutes trying to get an answer. Admittedly, she's not too good on her pins, but she could have walked it in ten minutes, killed Moon, and been home again by just after half past eight. The times are tight, but not impossibly so. How long does it take to bash someone's head in, after all?'

'You paint a convincing picture,' Llewellyn commented, then spoilt his remark with the reminder, 'but it's still just supposition. We have no more proof that she murdered him than we have that any of the other suspects did so. Besides, why go back later to tackle him? He was alone earlier; she could have spoken to him then.'

'Yes, but she had another job to go on to and not much time. Ellen Hadleigh takes her responsibilities seriously. She'd waited nearly thirty years for her revenge; another few hours wouldn't make so much difference. And I know it's not proof as such, but surely you of all people have thought more on the psychological angle? How likely is it,' Rafferty asked, 'that a woman with the gumption to physically attack him years ago was now so changed in character that she hadn't even *verbally* assaulted Moon that evening? It explains why she felt unwell at the Astells' and had to leave early. Her mind and stomach must have been churning in anticipation of tackling Moon.'

Llewellyn went to break in, but Rafferty, carried away on a wave of his own rhetoric, wasn't about to allow any interruption. 'Her son hadn't told her the truth about the assault, but supposing, when she returned and bearded Moon in his office, he had made her listen while he told her what had *really* happened all those years ago? That her son had lied to her, lied to the police, lied to the courts, lied to *everyone* about what had happened between him and Moon. What mother would be likely to believe him? And, if there *is* something in your psychological theory, what mother would be *willing* to believe him? It strikes me that the more he tried to convince her, the angrier she would become. It would be the work of moments to pick up the ball when Moon's head was turned away and to express the extent of her fury by bringing it crashing down on his skull.'

Satisfied that not only was he on the right track at last, but that he had laid out his case with sufficient logic for even Llewellyn's tastes, he added decisively, 'Get the squad to ask around and find out what Ellen Hadleigh was wearing that night, Dafyd. If she killed Moon, it's possible there are traces of blood on her clothes and as there are no open fires in those flats she couldn't get rid of the evidence easily. She'd have had to dump her clothing somewhere.' He frowned. 'Find out when the refuse collections are made at the flats. She might have thrown them down the rubbish chute.' He hoped not. He could just imagine what Bradley would say when he asked for a large team to search the Council dump.

Llewellyn hadn't been gone five minutes when a visitor arrived to see Rafferty. A most surprising visitor, as Ginnie Campbell hadn't impressed him thus far with her eagerness to talk to the police.

'Mrs Campbell?' Rafferty opened the door to the front office and beckoned her over. 'What can I do for you?'

'It's more a case of what I can do for you, Inspector,' she told him. 'Perhaps we should go to your office?'

Intrigued, Rafferty held the door for her to walk through and led her up to his office. 'Now,' he said, when they were both seated. 'What's this about?'

'Just something that I overheard that I thought you should know. I – forgot about it till now.' She stared at him, daring him to call her a liar. 'It must have been the shock of finding Jasper dead. It knocked everything else from my mind.'

Rafferty doubted it. She'd had sufficient presence of mind to remember to collect the money from Moon's cashbox. Sufficient, too, to lie about it. All her actions since finding Moon's body had been from callous self-interest. He wondered how what she had to tell him would further her interest. 'Go on.'

'It concerns the professional invalid, Mrs Ailing Astell. Her of the hundred and one illnesses, none of which anyone can put a name to.' She leaned back in her chair, a hint of a smile on her ruby-red lips. 'Ask her about the day she telephoned Jasper. She really laid into him. You should have heard her. There didn't sound much wrong with her then, I can tell you.' Her gaze avid, she added mischievously, 'If she could have got her hands on him that day I think she'd have killed him.'

Rafferty thought he understood now why Ginnie Campbell had decided to tell them about the phone call. He was willing to bet she'd hoped to make Mrs Astell buy her silence on the matter. But, he realized, she was also capable of making the story up just to cause trouble and get them off her back. Now he asked, 'If they were on the phone, how do you know what she said to him?'

She shrugged. 'It was an accident,' she told him, her manner implying he could believe what he liked. 'That Peruvian bitch was at lunch and I was covering the shop. Jasper had a new phone system installed recently. I haven't had much practice at transferring calls on it and I thought I'd cut her off at first. Anyway, I must have made the connection correctly because Jasper came on the line and she just laid into him. I didn't mean to listen to their conversation, but I was so shocked at her language that I was more or less hypnotized. Besides, it was odd that she should ring Jasper at all. She never has before, as far as I know. She didn't like him.'

'So how much of this call did you overhear?'

'Quite a bit.' She held his gaze for a while, and then laughed in that curiously abrupt way she had. 'All right, I admit it. I listened in. So what? I was curious. So would you have been if you'd heard her.' Now that she had dropped the pretence that her eavesdropping had been accidental, she allowed a little acid to creep into her voice. 'I could hardly believe my ears. I wouldn't have thought the dying swan knew such language. Such lady-of-the-manor airs she gives herself. Edwin came from a much poorer background, I gather, and is sensitive about it – thinks she married beneath her. But he might have changed his mind if he'd heard her that day.'

Her lip curled. 'Not that she'll be able to think herself so high and mighty now, anyway. I suppose you know she was a Lloyd's name?' This was news to Rafferty, but he nodded, hoping it would encourage more information. 'Then you'll know she's lost a packet in the last few years, nearly everything that her grandfather left her.'

'Even so,' Rafferty objected, 'she must still be a relatively rich woman. Her father was wealthy. Are you saying that whatever he left her has gone too?'

'He left her nothing in his will, apart from his old journals and film equipment. His money went to a cousin. They've had to mortgage the house.' Her smile was vindictive. 'That must have brought her down a peg or two.'

'How do you know all this?'

She shrugged. 'I keep my ear to the ground. Besides, Edwin has been to and from the accountants for months. Jasper offered them a loan, but Edwin turned him down. Said he did enough already by paying the bulk of the partnership bills.'

Rafferty nodded. It was strange that Sarah Astell's father had left her nothing. Of course, with his extravagant lifestyle he might well have had little money to leave. Still, he decided, it might be worth checking out Carstairs' will. If what Ginnie Campbell had said was true, it was their first indication that the Astells were in financial difficulties. The accountant should be able to confirm it, as he'd discovered during his visit that Mr Spenny acted in a private capacity for Mrs Astell, though, unfortunately for her, he hadn't had control of her investments. Maybe he'd acted for her father also?

'What exactly did Mrs Astell say to Moon?'

'A lot of it was so garbled I couldn't understand it. But I think she was accusing Jasper of assaulting someone, though whether it was herself or someone else ... She seemed to think he would know what she was talking about, anyway. She threatened to make it public knowledge, ruin his career.'

Hadleigh, Rafferty thought. She rang him about Terry Hadleigh. 'How did Mr Moon react?'

'How do you expect him to react? He sounded really upset. When I went in to see him later, he was very quiet, brooding, not like himself at all. I asked him what was wrong, but he wouldn't say. And I could hardly admit I'd listened in to the call.'

'What did he say to her?'

'Very little at first. But then, when she started threatening him, he broke in and told her she had no idea what she was talking about and that she should take care. He began to explain that whatever she was talking about had been little more than a misunderstanding, but when she shouted him down and refused to listen to what he had to say, he began to shout a bit himself. I remember his exact words. He said the past often concealed more than it revealed, and that if she was determined to pry into it, she might discover more than she bargained for.'

'And did she say she would carry on, anyway?'

'She did. She sounded very determined. She certainly wouldn't listen to his explanation, whatever it was.' Ginnie Campbell gave another careless shrug. 'I didn't hear the rest. A customer came into the shop, so I had to put the phone down.'

'And when, exactly, did this conversation between Mr Moon and Mrs Astell take place?'

Obviously she had deliberately saved the best bit till last. Her eyes darker than ever, she told him, 'The day before Jasper died.'

Although Rafferty judged Ginnie Campbell to be more than capable of lying when it suited her, he thought that the gist of what she had told him had been truthful, even if she had held back the

162

rest of it for purposes of her own. He certainly didn't believe that she had replaced the receiver when the conversation had been so riveting. She would think nothing of letting a customer wait, he was sure.

Soon after he had shown her out, Llewellyn returned. Rafferty told him what she'd said. 'I wonder what Moon thought Sarah Astell might discover that she would rather not know?' he mused. 'Do you reckon Astell and Moon might have had a thing going? Moon was certainly very generous to him.'

Llewellyn shrugged. 'Possible, I suppose, but unlikely. I would say that Astell is more into the cerebral than the physical. I really can't see him and Moon . . . No, it's what Mrs Campbell *didn't* say that interested me. We know she's deeply in debt. She certainly overheard more than she admitted. Possibly she hoped to extract a profit or at least a partnership from Moon for keeping silent about whatever she had just learned.'

Rafferty nodded. Of course, Ginnie Campbell knew that Sarah Astell was broke; any calls to her would be more for pleasure than profit. But, if she had believed Moon had something to hide – like the Hadleigh case – he would be the natural target for blackmail. But Ginnie Campbell hadn't been as clever as she thought. What she had told them didn't only put Sarah Astell under the spotlight, it further incriminated Ginnie Campbell herself. 'She'd worked there for a year. Maybe, given her propensity for eavesdropping, she had come across other sensitive information concerning him.'

Llewellyn nodded. 'She took some time off from the shop immediately after that phone call. I know she claimed she and her boyfriend went to the races last Thursday but, once in the bar, it's likely the boyfriend gave more attention to his glass. She could have gone anywhere.'

'And seen anyone,' Rafferty added. 'Depending on what else she found out, she could certainly have gone to see Moon that Thursday evening and threatened him with exposure. In turn, Moon could have threatened her with the sack and arrest. Her quick temper would do the rest. But that's all just more speculation at the moment. Another little chat with Mrs Astell would seem indicated. But first,' he picked up the phone, 'I think the accountant should be able to clear up a few points.'

Mr Spenny confirmed what Ginnie Campbell had told them; not only had Alan Carstairs left his money – quite a substantial sum – to a cousin, but Sarah Astell's maternal inheritance *had* largely gone to pay off her commitments at Lloyds. There was very little money left and what there was came from the business.

'Sorry, Daf,' Rafferty apologized as he put the phone down. 'In all this excitement I didn't ask what you found out about Ellen Hadleigh.'

'The refuse from her flats is collected on a Friday, so if she killed Moon she could have got rid of any stained clothing the very next day.'

'Handy. Have you set the squad to asking around to find out what she was wearing the Thursday night?' Llewellyn nodded. 'Right. Perhaps we should see what Sarah Astell has to say for herself before we tackle either Ellen Hadleigh or the Council dump. Come on.'

Their reappearance so soon after their previous visit seemed to make Sarah Astell edgy. Her thin hand clasped her chest as though to calm an erratic heartbeat. 'What is it this time, Inspector?' she asked. 'If you came to see my husband, he's upstairs.'

'Actually,' Rafferty replied, 'it was you we came to see.'

'Me?' Her gaze flickered anxiously between them. Her attempted smile faltered and she stood back. 'Perhaps you had better come in.'

As he made to follow her through the hall, Rafferty paused as he recognized a profile amongst the gallery of photographs in the hall. 'I didn't realize your father knew Nat Kingston, Mrs Astell.'

'They were friends for years,' she told them briefly. 'Of course, they were both artists, of a sort.'

'We actually met Nat Kingston the other day,' Rafferty told her. 'He's a sick man. Though Eckersley, his secretary, makes a good nurse. He's very protective of him.'

She nodded. 'Jocelyn Eckersley always cared far more about Kingston, his fame, his reputation, than Kingston himself. He couldn't have a more attentive nurse.' Fiddling with a pearl-like stone at her neck, she added softly, 'Jocelyn always did keep the vultures at bay. I imagine he'll do that till the end.'

She led them to her sitting room. From behind them came the

164

sound of footsteps on the stairs and, wheezing a little as though still troubled by his bronchitis, Edwin Astell entered the room. He must have heard them at the door.

The room was taken over by photograph albums. They were scattered on the floor, on Sarah Astell's chaise. One was open at a particularly large picture of her father as a very young man. On the opposite page was another picture of him. They had both been damaged and had jagged rips through their centres, from top to bottom, as if someone had torn them in a rage. Sellotape now held them together. The second picture showed him with his arm flung round a friend's shoulders and, as in so many of the photographs of Carstairs, he was staring straight into the camera. The friend was in profile, his large nose jutting towards Carstairs as if he intended to peck him to death. Their laughing faces exuded the unshakeable youthful conviction that immortality was theirs.

A depression descended on Rafferty as he realized that not only were they *both* probably dead, but that, at nearly thirty-eight, over half his own expected three score years and ten had passed. And all he'd got to show for it was one failed marriage. His gaze caught the swirling leaves in the garden and his thoughts turned morbidly poetical. That's us, he reflected bleakly. Like leaves, we are cast up, then down, upon the whims of fate. No one hears us, heeds us or delivers us. Such is life. He came back from his wretched musings to find Llewellyn and the Astells staring at him and he wondered if he had spoken aloud. But, as no one was ringing for the men in white coats, he thought not. His gaze dropped back to the photograph of the youths, and he frowned as a fleeting sense of *dejà-vu* came to him and as quickly vanished.

After tidying away the albums, Mrs Astell invited them to sit down. 'So what did you want to speak to me about, Inspector?' she asked, when they were all seated.

'It's about a telephone call you made to Jasper Moon, Mrs Astell.' Rafferty had half expected her to deny ringing Moon. Indeed, he could see the words of denial hovering on her lips. But obviously she thought better of it. Perhaps, Rafferty mused, she had remembered that it had been Ginnie Campbell who had put her through when she rang that lunchtime? She would be aware she couldn't expect discretion from such a source. Or maybe she was hoping that Rafferty didn't know any details of the call and had merely checked with the telephone company? If so, he immediately dashed such hopes.

'Perhaps I ought to tell you that your telephone conversation with Jasper Moon was overheard.' Edwin Astell, his gaze fixed anxiously on his wife, made a sound of dismay, but otherwise said nothing.

'I see.' She clasped her hands in her lap, and gave them a faint smile. 'So that's what Virginia Campbell wanted to speak to me about. She's rung several times, but I refused to speak to her. I don't like the woman, she's so dreadfully coarse. I suppose she thought I would be willing to pay her to keep quiet about it.'

Rafferty made no comment. 'Perhaps you would like to tell me your version of the conversation?' he suggested. 'We like to be accurate.'

She sat up straight. 'I'm not ashamed of what I said to him. Someone needed to say it. I'm afraid that after Mrs Hadleigh left last Wednesday I still felt so strongly; I knew I had to do something positive. At first, I didn't know what. Then I realized there was one thing I could do: I could tell Moon exactly what I thought of him. So I rang him. I felt I owed her that.'

'So you never really intended making the court case public?'

'How could I, without hurting Mrs Hadleigh and her son further? I took care not to let Jasper Moon know that, though. Edwin was unwell that day and in bed. When I told him what had happened, he tried to dissuade me from ringing Moon.' Understandably, she gave her husband a propitiating glance. 'He didn't say so, but I realize now that he was worried Moon might take it out on him in some way, even break up the partnership, but at the time I didn't think of that aspect. I felt too strongly about it.'

'I wasn't really worried that Jasper would end our partnership,' her husband broke in. 'I was more concerned for you. You know how badly any upset affects you.'

She gave him another tremulous, apologetic smile. 'I wish now I'd listened to you. But at the time I felt it was something I had to do. And your poor head was aching too much for you to have the energy to dissuade me.'

She glanced at Llewellyn's expressionless countenance, as though she detected disapproval. It was a feeling with which Rafferty was familiar. Even with his features blank and his tongue still,

166

Llewellyn's thoughts somehow communicated themselves. They frequently caused an unwise retaliatory outburst from Rafferty.

It seemed they had the same effect on Sarah Astell, for now she gave a defensive laugh, and told them, 'Of course, I calmed down later and felt cross that I'd let Moon distress me so much.' Her lower lip trembled. For a moment, she seemed to hover between rage and tears, a frown creasing her brow as if she was confused by her own strongly contradictory emotions.

'I'm surprised that after such a conversation Jasper Moon should still send you a birthday present,' Llewellyn remarked. 'He *did* still send it, I understand?'

Sarah Astell blinked. 'Yes. He gave it to Edwin before he left the office on Thursday evening. I put it straight in the bin. I didn't want his presents. Especially—' She broke off and glanced across at her husband. 'Edwin found it and made me take it back.'

'I gather he'd sent you a video?' Llewellyn went on. 'I—'

She stared at him, eyes wide. 'How do you know that?'

'He'd left the wrapped parcel on his desk earlier in the week, Mrs Astell,' he explained. 'Not difficult to guess what it was.'

'I see.'

'I hope it was to your taste?'

'I've no idea, Sergeant. I didn't watch it.'

Llewellyn, who seemed to have the bit between his teeth, paused before he changed tack. 'During your conversation, I understand he mentioned something about you finding out more than you bargained for if you dug into the past. Have you any idea what he meant?'

'None. I took it for granted he was merely trying to intimidate me with non-existent will o' the wisps. But as I had no intention of causing Mrs Hadleigh more upset, I didn't think any more about it.'

Llewellyn seemed to find her answer a bit hard to swallow, but as he appeared to have run out of steam for the present Rafferty called a halt and made for the door. 'We may need to speak to you again,' he warned and caught the anxious glance the Astells exchanged. 'Come along, Llewellyn.'

'But—' Llewellyn strangled his protest for the time being, but when they reached the drive, he complained, 'You were very easy on them, weren't you? Doesn't it strike you as odd that Moon should still send her a birthday present after that telephone call? Surely—'

'Of course it's bloody odd,' Rafferty retorted. 'But I can't see that badgering Sarah Astell about it is likely to explain the oddity. It's clear she didn't want Moon's gift. But being on the receiving end of unwanted presents is hardly a hanging offence, and as he's not about for me to ask why he sent it, there's not a lot I can do to find out. It's not as if she's even got any sort of motive that we've been able to discover; being repelled by homosexuals is scarcely reason enough for murder, or half the population would be at it.'

'But even so—' Llewellyn began again.

Rafferty interrupted him to demand, 'What did you expect me to do? Sit there for the rest of the day till she'd explained Moon's thick skin to your satisfaction?' He got in the car and turned on the engine. 'I tell you what I *am* going to do,' he said. 'I'm going to get a bite to eat. I'm starving.'

The Astells' house was situated on the southern outskirts of Elmhurst. Rafferty had already noted that it was only a five-minute run in the car to one of his favourite riverside pubs, the Black Swan, and now, with a frown, he nosed the car towards it. 'I hope we're not too late for the fish dish. So far this case seems to have twisted and turned like an eel with the runs. If we're to get a firm hold on it I reckon we're going to need all the brain food we can get.'

The sweeping branches of the weeping willow trees in the pub garden were only now losing their delicate, lance-shaped leaves. They still provided a pleasant shade from the suddenly fierce October sun. At one time, autumn had been his favourite of all the seasons, Rafferty mused, as he sipped his bitter. The season of mellow fruitfulness, as some dead poet had it; the time of bright Indian summer skies when, as today, the sun, as if guided by some Old Master's hand, burnished the rusts, russets and ambers of the shedding leaves to glowing life. But he had long ago realized that this appearance of vivid life was counterfeit. Like the photo of the young and long-dead Carstairs and his laughing friend, it served more as a reminder of one's own mortality. Because once the fruit was harvested, the glow faded and even the most beautiful autumn was merely the precursor to the death and decay of winter.

Rafferty was a realist, and as his childhood belief in an afterlife, of heaven and hell and soaring angels, had diminished to a vague hope of *something* to follow, he had transferred his allegiance to spring. To a policeman who had to deal with yet another sudden and violent passing, spring, with its vigorous renewal, was an infinitely more comforting season.

Still, it was a glorious day, he acknowledged as he leant back against the bench; he was getting used to snatching relaxation when he could get it. The recent prolonged rain had filled the sluggish River Tiffey after the long drought-ridden summer and it sparkled with the lustre of a thousand love-bright solitaires in the sunshine. Running fast and sweet, it had shaken off any lingering summer odours.

Llewellyn was just coming towards him across the grass with his second half of Elgood's and he sighed contentedly, silently congratulating himself for convincing Llewellyn of the superiority of pub lunches. He felt pleasantly full, having just got outside a particularly generous plateful of ploughman's – as he'd anticipated, the fish dish had long since been finished. But the ploughman's lunch had been a more than adequate substitute; he could still taste the crusty bread, the great wedge of mature Cheddar served with a pickle with the bite of a Doberman. Apart from finding the solution to the case, he asked himself, what more could any man want?

'We ought to make this the last, sir,' Llewellyn suggested, bringing, along with Rafferty's beer, the unwelcome reminder that in spite of an abundance of suspects, he had yet to solve the case.

Rafferty wished, not for the first time, that his sergeant was less the dutiful Methodist, less into keeping both their noses firmly fixed to the grindstone and more into indulging in the occasional bout of hookey. It remained to be seen whether his introduction to Catholicism and possible entry into the Rafferty family would loosen him up a bit. If it ever came off, that was. Llewellyn's cautious streak seemed to come from the bone. If she wanted to marry his sergeant, Rafferty suspected Maureen might have to do the proposing herself, and then kidnap her bridegroom as they used to do with well-dowered brides years ago.

Llewellyn murmured, 'I don't mean to rush you, sir,' as he

watched Rafferty resignedly pick up his glass, 'only I've just realized something that could have an important bearing on the case.'

'Oh yes? What's that, then? The name of the murderer?' he suggested sardonically before draining his glass.

'Maybe.'

Llewellyn's answer nearly made him choke on his bitter. Slowly, he lowered his glass and stared at the Welshman.

'I've just realized the identity of one of the boys in that old film that Moon had hidden in his wardrobe,' he explained. 'If I'm right, I believe it gives one of our suspects a very good reason for wanting Moon dead.'

Chapter Thirteen

Llewellyn was right. It *was* Carstairs on Moon's hidden video. Rafferty rewound the film and began to watch it through again.

'Now I know why, when I saw that veritable gallery of photographs Sarah Astell has of him, I had a feeling of familiarity. Of course, the film's very poor quality, and he's much younger.' Rafferty excused his own lack of observation. 'So much for his lady-killer reputation. That and his marriage must have made a pretty effective smokescreen for his real preferences.' He froze the film and nodded at the screen. 'And now I recognize the other young man, too. It's Nat Kingston. Mrs Astell told us he and her father had been close friends.'

'Whether or not the other youth is Kingston is hardly significant,' said Llewellyn briskly, as if reluctant to accept that his hero had other human weaknesses, apart from the reluctance to visit a doctor that he had already admitted to. 'But what *is* significant is my conviction that, after her cold-shoulder treatment, her abusive and threatening telephone call must have been the last straw for Moon. And he retaliated by issuing a threat of his own, to make this film public and turn her homosexual prejudices back on herself. He must have contemplated doing something of the sort even before she made that telephone call, otherwise why have four video copies made? Her phone call just provided that extra spur to a decision already more than half made.' Llewellyn paused for a moment and then added, 'And if, as I suspect, Carstairs had been the great love of Moon's life that young man in the Troubadour mentioned, it would explain his possession of this film. Carstairs was good-looking, sophisticated, experienced, travelled, and – as we now discover – homosexual. Moon would have been dazzled if Carstairs paid him attention. Moon was a good-looking young

171

man himself, on the spot, living in Carstairs' house.' Llewellyn's sallow skin positively glowed as, with an unaccustomed vigour, he laid out his arguments.

'If I'm right, it must have been Moon's first serious love affair; we can discount his half-hearted male–female romances. They were simply attempts at convincing himself he was other than homosexual. And then he discovered Carstairs had another lover Nat Kingston; a relationship that had endured for years. Can't you just imagine how devastated Moon would feel, the acrimony of the split when Moon found out that he had been little more than a plaything to Carstairs?'

Rafferty tried to break in, but Llewellyn hurried on. 'Don't you see? It would explain why Moon had this film. Carstairs seems the type who would have taunted him with it, thrown his love and the film in his face when Moon challenged him. Probably Moon took the film to torment himself, to remind him, should he ever forget, that great love often brought great pain and to keep clear of it in future. Moon was very young, sensitive about his own homosexuality, probably fearful about it becoming common knowledge. He must have felt a terrible sense of betrayal when he discovered that Carstairs had been cheating on him. And being so young, he was probably even more prone to melodrama then than when he was middle-aged. It would explain everything, including why he left Carstairs' employ.'

Rafferty had listened to Llewellyn's impassioned theorizing with growing astonishment. When he finally got a chance to get a word in, all he could find to say was, 'My God, you're a a bit of a drama queen yourself, aren't you? I never suspected.'

Llewellyn flushed. 'If you read the classics rather than those trashy novels you'd have more understanding of deep love and its passions. It can change history, create war, death, destruction. You must have heard of Helen of Troy, Tristan and Isolde, Romeo and Juliet. Surely even you can see that the homosexual world also have their great love stories?'

It was Rafferty's turn to flush. He supposed he should be grateful that Llewellyn had stopped short of accusing him of being wilfully blinded by his own prejudices.

'Could be one reason why Moon finally settled on Christian Farley rather than one of the gilded youth he could have chosen. You said yourself Moon's choice surprised you.'

Rafferty frowned. He suspected he knew in which direction Llewellyn's mind was going. And, in spite of the Welshman's eloquence, he still thought Ellen Hadleigh the more likely suspect. But this time he didn't attempt to interrupt.

'We know Sarah Astell disliked Moon even before she learned of his assault on Terry Hadleigh. Obviously, she never suspected when she threatened Moon that he had this film of her adored father, or she wouldn't have dared anger him. You must admit, Moon's possession of this film gives Sarah Astell a strong circumstantial motive for murder. It's not as if it's the only copy. We know he had more made. We also know he sent her a video on the evening of his death.'

Rafferty conceded the point. 'It would be more believable if she persuaded Astell to kill him for her. Trouble is, I can't see Astell committing *this* particular murder. It simply doesn't fit his character.'

'But it fits *hers*,' Llewellyn insisted and Rafferty had to agree. 'You said yourself that it was a spur-of-the-moment murder. She's just the type of highly emotional woman to act in such a way. No rational male – and Astell's certainly that – would be prepared to risk his livelihood over an ancient scandal that would be no more than a five-minute wonder. Most of Sarah Astell's money has gone to pay for her commitments at Lloyds. Even if his wife refused to face it, Astell would know that their future financial security rested with Moon. They needed his friendship. Once tempers had cooled Astell would have been likely to persuade his wife to eat humble pie and apologize to Moon. Any other course of action would have been foolish.' Llewellyn paused, before he added softly. 'Of course, the difficulty would be getting Sarah Astell to agree. She's capable of ignoring the financial angle to protect her father's reputation. She had the motive. She also had the opportunity, as she was almost certainly alone for some time that evening. Even if Astell and Mrs Moreno came in and discovered her missing from her sitting room, they would assume she was in the bathroom. And if Astell *did* check on her, as he claimed, and found her gone from the sitting room, how likely is it he would have betrayed her? He agreed with her alibi readily enough. He's been trying to protect her, can't you see that?' Llewellyn took a breath and went on.

'There's something else. I didn't mention it before, but while I

173

was talking to the people from the taxi firm I learned that one of their drivers moonlights from his regular job driving for the bus company. He remembered picking up a middle-aged woman from the stop outside the Astells' house at around five past eight that same night. It's only a five-minute drive to the High Street. She got off at the stop outside the Psychic Store and stood gazing in the window till the bus moved off. He noticed her particularly, because even though it was such a wet night she didn't seem in any rush to get out of the rain. Said she seemed all hunched up and furtive.' Llewellyn ventured another opinion. 'I wondered if it might not be Sarah Astell.'

Rafferty raised his eyebrows. 'So why didn't you mention this before?'

Llewellyn shrugged. 'What was the point of mentioning this woman when I didn't have anything to connect her with the case? You'd have pooh-poohed me if I'd said she might be Sarah Astell. After all,' he conceded, 'she could have been anybody.'

'Still could, for that matter. Anyway,' Rafferty pointed out, 'Sarah Astell's not exactly middle-aged. She's no older than I am. There's the first flaw in your argument.'

Wisely, Llewellyn made no comment regarding Rafferty's maturity – or otherwise – and merely pointed out, 'But she looks a lot older than her years. The driver says this passenger was bundled up in scarves, so he didn't get a good look at her face, but Mrs Astell doesn't move like a young person, does she? The driver could easily have thought of her as older because of her slow gait.'

'Surely Astell would have seen her going out the front door? It's at the end of the hall opposite the kitchen.'

'But she didn't need to use the front door,' Llewellyn pointed out reasonably. 'Her sitting room is at the side of the house and has french windows. She wouldn't even have needed to walk down the illuminated driveway as she could simply have walked through the shrubbery surrounding the house. It continues right up to the gates at the front, which had been opened for the guests. Then, all she had to do was wait for the five past eight bus.'

Rafferty shook his head. 'Bit risky. What if someone had recognized her?'

'Unlikely. She rarely goes out, so who would be likely to recognize her? Even when Mrs Moreno returned for her gloves, she wouldn't have passed the stop as she lives in the opposite direction. It was a wet, chilly night, not many people about. Astell said it was her custom to spend time alone on the night of her father's anniversary. She would feel herself safe for some time. She presumably wore an old coat over her dress and carried an open umbrella well down over her face to protect her hair from the wind. You remember forensic picked up an inside-out umbrella from the gutter outside. I wonder if it was hers?'

Rafferty wasn't convinced, but he conceded that point. 'I'll get a full description of it from them and see if anyone recognizes it. But I still don't think you're on the right track. The woman's a semi-invalid, after all. And she's so nervy, she'd jump at her own shadow. It was an appalling night. I can't imagine that someone who took her ailments as seriously as Sarah Astell would consider venturing out in such stormy weather. Apart from anything else, do you really think she had the mental or physical strength to kill Moon?'

'I know that *everyone*, including herself, behaves as if she were an invalid, but that doesn't make her one. As Juvenal warns us in his Satires, "*Fronti nulla fides*". Never judge a book by its cover,' he quickly translated as he noted Rafferty's expression.

'If you must throw these endless quotes at me, could you at least manage to drag yourself a bit nearer the twentieth century? There's something from Gilbert and Sullivan that might suit. "Things are seldom what they seem, skim milk masquerades as cream." Though, according to you, in Sarah Astell's case it should be the other way around: full-bodied cream pretending to be something weak, thin and far less deadly.'

'Exactly.'

'Come on, Dafyd. She's had poor health for years, we know that. It's not something she's just invented to help her get away with murder.'

'I'm not saying she has. But Astell himself said the doctors had been unable to diagnose what was the matter with her. Perhaps that's because, as Ginnie Campbell implied, there was nothing much to find in the first place? She wouldn't be the first person to find ill-health convenient. How much more convenient it would be if she could use it to get away with murder. You were the one

175

who said that police officers should suspect everyone, Llewellyn reminded him, when Rafferty expressed scepticism at his conclusion.

'All right, all right. I take your point. There's no need to hammer it home. But now's not the time to change the habits of a lifetime and go rushing off half-cocked.' Rafferty gave a self-mocking smile. 'That's my role, remember? Besides, the evidence of this film brings up another suspect. One we hadn't really considered before. Let's face it, if Moon used this film to expose Carstairs and hurt his daughter, he would also expose—'

'Not Kingston,' Llewellyn protested. 'I thought you agreed that he—'

'No,' Rafferty agreed. 'Not Kingston. Although this film exposes his homosexuality as well as Carstairs', it's debatable whether he would greatly care how he's judged by a world he is, anyway, soon to leave. He seems to have developed a fine contempt for it and its petty concerns. Besides, even if he did care, he's obviously far too ill to do anything about it. No, I was thinking of someone in their prime, someone who would care and care enormously if Kingston's reputation was tarnished by cheap sensationalism about his youthful sexual exploits: Kingston's zealous, over-protective secretary, Eckersley. Neither of us even thought of asking him for an alibi.' He took the video out of the player and handed it to Llewellyn. 'Maybe we ought to find out whether or not he has got an alibi before we tackle either of our favourite suspects.'

It was only a short drive to Nat Kingston's home. They arrived to find the gates wide open and an ambulance parked at the front door. Rafferty pulled up outside the gates and waited.

Five minutes later, the front door opened and the ambulance crew appeared carrying a stretcher. Its occupant was obviously dead, as a blanket covered the face. And after seeing a shattered-looking Eckersley trailing the little procession, Rafferty didn't need two guesses as to who lay under the blankets. Now was obviously not the time to question the secretary. After glancing at Llewellyn's shuttered face, Rafferty sat and watched, without speaking, as Eckersley climbed in the back of the ambulance. The doors closed, and it made its way at a suitably funereal pace out through the gates.

Rafferty crossed himself in an involuntary Catholic obeisance to the dead, unaware he had done so till, out of the corner of his eye, he saw Llewellyn follow his example. Amused to find that his ma's religious indoctrination of the Welshman was bearing fruit, some of his grim mood lifted.

They sat for a few more moments, silently paying their respects, while the sea, crashing on the rocks far below, paid its own thunderous homage. Then Rafferty turned the car round and they returned to Elmhurst.

Rafferty still felt that Ellen Hadleigh was their strongest suspect. And although Llewellyn had laid out a good case for Sarah Astell being the murderer, he remained unconvinced and was determined to pursue his own line before any other. Llewellyn raised no objection when Rafferty told him his decision; Kingston's death had affected him deeply and he had not said a word all the way back to town, not even to criticize Rafferty's driving.

Unfortunately for Rafferty's theory, no one who had seen Mrs Hadleigh on the night of the murder had been able to recall *what* she had been wearing. It seemed she had an assortment of nondescript dresses which she wore for her work and they all looked much the same: dark, drab and practical. There was no help for them there, Rafferty realized. But, he thought, before he went cap in hand to Bradley to have the tip searched he wanted another go at getting the truth out of her. As he'd already discovered, telling lies didn't come easily to her. Maybe, if she *had* killed Moon, the strain of having to tell more would prove her undoing.

It was clear when they visited her at her shabby flat, however, that Ellen Hadleigh wasn't about to confess to murder just to give Rafferty the satisfaction of being right.

'Do you deny challenging Moon that night?' Rafferty asked again, having received no reply to his earlier question on the point. 'You had only discovered his true identity the previous day. Do you really expect us to believe you were prepared to forgive and forget?'

'No,' she admitted. 'I *was* going to tell him what I thought of him; tell him exactly what damage he'd done to our lives. I'd had long enough to decide what to say.' She raised her hands for a moment, before dropping them back in a gesture of hopelessness. 'But then, I thought – what was the point? What could I expect to come of it, bar me getting the sack, that is? Would it have changed my Terence back into the boy he used to be?'

Her eyes fixed steadily on Rafferty's. 'He's forty-one, Inspector, not a boy any more. Moon may have tried to force my son to his own unnatural ways, but do you think I don't realize that Terence has continued with them willingly enough?'

Her answer sounded logical enough to convince Llewellyn, thought Rafferty. But he found it difficult to accept that logical reasoning would come naturally to a loving mother in such circumstances and he decided to try another tack. Although her answer to his next question wouldn't prove anything either way, as it now seemed pretty conclusive that Moon had still been alive when she left the offices after work, if he could wrong-foot her on an unimportant aspect it might unnerve her sufficiently to betray herself on something that *did* matter.

'I understand you finished work at seven p.m.?' She nodded. 'Yet you didn't arrive at the Astells' house till seven thirty-five. It's less than a five-minute ride. There's a bus from the stop along from the offices at seven ten, yet obviously you weren't on it. Can you explain why?'

'I *did* finish work at seven o'clock, as I told you,' she insisted. 'But I couldn't go to the Astells' house on such an important evening in my old cleaning dress. I know from previous years that even if I'm only there to remove glasses and load the dishwasher I'm still expected to make an effort, to show respect for her father's memory. Can you just imagine what Mrs Astell would say, and her in her expensive black glittery get-up, if I turned up in something worn out and shapeless? I had to have a wash and get changed.'

Rafferty stared at her. 'What did you just say?'

'That I had to get chang—'

'No. Not that bit. What you said about Mrs Astell's dress. Describe it to me.'

Ellen Hadleigh looked at him as if he had just gone mad, but did as he asked. 'She had a thin black dress on. Cashmere, she told me it was. It had glittery silver threads that caught the light. I told her she'd catch her death in it.'

Mrs Hadleigh had been wrong, Rafferty thought grimly. And so had *he*. It had been Moon who had caught his death. But Mrs Hadleigh's description of the dress made him swiftly cast aside his ruminations on mortality. Because its make-up sounded suspiciously similar to the few threads that had caught on Moon's desk. And Sarah Astell had said she had never been to the offices . . .

Rafferty sneaked a glance at his sergeant's face as they left. It was as expressionless as ever and Rafferty's conscience started up in fine heckling style. *You should be ashamed of yourself*, it chided. *Making Dafyd feel he has to cloak his triumph with tact just to soothe your bloated ego. If it had been you*, it told him, *you'd have been crowing from the rooftops.*

As usual, his conscience managed to hit the target. Rafferty cleared his throat and said, 'Come on, Daff. You're allowed to say "I told you so." ' With a rueful grin he added, 'Only once, mind.'

Llewellyn's dark eyes met his and his thin lips turned up a millimetre. 'In that case, I'll wait till the court gives me the go-ahead, if you don't mind.'

Rafferty shrugged. 'Suit yourself.' I *tried*, he told his conscience, before it had the chance to have another go at him. It's not my fault if he doesn't know how to relish his triumphs.

Further questioning of Ellen Hadleigh had revealed that the dress had cost £150. As they made their way down the grubby stairwell to the car, Rafferty recalled Mrs Hadleigh's scandalized voice as she had told them this. Understandable, of course, in a woman who must exist on a similar amount for the best part of a month. 'And there was nothing of it,' she had said. 'Just this plain black cashmere with silver metal threads woven through it. Not a patch on my good black jersey.' Sarah Astell had bought it, just before the anniversary evening, at Chez Sophie, an up-market dress shop in Elmhurst.

'Do you want me to go to Chez Sophie and ask them to let us have a similar dress?' Llewellyn enquired when they returned to the station.

179

'No,' said Rafferty decisively. 'I'll do that myself. You go and light a candle for Nat Kingston.'

An hour later, Rafferty let himself out of the tastefully discreet door of Chez Sophie and patted the silver carrier bag. Mission accomplished.

The dresses were a new line imported from France for which Chez Sophie had sole selling rights in the county. They'd taken two dresses in four slightly different styles, two each in black, midnight blue, scarlet and gold. The black were the only ones with silver thread; the others had toning threads. So far, the proprietor assured him, they had sold only one of the black – to a local lady – Mrs Astell. The credit card slip confirmed it.

Now all he had to do was drop the dress off with Appleby at forensic and wait for the results of their tests to see if they matched the fibres removed from Moon's desk. With luck – even if it was no thanks to him – the end of the investigation was in sight.

Back at the station, Rafferty told a slightly happier Llewellyn, 'If Appleby comes up trumps, I think we'll have enough to get a search warrant and—' He broke off as the phone rang. Two seconds later he shot up in his chair, fingers clutching the receiver tightly as he demanded, 'When did this happen? Which hospital?' Having got answers to his questions, he deliberately broke the connection. After asking the desk sergeant to get him the hospital on the line, he told Llewellyn grimly, 'Guess what? That was Edwin Astell. His wife tried to kill herself this afternoon.'

Chapter Fourteen

'What was it?' Llewellyn asked. 'An overdose?'

Rafferty nodded. 'The little girl's nanny found her in time and she's had her stomach pumped out.' He met Llewellyn's eye and smiled wearily. 'I'd say this clinches the case against her, wouldn't you?' The phone rang again. It was the hospital. Quickly Rafferty got put through to the doctor looking after Mrs Astell and, after a bit of persuasion, managed to get him to agree to let them see her for a few minutes.

Sarah Astell was pale but dry-eyed. She was sitting up in her hospital bed when they arrived and appeared surprisingly calm, as if her recent brush with death had insulated her from earthly troubles. Astell, in the chair beside the bed, tried to prevent them questioning her, but when Rafferty over-rode him he subsided.

Sarah Astell's unnatural calm deserted her when Rafferty tried to get her to admit the reason for her attempted suicide. She quickly became hysterical, and Astell protested again. 'Surely you can see she's in no fit state to be questioned? For pity's sake, she's just tried to—' Astell broke off and glanced guiltily at his wife, as if he had been about to mention a forbidden topic.

'I'm aware of that, sir,' Rafferty told him, his own guilt making his voice sharper than he intended. He should have guessed Sarah Astell might attempt suicide, he told himself. She had already attempted a form of self-destruction in her youth, so the seeds were there. Being suspected of murder was a far more pressurizing influence than the indifference of a parent. But Astell was right, he realized. Now was not the best time to question her. But before he could say so, Sarah Astell herself calmed down sufficiently to answer his question.

181

'Surely you know of our money problems, Inspector?' Her voice, though flat, was tinged with irony, as if she didn't really expect him to believe that was the reason for her attempted suicide and was just going through the motions.

So, Rafferty thought, that was how they were going to play it. Astell, although failing to inject his wife with conviction, had at least managed to make her primed response both reasoned and reasonable. 'So you took all those tablets because of money worries?'

She gave a brief nod and began to warm to her story. 'I was a "Name" at Lloyds. I've lost a lot of money. We've had to mortgage the house, sell some of our most precious possessions. I was afraid, so afraid I'd lose – everything.' She swallowed hard, her expression bleak. 'And then – with Moon's death, Edwin made me see that the bulk of our income had gone also. He explained that the house would certainly go. I – hadn't realized. It was the end, I knew that then. I couldn't bear it any longer, waiting for the worst to happen.' Her fingers began folding the sheet, gathering it into a neat fan shape, as if its precisely matching folds were the most important thing in the world to her.

'I see.' Rafferty paused. Her elaborate explanation sounded yet more reasonable than the simpler version. And, even though both Llewellyn and the evidence had convinced him of her guilt, but for that ironic tone he might have believed her. More plainly than the truth shouted loud from the hospital roof, it betrayed her appreciation that, in murdering Moon, she had brought about her own ruin. He tried to get her to admit it. 'And there was no – other reason for taking the overdose?'

'Other reason?' She stared back at him, her chin coming up a fraction. 'What other reason could there be?'

Whatever Astell had said to her had been effective, Rafferty realized frustratedly. It was obvious they would get no confession out of her today. But, even if she *did* confess, it would probably be inadmissible. She was in hospital, in a vulnerable state; not the ideal confession from the police point of view. Not that it mattered, he reminded himself. They had the evidence. All he was waiting for was Appleby's confirmation. And it would be better if she were in custody when she learned of the rest of the evidence against her. Just in case she attempted a second suicide. Instead

182

of answering her question, he asked one of his own: 'When do you expect to go home, Mrs Astell?'

She stiffened, as if in recognition that home would be a luxury she wouldn't have long to enjoy. 'In a few days, I suppose.' All the colour seemed to have been drained from her face. The skin under her eyes was a dirty putty colour. 'They want me to see a psychiatrist.' Unexpectedly, she laughed, a harsh, broken sound that expressed the depth of her despair more effectively than mere words. 'Though I fail to see how that would help.' She blinked and the precariously balanced tears tumbled over.

They left before Astell could voice any more of the protests Rafferty could see welling up in him. On the drive back to the station, Rafferty mused, 'I wonder why she chose that particular night to kill Moon? When she was all dressed up in her expensive frock.' When Llewellyn failed to respond, he supplied his own answer. 'I suppose it must have seemed particularly appropriate. What better night to rid herself of the man who threatened her father's reputation than the one that held most poignant memories of him?'

'I doubt if she chose it for that reason,' said Llewellyn. 'In fact, I doubt if she chose it at all. Moon must have insisted he had to see her that night. He would know how much that evening meant to her; obviously, it was a case of come or take the consequences.'

'She'd have done better to take the consequences,' was Rafferty's opinion. 'They'd have been, what? A five-minute and soon-forgotten sensation in the press. Even someone like Sarah Astell could get through that; damn sight easier to endure than a murder trial with months of headlines parading your father's homosexuality. Can she really have thought anyone but herself would care what her father did with his body?'

'I'm sure she did. Old prejudices don't die,' Llewellyn told him. 'They simply go underground.' His voice deceptively soft, he added, 'Not everyone's as broadminded as you, sir.'

Rafferty had the grace to blush as Llewellyn went on. 'After all, it's not so many years since all homosexual acts were classed as criminal offences, punishable by prison. Hadleigh told us that Moon himself had kept his homosexuality secret as a young man, said he'd even tried to deny it by having one or two heterosexual

183

affairs. Carstairs went even further. He got married, produced a child.'

Llewellyn slowed to cross the bridge at Tiffey Reach. 'Sarah Astell admitted she was repelled by homosexuality. There's usually some cause for these unreasonable prejudices, and my guess would be that she had seen her father with another man as a child and pushed it to the darkest corner of her mind. Maybe the psychiatrist will get it out of her? But if she regarded it as so secret that she couldn't even admit it to herself, imagine how she'd feel to have Moon – a man she had come to hate – knowing all about it, sneering and making threats.'

Llewellyn turned left into Cymbeline Way, past the ruins of the old priory. 'Of course, adult homosexuals no longer risk imprisonment, but in other ways things haven't really changed so much since Carstairs' youth. Many careers still demand marriage; employers think it "steadies" a man. Even a society photographer in the fifties would do well to keep his real traits hidden. Carstairs was obviously deeply ambitious, he wanted fame, to be respected as a man and admired for his work, not sniggered over in corners because of his sexual preferences, which, if they had got out, could have cost him work, the world-wide reputation that he craved. So, as I said, he married, fathered a child, which "proved" his heterosexual credentials in the eyes of society. Unfortunately, in his youth he hadn't been quite so cautious or he wouldn't have permitted that old film to be made. I imagine that until Moon sent Sarah Astell the video she had pushed the realization of her father's homosexuality so deeply into her subconscious in determined denial that it was effectively buried.

'But Moon made her face that denial. As part of the price for not revealing her father's homosexuality. Can you imagine what it must have done to her to see that film of her father with another man when he had shown her so little affection? I think she became temporarily insane when Moon made her watch the video in his office. It must have brought it home to her that she had adored a man whose indifference had turned her into a neurotic invalid, ruined her life. I think in that instant her obsessive love for her father turned to hatred, and Moon received the full force of that hatred at its birth. She needed to punish someone, and he became the focus of that hatred.'

'But Moon knew Terry Hadleigh was due for his painting lesson

184

that same evening,' Rafferty suddenly pointed out. 'Why would he tell Mrs Astell to come to his office at virtually the same time?'

'I imagine he wanted Hadleigh to tell her that he had lied about Moon's supposed attack on him all those years ago. Perhaps he wanted to force an apology out of her? We'll never know for certain now, but I'd guess that was what it was.'

Slowly Rafferty nodded. None of Mrs Astell's fingerprints had been found in Moon's office, but that wasn't surprising if this was a one-off visit. It had been a chilly night and she would have been wearing gloves. He could imagine her sitting, determinedly upright in her chair, still dressed in her outdoor clothes, as Moon put the video in the machine.

Llewellyn continued. 'Moon was expecting her. You remember he called the Astells' house from his office earlier that day? Astell, of course, said Moon had spoken to him to find out if Sarah Astell had liked her present. But I believe it was *Sarah* Astell he spoke to. Astell said Moon called in the early evening, just before the anniversary guests were due to arrive. I think Moon rang as soon as he could be certain she had received his birthday present. She denied opening it, but Moon would have told her she'd better do so. He would have also told her she was to come to his office that evening. He would have given her little choice. The rest we can guess.' Llewellyn fell silent.

Rafferty felt rather sorry for Sarah Astell. In her own way, she had been as unlucky with the men in her life as Ellen Hadleigh. She had adored a father who had been indifferent to her and she had then married a man who, while he had done his best to protect her from the consequences of her own folly, had obviously failed to answer her emotional needs. If he had, her desperate love for her father would have faded naturally as she matured. But, instead of fading, it had taken her over – that and her pitiful obsession with her own health, which she appeared to cling to like a child clung to its security blanket. She'd have security of another sort soon enough, though, complete with bars and warders. All they were waiting for now to make her arrest inevitable was the evidence from Appleby. Rafferty wished he could find some pleasure in the prospect.

Rafferty, in danger of feeling sorry for Sarah Astell, was relieved when, later, with hindsight's godlike vision, he saw clearly an aspect of the case that he and Llewellyn had *both* missed. One that provided Sarah Astell with an even stronger and – from Rafferty's point of view, anyway – far more satisfying motive for murder: greed.

This indication that she hadn't been prompted entirely by a misconceived but entirely understandable concern for Carstairs' reputation instantly gave Rafferty much more relish for his job. Even better, Llewellyn would be annoyed that he'd spotted the large clues while missing the more subtle ones. But, as he picked up the phone he cautioned himself, he'd better try to check his facts *before* he shared his suspicions with the Welshman.

Fortunately, the phone call supplying the required answers to Rafferty's questions came before Llewellyn returned.

Rafferty waited till his sergeant was seated comfortably before he began. 'We assumed that Moon had an affair with *Carstairs*. What if we were wrong? And it was *Mrs* Carstairs with whom he had the affair and Sarah Astell was the result? Mrs Astell told us her arrival caused a bit of a stir as she wasn't born till her parents had been married for ten years.'

Llewellyn, of course, was inclined to pour cold water on his idea. 'It's something of a wild leap, isn't it?' he criticized, obviously more than content with his own theories and unwilling to have them mucked about. 'Have you any proof to back it up?'

'Not proof as such,' Rafferty admitted. 'Not yet. But I've got the next best thing. I did a bit of arithmetic, and, for once, my sums added up. Was it just coincidence, do you think, that the young Moon worked for the Carstairs nine months before Sarah was born? Mrs Carstairs must often have felt lonely. Not only did her husband spend most of his time careering round the world, but she must have suspected he had only married her as a cover for his real inclinations. And then there was Moon – a young Moon, fearful of his own homosexuality. What could be more natural than that two unhappy people should comfort one another? She was lonely, Moon was young and desperately trying to deny his true nature.'

'Surely, if Mrs Carstairs knew that Moon was Sarah's father, she would have told her, not left her in ignorance for years?'

186

'I doubt it. But until I have some more solid evidence, I don't want to ask Sarah's mother about it and give my hand away. Look at it this way: Sarah Astell adored the man she had thought of as her father. How could her mother tell her the truth? It would have become more difficult, not less, as time passed. Besides, there are a few other things that point to me being right. For instance, although Carstairs died a wealthy man, he didn't leave Sarah anything in his will, but left the bulk of his money to a cousin. Admittedly, it might have been that he thought she didn't need it as she had inherited from her maternal grandfather, but still, you'd think he would have left her more than his old journals and films. My theory would explain why he didn't.

'And then there's Moon's inexplicable behaviour. I know he was supposed to be sentimental, but that was over people he had actually *known*. He had never known Sarah as a baby. He had left Carstairs' employ months before she was born. Had probably never suspected that Mrs Carstairs had been pregnant until years later. It's my guess he only realized Sarah must be his child when he saw that picture of her at her twenty-first birthday party in Jubilee Year, asked Henry at the pub a few questions, and worked out the dates. Remember it was around that time that he offered Astell a job. It was probably an attempt to get close to Sarah. He must have helped himself to that photo of her as a baby on one of the rare occasions he managed to get his foot over the door. Why would any normal person feel anything but dislike for someone who treated them as badly as Sarah Astell treated Moon? They'd hardly carry their photo around, unless it was to stick pins in it. No, I'm convinced she was his natural child.' Llewellyn still looked sceptical and Rafferty produced his trump. 'According to Sam, Moon was "AB" blood group. So is Sarah Astell.'

Llewellyn raised his eyebrows. 'How did you come by that information? Medical records are—'

'One of the easiest things in the world to gain access to. I know, I know. It's unethical. But I've got a murder to solve, Dafyd. I can't be doing with pettyfogging rules and regulations. I got Sam to make a few discreet enquiries at the local hospital. Luckily, Carstairs and Sarah have both been treated there. As I told you, Sarah Astell is "AB" group. Carstairs was "O" blood group. And according to Sam, it's impossible for an "O" blood group parent to have an "AB" child, *no matter what the blood group of the other parent.*'

Llewellyn digested this latest information. 'Very well. I agree that means Carstairs couldn't have fathered her. But it still doesn't prove that Moon did.'

'True, but it's certainly a coincidence that both Moon and Mrs Astell were "AB" group, especially as only about three per cent of the population come from that particular group.'

Llewellyn pointed out that three per cent of 56 million people was still quite a large number.

'But how many of them had the run of the house at the appropriate time, as Moon had?' Rafferty demanded. 'You must admit it explains Moon's interest in Mrs Astell. It also explains why he carried that baby photo of her round with him. Ginnie Campbell said he stuffed his wallet with photos of friends, clients and relations. And as she certainly wasn't numbered amongst the first two, she must be one of his kith and kin.'

'Suppose you're right. What difference does it make?'

'It means that I'll feel a whole lot better about arresting her, for one thing,' Rafferty told him.

If he *was* right in his conclusions, there was one other thing that Rafferty now expected to happen. The very next morning, it did.

Moon's solicitor rang him with some interesting news. As Rafferty had anticipated, Jasper Moon's will had finally turned up. Also, as anticipated, it was a DIY job. And, although Soames, the solicitor, appeared to find it perfectly understandable that Jasper Moon should elect to trust him above all others to execute his will, he did express slight reservations over the late arrival of the document. However, his concern was easily assuaged. As he explained to Rafferty, 'We've all read of cases where mail arrived weeks, months, even *years* after posting. Besides, there's no doubt that the will is genuine. It's certainly Mr Moon's handwriting. I recognize it and his signature. And considering it's an, ahem,' he paused, '*amateur's* effort, it's more than adequate.'

Rafferty smiled at the thought that Moon's lack of confidence in the legal profession was more than borne out by the solicitor's easy acceptance of the document. Although he shared Soames' confidence that the will was genuine, he considered it rather more than a *bit* odd that it should arrive now. Still, he reminded himself, there are gullible fools in every profession.

A tart voice that was never slow to express an opinion echoed in his head, *Mr Soames has arrogance and age as his excuses. What are yours?* Rafferty told the voice to shut up and asked Soames, 'Who's the beneficiary?' Soames told him and Rafferty nodded. It was as he had expected. Even Soames, a man of discretion, couldn't hide his astonishment that Moon should have called Sarah Astell 'my beloved daughter', and Rafferty smiled his satisfaction.

'I imagine you'll want the beneficiary's address? It's—'

'It's OK. I know the address. Could I have a copy of the will?'

'It's rather unethical. It hasn't even been read yet.'

Rafferty managed to persuade Mr Soames to forget his ethics.

'Of course, we still have no confirmation other than the chain of coincidences, his inexplicable affection for her, and that will saying that *Moon* was Sarah Astell's father,' Rafferty admitted to Llewellyn. 'But what a motive the will gives her.'

Llewellyn was still playing hard to get. 'We can't be sure she even knew about it.'

'Oh, come on, Dafyd,' Rafferty protested. 'I imagine that was part of the reason Moon wanted to see her. If I'm right and I'm sure I am, he must often have longed to tell her the truth. She was his only child, for God's sake. The only one he was ever likely to have. I reckon he must have decided it was time she knew the truth. I'm sure his motives were mixed, confused. And he must have been anxious to demote Carstairs from his pedestal. That film put him and Moon on a par, if you like. It was a start. I doubt he would have expected much at that stage. But he must have fantasized about it so often that it would be easy to substitute her real reaction with his imagined one. There are times when we all see what we want to see. Even professional seers, like Moon, aren't immune.

'He would have told her about the will then, in a misguided attempt to make her accept him. He knew she risked losing her beloved childhood home. He must have thought he could use that as a lever. I doubt it crossed his mind that she would attack him. As I said, once he told her she was his beneficiary that would give her even more reason to kill him. About five hundred grand's worth of reasons. I checked with Moon's publishers; his last book's selling very well, and not just in this country. Its worldwide sales so far put it in the best-seller class.

'We know that Mrs Astell's lost a pile at Lloyds. They'd already mortgaged their house. But as the debts grew she risked losing the childhood home that meant so much to her. She said herself that she was scared she would lose everything. Don't you think she would be prepared to do anything – anything at all – rather than risk losing that? Then she discovered she was Moon's daughter, his sole beneficiary and in a moment's unthinking anger, greed, call it what you will, she killed him. Patricide, Llewellyn; a truly appalling crime. I imagine it was only later that she came to appreciate the enormity of what she had done. No wonder she couldn't bear to live.'

Rafferty snatched up the phone. 'I'm going to ring Appleby and put us all out of our misery. He must have the results of those fibre tests by now.'

Appleby had come up trumps. The fibres taken from the desk were an exact match with those of the dress that Rafferty had obtained from Chez Sophie, identical in every way to the one which Mrs Astell had worn on the night of Moon's murder. Even the umbrella found in the gutter the morning after his death had been identified as hers. The net was closing in and now Rafferty felt he had enough proof of her guilt to charge her. She was out of hospital and was presumably physically well enough to be charged. Even if, as seemed probable, her mental state was less than healthy, at least in custody she was unlikely to be able to attempt a second suicide in order to escape justice, if such was her intention.

Now that he had the evidence of Moon's will, Rafferty tried to contact Sarah's mother to get her to admit the truth of her daughter's paternity. Unfortunately, she was uncontactable, being, at that moment, on the shuttle flying to be with her daughter.

Rafferty got Llewellyn to organize the search warrant. Of course, it was unlikely they would still find the dress. She would surely have destroyed it by now. But she had paid for Chez Sophie's frock by credit card, so the purchase could be easily proved.

A little while later, Rafferty nosed the car out of the police car park and turned it in the direction of the Astells' house, accompanied in the car by Llewellyn and two other officers. WPC Green and Constable Hanks followed in another vehicle.

Astell answered the door. He didn't seem surprised to see them. 'Inspector.' With a frown, he took in the other officers, before returning his gaze to Rafferty. 'What's going on?'

'I think you know, sir. Is your wife at home?'

'My wife? Yes, of course. She only came out of hospital yesterday. But why do you want to see her? She's hardly up to receiving visitors at present. I really can't allow—'

'I'm afraid you have no choice, sir.' It was the sort of situation Rafferty hated and he forced his voice to sound firmer. There was no doubt that Sarah Astell was a sick woman, maybe not even totally responsible for her actions, but, if so, that was for others to decide. His job was to take her into custody. For himself, he believed her actions had been at least half prompted by greed, and this conviction firmed his voice still further, as he added, 'I really must insist.'

For a few seconds more Astell barred their way and then, as if recognizing the futility of his delaying actions, he stood aside and, with a defeated air, told them, 'She's in her sitting room.'

Rafferty, by now familiar with the layout of the ground floor, led the way. After knocking firmly on the door, he thrust it open. Sarah Astell was reclining on the chaise longue, just as she had been on the occasion of their first visit to the house.

'Inspector?' She sat up straight and looked at him, her expression curiously blank. 'My goodness. So many policemen. Whatever do they want, Edwin?'

'I think you know,' Rafferty told her. He paused for a moment, to gain strength for the inevitable hysterics, before he cautioned her. She simply stared dumbly at him, as if unable to believe what was happening, and it was left to Edwin to make the denial.

He did so swiftly, stepping forward protectively in front of his wife. 'You can't suspect my wife of murdering Jasper. The idea's insane. She was here all that evening.'

'I don't think so,' Rafferty told him. 'In fact, we have evidence to the contrary. And a warrant to search this house.'

'But you can't just come in here and arrest my wife,' Astell protested. 'What about your other suspects? Ellen Hadleigh, for instance. After what my wife discovered about Moon and her son, I would have thought she had a particularly strong motive. What about her?' Even now, Astell's olde-worlde manners didn't desert him. 'You must excuse me for being so blunt, Inspector, but when you turn up here to arrest my wife – my *wife* of all people – I must question your competence and your judgement.'

Rafferty flushed. But before he could make some possibly unwise reply, Llewellyn interposed himself between them.

'I think the Inspector will permit me to tell you that your own evidence exonerates Mrs Hadleigh.'

'*My* evidence? What do you mean, Sergeant?'

Rafferty, unwilling to admit that he was as bewildered by Llewellyn's claim as Edwin Astell, waited, intrigued to discover what he had missed.

'You told us yourself that, as well as trying and failing to speak to Mr Moon on the telephone that night, you also telephoned Mrs Hadleigh.'

Light seemed to be dawning behind Astell's eyes. After a worried glance at his wife, who had collapsed back on to the settee, he admitted it.

'Would you mind telling us what time you spoke to her?'

Astell hesitated. Rafferty broke in quickly. He now understood that Llewellyn was playing a game of double-bluff and he was scared the Welshman, not being a gambling man, might overplay his hand. 'Please think very carefully before you answer, Mr Astell. It wouldn't be a good idea to lie to protect your wife. It can easily be checked.' But as Llewellyn had guessed, it seemed probable the call had been made around the same time as the one to Moon; either just before, or just after.

Thirty seconds passed before Astell, his voice dull, defeated, told them, 'I rang her just before eight twenty-five.'

'In other words, after you had tried and failed to ring Mr Moon, whom we, as you know, have reason to believe was dead by then. You must see that your evidence clears Ellen Hadleigh. We know she didn't take another taxi to or from Moon's office – I had that checked out. She couldn't have walked from her home to Moon's office, killed him and then returned home in time to take your call.' Rafferty cleared his throat. It sounded unnaturally loud in the now tense silence. 'But, while your evidence clears the person you yourself considered the main suspect, it points the finger even more firmly at your wife.'

Astell sank down on the nearest chair and, briefly, put his head in his hands. Rafferty turned to Sarah Astell, who had remained silent throughout. She seemed bewildered by the turn of events, and shrank back in her chair as Rafferty gestured for WPC Green and Hanks to come forward.

'These two officers will accompany you to the station, Mrs Astell. I'll be along shortly.' Even though it wasn't strictly necessary for him to be present, Rafferty was anxious to begin the search for the incriminating dress. He wanted to find out if it was still in the house before he began interviewing her.

'No!' Sarah Astell gripped the back of her chair as the officers approached. 'Go away! Edwin, stop them. Make them understand I didn't do it.'

Astell's only answer was to put his head in his hands again, as if to shield himself from the sight and sound of his distraught wife. But her next imploring wailing of his name brought him to his feet, white-faced now, and he pulled her up. 'I think you'll have to be brave, Sarah. At least for a little while.' She swayed in his arms and he told her in a tone intended to encourage, 'Come along, my dear. You'll have to go with them. It'll only be for a short while, I promise. Try not to worry. I can't believe they have a case against you. They'll soon find out their mistake. Anyway, I understand they can only hold you for a limited time before they must either let you go or arrest you, and I doubt they'll be able to do that.'

At the word *arrest*, she clutched at him and let out a frightened cry. 'They can't arrest me, Edwin, they can't. You mustn't let them. You know I'm not well . . .'

Somehow Astell managed to calm her. 'I can't stop them taking you, but you'll be back home very soon, I'll make sure of it. Just promise me you'll say nothing until I can contact our solicitor and get him to the police station. Promise me?' His long, gloved fingers cradled her head on either side while he gazed at her, his expression that of an anxious parent trying to imbue a weak and easily swayed child with some of his own strength.

His voice, with its sensible advice and measured tones, seemed to calm her, for, after gazing uncertainly back at him, she nodded, the action sending the tears in her eyes cascading over their rims. 'I promise.'

'Good girl.' After helping his trembling wife into a warm coat, he had more words of comfort for her. 'I'll get straight on to Courtney and then follow you on to the police station. We'll be with you very soon.'

'But what if he can't come, Edwin? What if he—?'

Her shushed her. 'He'll come. I don't care what it costs, or how inconvenient he finds it to do so. I want you home here with me, not locked up in a police station. And the sooner the better.'

In spite of her distress, a creeping flush of pleasure stole into Sarah Astell's pale cheeks. She reached out a trembling hand and touched his face, gazing searchingly at him, murmuring his name softly before he released her.

Chapter Fifteen

As soon as Mrs Astell had been driven off to the station, Rafferty wasted no time. He called more officers, and when they arrived five minutes later he led the way upstairs. Once in the Astells' bedroom, he instructed them to begin searching. They started with the wardrobes; Astell's wardrobe was half-empty, but Mrs Astell's was full to bursting. Rafferty watched impatiently as the clothes in each were checked. To his surprise, Mrs Astell *hadn't* destroyed the dress. It was very foolish of her, but also very natural. It had been expensive. Even if it was likely to incriminate them, not many women would be able to bring themselves to throw away such a beautiful gown. After he examined the hem and discovered it *did* have several pulled threads, he had it carefully bagged up and labelled.

Father and daughter seemed to favour the same hiding places for their secrets. Because, hidden at the back of Mrs Astell's wardrobe, they found the twin of the Memory Lane video they had found concealed in Jasper Moon's wardrobe. After killing Moon, she would have taken and destroyed the video Moon played in his office, but she would have realized he would have another copy hidden away. In desperation, she had ransacked his office. Unfortunately for her, Moon had taken the precaution of hiding it at his flat.

Rafferty frowned. He was missing something. What was it? But, he realized, it hardly mattered. They had the dress and the video; with the rest of the case against her, they had more than enough for a conviction. Now he had the evidence, Rafferty was content to leave the other officers to continue their search. With a nod to Llewellyn, he led the way downstairs and into the sitting room. There was one more thing he needed. He thumbed along the spines of Carstairs' journals till he found the one he wanted. Quickly, he hunted through the first quarter of the journal for 1956. It was as he had thought – Carstairs had been continuously abroad throughout that period. It was just another piece in the jigsaw, because they already knew he couldn't have fathered Sarah.

Astell had been speaking to his solicitor on the telephone when Rafferty came out into the hall and had just put the phone down when someone rang the front door bell.

It was Mercedes Moreno, a large bouquet of flowers in her hand and a concerned expression on her face.

'I'm afraid Sarah isn't here,' Astell told her. 'The police have taken her to the station for questioning over Jasper's death.' He attempted a bleak smile. 'They seem to think she killed him.'

'What nonsense is this?' Mrs Moreno demanded, turning to Rafferty. 'You think that poor, sick lady could have killed Jaspair? Is stupid. She could not have even left the house,' she insisted. 'I know this as Edwin and I, we were both in the kitchen the entire time, and would have seen her leave the sitting room.'

'Not if she left by the french window in her sitting room,' he told her. Edwin Astell must have momentarily forgotten his earlier story, he realized, because when Mercedes Moreno had stated that neither of them had left the kitchen once she had returned to collect her gloves, but had stood chatting to her, he had nodded his head absently in agreement.

Rafferty quickly picked up the discrepancy. 'I thought you said before that you had popped in on your wife twice during that time?' he said to Astell. 'Mrs Moreno has already told us that she arrived back to fetch her gloves just before ten past eight and she's now let slip that you were both in the kitchen the whole time. Perhaps you'd care to explain?' he invited. Behind him, he heard Mrs Moreno's gasp of dismay. 'Perhaps it's time you *both* told me the whole truth. Mr Astell? I'm waiting.'

'I–I.' Astell cleared his throat his shoulders slumped, and, with an unhappy sigh, he admitted, 'All right, I lied. I was worried about her. Worried that when you learned of that foolish telephone call she made to Jasper you might suspect what you evidently *do* suspect. I thought by saying I had popped in on two occasions between eight and eight-thirty I would be able to supply her with an alibi. It was obvious that Jasper must have died during those times.'

'I see. Thank you for at last confirming what we've long suspected.' As Llewellyn had said near the beginning of the case, those two visits Astell had claimed to have made to his wife's sitting room hadn't quite rung true. 'You realize that now we've finally got this information it strengthens the case against your wife considerably?'

Astell only managed an unhappy nod in reply, all his earlier bluster quite gone.

Rafferty had expected Sarah Astell to go to pieces during questioning. Instead, to Rafferty's astonishment she had shown sufficient sense to take her husband's excellent advice to heart and had said nothing until her solicitor arrived. Even then, when Rafferty pointed out that the alibi she and her husband had concocted for her hadn't stood up to deeper investigation, she had merely asked, 'What alibi? I don't know what you're talking about,' refused to discuss it any further, and again insisted she was innocent.

Exasperated by her continuing denials, Rafferty took the video out of his pocket, put it in the machine, and pressed the 'play' button. 'We know you went to Moon's office,' he told her. 'We know what happened there.'

As the naked images began playing on the screen she screamed, making Rafferty jump. 'What are you doing to my daddy?' she shouted at the writhing bodies on the film. 'Don't you hurt my daddy. Get off him, get off him.' Her voice had taken on the lisping tones of a little girl and she leapt at the screen as if she intended to destroy it and the evidence it showed. Stunned, it was a few seconds before Rafferty reacted and when he tried to restrain her he found she was stronger than she looked. With difficulty, he managed to force her back in her chair.

She blinked, and Rafferty, thinking she had got herself under control, moved away. But as she caught sight of the still-playing film, she began screaming again.

Courtney, the partner in Soames' legal practice who specialized in criminal law, and the soul of urbanity till now, banged on the table and shouted above the noise, 'I really must protest, Inspector Rafferty. Protest in the strongest possible terms. What do you think you're doing, showing my client a pornographic film? I really must protest,' he began again, like a stuck record. But his voice was cut off in mid-stream as his client leapt to her feet, one hand landing inadvertently on the solicitor's paunch, effectively robbing him of breath, much to Rafferty's relief.

'Make them turn it off,' she demanded of Courtney, as she put her hands over her face. 'Make them turn it off. Where did they get that filthy thing?'

'You know where,' Rafferty told her. 'It's the video Moon sent you for your birthday.'

She denied it, of course. 'It is not! He sent me one of the classics.' She paused as she stumbled for a name – any name, Rafferty thought. 'He sent me a video of *Jane Eyre*, I tell you. Not this . . . this . . . abomination. Edwin will tell you it's the truth.'

Rafferty didn't doubt it. 'And where is this other video?'

'It's at home in the rack,' she told him sullenly. 'Edwin wouldn't let me throw it away, as I had intended. But I had no intention of playing it. You'd think he would have realized I didn't want birthday presents from *him*.'

Rafferty frowned. They were getting nowhere. It was evident they were further away from a confession than ever. He switched the video off, hoping it would calm her, and sat beside her. 'We understand how you must have felt, especially when you learned that Alan Carstairs wasn't your father.' He had left an officer at the Astells' house to await the arrival of Sarah's mother. She had insisted on coming to the station and Rafferty, after a little persuasion, had persuaded her to tell them the truth about Sarah's parentage. But it was plain her daughter wasn't about to admit she had discovered her mother's secret. At Rafferty's words, she took refuge in her semi-invalid status and slumped to the floor in a swoon.

They swiftly revived her. After giving her a glass of water, Rafferty said, 'Please, Mrs Astell, acting like this isn't helping you. I can understand that you've had some tremendous shocks recently. First that video and learning that Moon was your father.'

She stared at him. 'Moon my father? How dare you say such a thing? Of course he wasn't my father.' With a naive scorn, she asked, 'How could such as he be anyone's father?'

Rafferty tried to make her see that she was only harming herself by her insistent denials. 'Look, Mrs Astell, this behaviour isn't helping you. I'm sure, when the case comes to court, the judge will be sympathetic. But it would still be better for you to start to co-operate, you know. You must tell us the truth.' He paused. 'Now, perhaps we can start again?' He nodded at Llewellyn to turn the tape recorder back on. Quickly, he repeated the details into the machine, before turning back to Mrs Astell. 'We know you went to Moon's offices that night, so why don't you admit it?'

'But I *didn't*, I tell you.' She appealed to her solicitor. 'Why won't they believe me?'

A little breathlessly, Courtney told her, 'They believe they have evidence that you *were* there that night.'

'Evidence? But how can they have? What evidence?'

Rafferty told her. 'Unfortunately for you, that expensive cashmere dress with the silver threads snagged on Moon's desk. It's a very distinctive dress, Mrs Astell. Perhaps you can explain how we found threads from it on the desk when you told us you'd never been to the offices?'

'But I wasn't wearing that dress,' Mrs Astell protested.

Rafferty sighed and stood up. Perhaps a few hours to think would bring her to see sense? 'It's useless to lie, Mrs Astell,' he told her as he made for the door. 'We know you *were* wearing it. In fact—'

'Oh *earlier*, yes, I did wear it. I admit that. Why shouldn't I? But I felt cold, so I changed into another dress.'

Rafferty paused in the doorway. 'Do you really expect us to believe that?'

'But it's true.'

A faint vein of scepticism threaded through his voice as he asked, 'If it's true, what time – exactly – did you change from the cashmere dress? And what – exactly – did you change into?'

Mrs Astell frowned. 'Let me see. It was just before Clara Davies left at eight o'clock. Mrs Moreno had already left. I'd said my goodbyes and gone upstairs to change. I'd felt chilly earlier standing at the step seeing Mrs Hadleigh into her taxi and decided to put on something warmer; a thick, cowl-neck dress in navy and white. I left Edwin chatting to Clara by the door. She'd just left as I came down the stairs after getting changed and Edwin had gone through to the kitchen. While I was upstairs I remembered I'd promised to let her borrow some of my father's photographs for the biography on him she's trying to write. I quickly took the album I thought most suitable and ran after her. She was just getting into the taxi. She must have seen me very clearly as the outside light was on. She'll be able to tell you what I was wearing.'

Bemused, Rafferty stared at her. Could they have been wrong, after all? But how could they be? There were too many other factors against her. She was simply trying to delay them for reasons of her own. He doubted Clara Davies would confirm what she said. But if she *did*, the case he had thought so strong would collapse around his ears; a little shiver of anxiety gripped his stomach. Because, if her story was confirmed, it was improbable she would have stolen upstairs a second time to change back into the chilly number specifically to creep out into the stormy night to murder Moon. Even if she'd had time, what would have been the point of such behaviour? 'Just as a matter of interest, Mrs Astell, how many people knew what dress you intended wearing that evening?'

'Well, all my acquaintances who had reason to come to the house that week, I suppose. It's such a beautiful dress, I couldn't wait for Thursday evening and the opportunity to show it off. I showed it to Mrs Hadleigh as soon as I bought it, and to that charming Mrs Moreno when she called round to see me earlier that week. It was a bit naughty of me, I know, but I wanted her to make that wretched Campbell woman jealous and I knew Mrs Moreno would be sure to tell her how expensive it was. I know *she* could never have afforded such a gown.'

Rafferty was surprised that Sarah Astell thought *she* could, given her own admitted money problems. But then some women always managed to find money for new clothes. His own late wife had been the same. 'Did you leave anyone alone with the dress?' he asked. 'Alone for long enough to remove some threads?'

Slowly, she nodded. 'Yes. Naturally I left the dress hanging in my sitting room when I went to the kitchen to make Mrs Moreno coffee. And Mrs Hadleigh is in and out of the bedrooms all the time. If she'd wanted to tamper with the dress she could have done so at any time. But . . .' Her voice faltered, and she went on uncertainly, 'You said Mrs Hadleigh was no longer a suspect, and as she's the only person who had reason to kill Moon . . .'

With her exoneration of Ellen Hadleigh, she seemed to come to a realization of her own position and her brief spark of animation died. She gazed pitifully at him, a mute plea in her eyes, before she managed to find her voice again. 'If – when – you find I'm telling the truth, will I be allowed to go home?' She clutched her handkerchief to her bosom as if the scrap of lawn and lace was the only thing keeping her from going to pieces. Her voice rose in agitation as she realized she might never go home again. 'Only, it's time for my medication, you see. I don't like to miss it.'

Rafferty cursed himself for a fool. He should have made certain he had her pills. Her brief would be sure to make something of that when it came to court. When and if Clara Davies failed to confirm her story, he'd have to send someone back to the house with Astell for them. He was about to offer her the panacea of tea, but realized she was long past the stage of being able to rely on that as a crutch. She had borne up surprisingly well, so far. But as he looked at her, it was obvious that her fragile calmness wouldn't hold out much longer. Her brittle fair hair had escaped its previously neat bun and stood up wildly, and under the red blotches her face was stark white, her eyes quite glassy. In a little while she would start to come apart at the mental seams.

Even though he had little faith in her claims being backed up, compassion compelled him to reassure her. 'If Ms Davies confirms what you say, I'll be able to let you go home very soon. Just give me time to make a phone call.'

He left her with the WPC. Followed by Llewellyn, he hurried along to his office. Picking up the phone, he paused and asked the Welshman, 'Have you got the telephone number of Clara Davies handy?' Llewellyn nodded. 'Let's have it, then. Perhaps once she denies Sarah Astell's tale, she'll be prepared to face facts. Then we can get on.' Quickly, he punched out the number.

Slowly, Rafferty replaced the receiver. He could barely believe it, but Clara Davies *had* confirmed Sarah Astell's story. And when he had questioned her memory and powers of observation, she had briskly reminded him that she had worked as a designer all her adult life; of course she noticed whether someone was wearing black, silver-threaded cashmere or navy-and-white wool.

Dispirited, Rafferty knew he had no more cards to play. They'd worked their way through the entire suspect pack, queens, knaves, even the odd joker. Before today, he'd believed – as the man said

– that once they'd done that, whoever was left, however improbable, must be the murderer.

The trouble was they *had* nobody left. They had eliminated every single suspect. Not only had the middle-aged woman on the bus whom Llewellyn had thought to be Sarah Astell turned out to be one of her neighbours, and the furtiveness explained by the reluctant information that she had sneaked out to meet her lover, but reliable witnesses had come forward to swear that neither Ginnie Campbell nor Christian Farley had been anywhere near Moon's office at the time of his death. They had actually been seen at the houses of the respective friends where they had claimed to be around the time Moon had died.

Even Jocelyn Eckersley had finally produced an unimpeachable alibi. He had been at a London literary awards dinner, picking up a special, lifetime's achievement award for Nat Kingston. Desperation made Rafferty reconsider the possibility that, after all, Kingston *had* killed Moon and had taken his secret, and the solution to Rafferty's investigation, to the grave. If so, it was probable he would never know the truth.

Rafferty wondered where the hell he went from here. The thought occurred to him that Superintendent Bradley might have some suggestions to make. Unfortunately, as he was seeing him in the morning, there was no way he was going to be able to avoid hearing them. Perhaps he should ask Mercedes Moreno to prescribe another stone? One that would render their ego-on-legs Superintendent full of sweet reason instead of the accusing diatribe that Rafferty was expecting. Trouble was, he doubted it would be any more effective than the other stone she had given him. The one that was supposed to help him solve the murder.

After he had seen Sarah Astell off home, Rafferty went to find Llewellyn. 'I don't know about you,' he complained to the still-alert-looking Llewellyn, 'but I've about had a bellyful today. I'm off home.'

Llewellyn nodded. 'I nearly forgot. Happy birthday, Joseph.'

Rafferty *had* forgotten it was his birthday. And given the way the day had turned out he wasn't in the mood to be reminded. Grim-faced, he demanded, 'Are you trying to be funny?' before he made for the door, slamming it behind him.

Rafferty opened the door of his flat, kicking aside a belatedly delivered, second-post birthday card as he did so. As near total despair as he could ever remember being over a case, he scowled at the mantelpiece and its bright display of family cards that he had opened that morning. Another year older and no smarter, he thought. Age was supposed to bring wisdom; his must have been taken away when they'd whipped out his impacted molars. He'd had the case wrapped up and now . . . Now he was back to square one. Worse, because at least when he'd been at square one the first time round, he'd had hope and enthusiasm. Now he had neither.

Disgruntled, he took himself and a bottle of Jameson's off to bed. But his dreams were filled with images of fortune-tellers, crystal-ball gazers and tarot-card readers, all predicting a dire future for him. Unsurprisingly, they all wore Superintendent Bradley's face.

Thankfully, the sadistic seers eventually tired of tormenting him and he fell into a heavy sleep, only to wake, shouting, 'But it should have been two!' as the radio alarm went off. He climbed reluctantly out of bed to greet both the new day and a splitting headache. After swallowing a couple of painkillers, he headed for the shower.

The post fell to the mat as he came out of the bathroom. He carried it through to the kitchen and opened it while he waited for the kettle to boil. Gas bill. Phone bill. The belated birthday card from some night club touting for members that he had kicked aside the night before. He threw it in the bin, took his tea through to the bedroom and got dressed.

He was halfway to his car when he stopped, clapped his hand to his head in astonishment at the idea that had just occurred to him, and sprinted the last few yards to his car, headache forgotten as he realized its implications. He broke all the speed limits on the way to the station and burst into his office like a kid on Christmas morning.

'Quick,' he said to a startled Llewellyn. 'Where's Moon's diary? Don't stand there staring at me, man!' he shouted as Llewellyn made no move to answer him. 'And don't tell me it hasn't come back from the accountants. I want it now. This could be important.'

Llewellyn went out without a word. He returned in five minutes, the diary under his arm. Rafferty snatched it from him and thumbed through to the appropriate page. When he raised his head, his eyes were shining. 'Gotcher.'

And now he also realized just what it was that had niggled him the previous day. Because his dream had been right. Unless Sarah Astell had inexplicably thrown one away, it *should* have been two.